Praise for

CITY SPIES

"Whenever anyone asks me for a recommendation about whose books they should read, I tell them, 'James Ponti.' I loved James's Framed! mysteries, and now with *City Spies*, he has upped his game. As is always the case with a James Ponti novel, the characters are intriguing and fun, the settings are fascinating, and the story is inspired. I couldn't put this book down—and more importantly, neither could my children. This is a must-read for anyone who loves adventure, intrigue, mystery, and humor."

—STUART GIBBS, *New York Times* bestselling author

"James Ponti is such a master of the fast-paced page-turner, I'd read anything he writes! Beware, *City Spies* may keep you up all night—reading!"

—CHRIS GRABENSTEIN, #1 *New York Times* bestselling coauthor of the Max Einstein series

"With a savvy group of teen spies running the show, expect rollicking good fun. James Ponti's latest middle-grade novel is packed with fast-paced action, endearing characters, and plenty of clever spycraft. The stakes are high as Brooklyn, Sydney, Kat, Paris, and Rio pursue a mysterious villain with evil intentions. Along the way, they learn to work as a team, relying on each other's strengths and forgiving each other's weaknesses. They might even be *friends*. Building to a nail-biter of a conclusion, *City Spies* will keep young readers glued to the page. Literally a one-sitting read! So, when do I get the sequel?"

—BETH MCMULLEN, author of *Mrs. Smith's Spy School for Girls*

ALSO BY JAMES PONTI

The Framed! series

Framed!

Vanished!

Trapped!

The Dead City trilogy

Dead City

Blue Moon

Dark Days

BY JAMES PONTI

ALADDIN
New York London Toronto Sydney New Delhi

This book is a work of fiction. Any references to historical events, real people, or real places are used fictitiously. Other names, characters, places, and events are products of the author's imagination, and any resemblance to actual events or places or persons, living or dead, is entirely coincidental.

ALADDIN
An imprint of Simon & Schuster Children's Publishing Division
1230 Avenue of the Americas, New York, New York 10020
First Aladdin hardcover edition March 2020

Book designed by Tiara Iandiorio
The illustrations for this book were rendered digitally.
The text of this book was set in Sabon LT Std.
Manufactured in the United States of America 1022 FFG
10 9 8
Library of Congress Cataloging-in-Publication Data
Names: Ponti, James, author.
Title: City spies / by James Ponti.
Description: First Aladdin hardcover edition. | New York : Aladdin, 2020. | Summary: "Sara Martinez is facing years in the juvenile detention system for hacking into the foster care computer system to prove that her foster parents are crooks. But then she gets a second chance when a mysterious man offers her a chance to join a group of MI6-affiliated spies"—Provided by publisher. |
Identifiers: LCCN 2019011804 (print) | LCCN 2019016515 (eBook) |
ISBN 9781534414914 (hardcover) | ISBN 9781534414938 (eBook)
Subjects: | CYAC: Foster children—Fiction. | Spies—Fiction. | Hackers—Fiction. | Conduct of life—Fiction.
Classification: LCC PZ7.P7726 (eBook) | LCC PZ7.P7726 Cit 2020 (print) |
DDC [Fic]—dc23
LC record available at https://lccn.loc.gov/2019011804

FOR DENISE: WIFE,
BEST FRIEND,
PARTNER IN CRIME

A Man Called Mother

SARA LOOKED AT THE WATER STAIN ON the wall and imagined it was an island. She wasn't sure if that was because it actually looked like one or just because she so desperately wished she were in some tropical paradise far from Brooklyn and this tiny room on the eighth floor of Kings County Family Court.

She sat across the table from her public defender, a massive man in a rumpled suit named Randall Stubbs. His bulky frame hunched over as he scanned her file. "This doesn't look good," he muttered, because stating the obvious was apparently something they taught in law school. "You're lucky they've made such a generous offer."

"They have?" Sara asked, surprised. "What is it?"

He looked up from the file and said, "You plead guilty to all charges and get thirty months in juvenile detention."

Two and a half years in juvie didn't sound generous to Sara, but it probably wasn't much worse than her last few foster homes. She was tough for a twelve-year-old. She could handle it.

"And, of course," he added, "you won't be allowed near a computer."

This, however, was unacceptable.

"For how long?"

"For the duration of your sentence. Maybe longer as a condition of your release. That'll be up to the judge."

"But all I did was—"

"What?" he interrupted. "Hack into the computer network for the entire juvenile justice system of New York City? Is that what you were going to say? Because that's not what I'd call an 'all I did' situation."

"I know, but I was only trying to . . ."

"It doesn't matter what you were *trying* to do," he said.

"All that matters is what you did. You're lucky you're twelve. If you were thirteen, they probably would've bumped you up to a higher court to make an example out of you."

The weight of this hit her hard, and for the first time she regretted her actions. Not because they were against the law. Legal or not, she had no doubt that she'd done the right thing. But she'd never considered that she could be banished from the one corner of the world that made sense to her. The only time Sara felt at home was when she was sitting at a computer keyboard.

"I'll never hack again," she said. "I promise."

"Oh, you promise?" he responded sarcastically. "Maybe you can cross your heart and hope to die once we get in court. I'm sure that'll fix everything."

Sara struggled when it came to controlling her temper, a diagnosis confirmed by multiple counselors and at least two school psychologists. Still, she tried to keep cool as she looked at the man who was supposed to be helping her. She couldn't risk angering him, because he was her only hope for a positive outcome. So she took a deep breath and counted to ten, a tip from one of those counselors whose name she'd long since forgotten.

"If I can't use a computer," she said, barely masking her desperation, "then I can't do the one thing I'm good at. The thing that makes me special."

"Yeah, well, you should've thought of that before you—"

She probably would've lost her temper right then and there if the door hadn't suddenly flown open, and into the room stepped a man who was in every way the opposite of her attorney.

He was tall and thin with a thatch of unruly black hair. His suit was impeccable. His tie matched his pocket square. And he spoke with a British accent.

"Sorry to interrupt," he said politely. "But I believe you're in my seat."

"You've got the wrong room," grumbled Stubbs. "Now, if you don't mind, I'm having a conference with my client."

"Except, according to this Substitution of Counsel form, she's my client," the other man replied as he showed Stubbs a piece of paper. This brought an instant smile to Sara's face.

Stubbs eyed the man. "That doesn't make any sense. She can't afford a fancy lawyer like you. She doesn't have any money."

"Of course she doesn't have any money. She's twelve. Twelve-year-olds don't have money. They have bicycles and rucksacks. This one, however, also happens to have an attorney. This paper says I've been retained to represent Ms. Sara Maria Martinez." He turned to her and smiled. "Is that you?"

"Yes, sir."

"Brilliant. That means I'm in the right place."

"Who retained you?" asked the public defender.

"An interested party," said the man. "Beyond that, it's not your concern. So if you'll please leave, Sara and I have much to talk about. We're due before a judge shortly."

Stubbs mumbled to himself as he shoveled his papers into his briefcase. "I'm going to check this out."

"There's a lovely lady named Valerie who can help you," said the British man. "She's with the clerk of the court on the seventh floor."

"I know where she is," Stubbs snapped as he squeezed past the man into the hallway. He started to say something else, but instead just made a frustrated noise and stormed off.

Once Stubbs was gone, the new attorney closed the door and sat across from Sara. "I've never seen that before," he marveled. "He literally left the room in a huff."

She had no idea who might have hired an attorney for her, but she was certainly happy with the change. "I've never seen it either."

"Now tell me," he said as he popped open the latches of his briefcase. "Is it true? Did you hack into the computers of the city's juvenile justice system?"

She hesitated to answer.

"You needn't worry. Attorney-client privilege forbids me from telling anyone what you say in here. I just need to know if it's true."

She gave a slight nod. "Yes. It's true."

"Brilliant," he said with a wink. He pulled a small computer from his briefcase and handed it to her. "I need you to do it again."

"Do what again?" she asked.

"Hack into the juvenile justice database," he said. "I need you to make me your attorney of record before Mr. Stubbs gets to the seventh floor and checks for himself."

"You mean you're not my attorney?" she asked.

"Never set foot in a law school," he said conspiratorially. "So, chop-chop. I've got an associate who's going to delay him in the hallway, but she'll only be able to do that for so long."

Sara's head was spinning. She didn't know what to think. "Listen, I don't know who you are, but the court's supposed to assign me a lawyer. A *real* one."

"And the chap with the mustard stain on his tie is the one it assigned," he replied, shaking his head. "I don't know about you, but I'm not particularly impressed. Over the last nine years, that same court has assigned you to six foster families and nine schools. It's been one botch job after another with them. What do you say we try something new?"

She looked at him and then at the computer. She was tempted, but she was also confused. "I don't think—"

"What did he say would happen?" he interrupted. "I bet he's already worked out a deal with the prosecutor."

"Two and a half years in juvie and I'm banned from using a computer."

He shook his head. "I can do better than that even without a law degree."

For reasons she didn't fully understand, Sara believed him. Maybe it was wishful thinking. Maybe it was desperation. Either way, she trusted her gut and started typing.

"Excellent," he said. "You probably won't regret this."

"*Probably?*" She raised an eyebrow. "Shouldn't you be trying to build up my confidence?"

"Only fools and liars speak with certainty about things beyond their control," he replied. "But I'm optimistic, so I'd rate your chances around . . . eighty-seven percent."

Sara smiled and continued typing. "What kind of computer is this?"

"Bespoke," he answered.

"I thought I knew all the computer companies, but I've never heard of that one."

"It's not a company," he said. "'Bespoke' means something has been tailor-made to the specific needs of an individual."

"Someone made this for you?"

He nodded.

"Well, whoever 'bespoke' it really knew what they were doing."

"Wait until you see the massive one," he said. "You're going to love it. That is, if we're not both behind bars by the end of the day."

Sara knew computers well, but she'd never seen one like this. It was fast and powerful, and she quickly shredded through the firewall that was supposed to protect the juvenile justice portal.

"They didn't even fix the backdoor I used the other day," she said in disbelief.

"Large institutions move slowly," he said. "Hopefully large attorneys do too."

It took her less than two minutes to reach the database for attorney assignments. She happily deleted the entry for Randall Stubbs and asked, "What's your name?"

"Excellent question," he said as he pulled three passports out of his briefcase. "Which sounds best?"

He read from the first one. "Croydon St. Vincent Marlborough the Third." He gave a sour face. "Seems a bit excessive, don't you think?"

She nodded. "Yes."

"We'll pass on that." He read from the next. "Nigel Honeybuns." This one made him snicker. "Honeybuns? I quite like that." He tucked it into a pocket in his briefcase. "I think I'll save that one for another time."

"We're kind of in a hurry," she reminded him.

"Right, right, here we go," he said, reading from the last one. "Gerald Anderson. That sounds like a proper barrister. Dull. Boring. Imminently forgettable. Which is exactly what we want. That's my name, Gerald Anderson."

He handed her the passport so she could check the spelling as she typed it into the database.

"I just click 'update,'" she said as she finished, "and we're all set."

He flashed a nervous smile and paused to listen. "No alarms." He opened the door and leaned out into the hallway. "No one rushing in to arrest us. Very nice work, Sara."

"Except now I have an attorney who's never gone to law school."

"I've watched a ton of courtroom dramas on the telly," he said. "I can handle an appearance before a judge."

"Don't you mean '*probably*'?" she replied.

He smiled at this. "Right . . . *probably*. First, though, I'll need details about the hack."

"I'm sure they're all in there," she said, pointing at the file.

"This only tells me what you did," he replied. "I want to know the reason."

"The lawyer, you know, the one who actually went to law school, said it didn't matter why I did it."

"It may not matter to him. It might not even matter to the judge. But it matters very much to me."

She thought about her answer for a moment, trying to

come up with the most straightforward way to tell it. She didn't want to get upset. She hated showing emotions in front of anyone. "My most recent foster parents . . ."

"Leonard and Deborah Clark?"

"Yeah, them," she said with a sneer. "They like to take in more kids than they have room for because the state pays them by the kid. More kids mean more money, whether they spend it on us or not. No one really checks that. We were crammed into bedrooms that were too small. Rather than give everyone a meal, they put food in the middle of the table, so it looked like there was more than there was. They called it 'family style,' which is a joke because they treated us like anything but a family.

"A new kid named Gabriel came about a month ago. He was scared. Sad. Lonely. Everything you'd expect from a five-year-old. He liked me because we were the only Hispanic kids in the house."

"You spoke Spanish to him?"

"Sometimes," she said. "Until they made us stop. Mr. Clark told me, 'You're in America now, so speaking English is something you're going to have to get used to.'"

The lawyer shook his head. "And what did you say to that?"

"I pointed out that Puerto Rico was already part of America, that I'd spent almost my entire life in Brooklyn, and that if *he* really wanted to speak English well, he shouldn't end sentences with prepositions."

The man laughed. "Cheeky."

"I'm not exactly sure what 'cheeky' means, but his cheeks turned red, so I guess so," she replied.

"Did you get in trouble?" he asked.

She nodded, the humor of the moment gone. "I could handle his punishment, though. It was Gabriel who couldn't."

"Why was Gabriel punished?"

She paused and saw him studying her expression. He wanted to watch her eyes as she spoke.

"One night he wet his bed," she answered, "and to punish him, they locked him in the hall closet. I could hear him crying. They didn't care. They would've let him cry all night. So, I got up and let him out."

"And then what happened?" he asked.

"Then they locked me in the closet with him. Told me I had to learn my place. So, I picked the lock from the inside and let us both out." She was on the verge of tears, so she stopped for a moment.

"And then?" he prodded.

"They locked us outside on the roof. They left us there all night. It was cold. It was terrifying. The next morning, I went to school, got a pass to the computer lab, and started working. First I hacked the juvenile justice database to see how many kids had been sent to the Clarks. Then I hacked their bank accounts to show how much money they were taking in and where they were actually spending it."

"You're not being charged with hacking the bank," he said, flipping through some pages.

She grinned. "Yeah, they dropped their complaint. I'm pretty sure they don't want the world to find out that a twelve-year-old girl beat their security system."

"Nice," he said. "I might be able to use that later. What'd you do with this information once you'd gotten it?"

"I sent everything to my social worker," she said. "And you know how stupid I am? When I saw the police coming up to the house, I thought they were going to arrest the two of them. For about forty-five seconds I was happy."

"But they arrested you instead?"

She nodded.

"The Clarks even had the other kids line up on the porch so they would see me being led out of the house in handcuffs." She closed her eyes tight, determined not to let a single tear fall. "They said, 'This is what happens to criminals.'"

He'd actually heard the story the night before, through a listening device. But he liked hearing stories twice. He wanted to see if they changed. That was always a good indicator of how truthful they were. Besides, seeing her face as she recalled it told him everything he needed to know.

"That's a good reason," he said. "I can work with that. I can make this a lot better."

"Don't you mean '*probably*'?" she asked.

He smiled warmly. "No, I'm certain I can. But I'll need you to do something difficult. Something the reports in this file say you're completely incapable of."

"What's that?" she asked.

"I need you to trust me," he said. "No matter what I say or do, I need you to trust me."

"How can I trust you?" she asked. "I don't even know your name."

"Sure you do. It's Nigel Honeybuns. It's Gerald

Anderson. Sometimes it's even Croydon St. Vincent Marlborough the Third. It all depends on the situation," he said with a shrug. "But my friends and colleagues, and I do hope that's a group you'll soon consider yourself to be a part of, they all call me Mother."

For the first time since she'd been arrested, Sara laughed.

"Mother? That's an unusual name for a man."

"True," he said, smiling at her. "But I'm an unusual man, wouldn't you say?"

Crunchem Hall

THE REPORTS IN SARA'S FILE WERE accurate. She didn't trust people. Especially adults. To be fair, not many had given her reason to do so. There'd been a few nice teachers along the way. And two good foster families. But that was about it. Now, as she sat in a holding cell waiting to be called into the courtroom, she was having second thoughts about trusting a man who called himself Mother and carried at least three phony passports in his briefcase.

"Rich girl, you gonna help me out?"

There were only three other girls in the cell, but it took Sara a moment to realize this one was talking to her. She almost laughed at the absurdity of it.

"I'm not rich."

They were sitting on blue wooden benches facing each other, about four feet apart. The older, much larger girl leaned closer.

"I saw your lawyer," she said. "Shiny suit. Expensive shoes. You've gotta have money to have a lawyer like that. Maybe he can help me out too. Or maybe I can look after you. Keep you safe once we get to juvie. It won't cost your family much."

"Leave her alone."

The warning came from an unlikely source, a girl named Emily who'd shared a cell with Sara the night before. Her perfectly manicured nails gave the impression that she knew her way around the salon much better than she did a jail cell. She'd told Sara that she'd been arrested for shoplifting and her mother was making her spend the night behind bars to teach her a lesson.

"No one was talking to you, princess," the first girl said.

"Well, if Sara needs anyone to look after her, I'll do it," Emily replied. "So thanks, but no thanks."

The first girl stood and towered over them, her

attention now fully focused on Emily. "How do you plan on protecting anybody?"

"Really, guys," Sara said, trying to calm the situation. "It's all a misunderstanding. I don't have any money. And I don't need any protection."

Emily ignored her and got up in the other girl's face. "I'll just use these," she said, flashing her thumbs.

"What? You gonna text someone for help on that phone you shoplifted?"

"No," Emily replied flatly. "I'm going to do this." With lightning speed, she jabbed her thumbs deep into the sides of the larger girl's rib cage, making her gasp for air and stagger backward. Sara stared in amazement as Emily reached over and carefully guided the other girl back to the bench, making sure she didn't fall.

"It'll hurt for a while, maybe bruise a bit, but there's no real damage," Emily said in a half-whisper. "I can't promise I'll go as easy on you next time, so you might want to think twice before you threaten anyone else."

Sara sat there amazed and was still trying to make sense of it all when a guard came to the door.

"Martinez, Sara," he announced.

She was too distracted to respond.

"Martinez, Sara," he repeated.

"That's me."

"Time for court," he said, unlocking the cell door.

Sara looked back at Emily, who said, "Good luck in there."

"Thanks," she replied as she got up and started to leave. She nodded toward the girl who was still catching her breath. "Thanks for that, too."

Emily smiled. "It's what cell sisters do, right?"

Sara followed the guard into the courtroom. Her mind was still distracted by what had happened between the two girls as she sat at the defendant's table next to Mother.

"You all right?" he asked when he saw her expression.

"Yeah," she said. "I'm fine."

"Good, because I need your full attention," he said. "And I need you to remember the part about trusting me."

She didn't know what to make of him, but there wasn't any time to figure it out. The bailiff stood and announced the judge's entrance.

"All rise for the Honorable Lyman J. Pancake. Court is now in session."

Mother smirked. "Pancake? Maybe I should've gone with Honeybuns after all. We would've been like a breakfast buffet."

Sara didn't laugh. She wasn't in a joking mood.

Neither was the Honorable Lyman J. Pancake.

He might've had a funny name, but the rest of him appeared completely humorless. Perhaps a lifetime of listening to flapjack jokes had worn away his good nature. His expression could best be described as puckered, as if he'd just drunk lemonade without enough sugar. What little hair he had left formed a semicircle of white bristle that started above his ears and met somewhere in the back. After some formalities he asked, "How does the defendant plead?"

Mother looked up from his briefcase long enough to announce, "Guilty, Your Honor."

Sara knew she was guilty but thought there'd be some negotiations before they admitted it. From what she'd seen on television, guilty people usually started off claiming to be innocent.

The judge turned to the prosecuting attorney and asked, "Is there a plea arrangement, Ms. Adams?"

The prosecutor was tall and lean with short blond hair. Her youthful face hinted that she'd only been out of law school for a few years, and her huge smile indicated she was delighted, if perhaps a bit surprised, to hear the guilty plea.

"No, Your Honor," she replied. "I had preliminary discussions with Ms. Martinez's original attorney, but no agreement was reached."

"She looks really happy," Sara whispered nervously. "I don't think you were supposed to plead guilty."

"Is that true, Mr. Anderson?" asked the judge.

Rather than respond, Mother kept shuffling through his papers. It took Sara a moment to realize that it was because he didn't recognize his phony name.

"Is that true, Mr. Anderson?" the judge repeated, this time a bit louder.

Sara nudged him. "*You're* Mr. Anderson."

"Oops," he whispered to her. "Told you it was forgettable." He turned his attention to the judge and asked, "Is what true, Your Honor?"

"That you have not reached a plea arrangement with the prosecution?"

"It's my understanding that opposing counsel has offered a sentence of two and a half years in juvenile detention," Mother said.

"That may have been discussed as one of several possibilities," the prosecutor replied with a Cheshire cat grin. "But like I said, there was no official agreement. And now that there's an admission of guilt in open court, I'm not inclined to let her off so easy."

Sara slumped in her chair. Things were going from bad to worse in a hurry.

"That's fine," said Mother. "Because we find that offer unsatisfactory."

"I guarantee you won't get a better one," she said.

"I don't want a better one," he replied. "I want one that's worse."

Now Sara was really confused.

"I'm sorry, what?" asked the judge.

"Thirty months just isn't enough," Mother replied. "My client compromised highly secure computer files. And, although it's not listed among the charges, she also hacked into the financial records of a multinational bank."

"Hey," protested Sara. "What about attorney-client privilege?"

"That would only apply if I was actually an attorney," he whispered. He turned back to the judge and continued, "Your Honor, this behavior is serious and calls for more than two and a half years. Personally, I think she should remain in custody until she turns eighteen."

"What are you doing?" Sara pleaded under her breath. "That's six years."

"One moment, Your Honor," he said, raising a finger. "I need to confer with my client."

Mother leaned over so that he was right next to Sara's ear. "As crazy as this sounds, this is the part where I need you to trust me."

"But you're arguing for a harsher penalty than they offered," she said. "That doesn't make sense."

"It will when I'm done," he replied. "Just give me ninety seconds." He unclasped his watch and held it up for her. "Then you can decide."

For the first time she noticed the back of his left hand was covered with burn scars. They continued up past his wrist and disappeared beneath his sleeve. Somehow, she'd overlooked them earlier.

"A fire," he said, reading her reaction. "I'll tell you about it when we get out of here. But now I'm asking for a minute and a half of trust."

Oddly, the scars were what swayed her. They hinted that there was more to him than fast talk and a nice suit. He'd suffered through something, which meant he was tough. Maybe even as tough as her.

She took the watch and examined it. "Looks pretty cheap for someone who's supposed to be a high-priced attorney."

"I keep meaning to get a posh one," he said. "Maybe we can take care of that once we're done here."

Finally, she nodded her assent. "Okay . . . but at ninety-one seconds I start telling the judge about fake passports."

"Attagirl."

"Your Honor, if I may?" interjected the prosecutor. "We can quickly draft an agreement placing Ms. Martinez in a supervised group home until her eighteenth birthday."

"Also unsatisfactory," said Mother.

"Aren't you the one who just said she should remain in custody until she becomes an adult?" she asked.

"Yes, but not at a place like that," said Mother. "All she'll do there is learn how to be a better criminal. I have an alternative in mind."

Sara watched the second hand intently. He was down to a minute and seven seconds.

"Where?" asked the judge.

"Crunchem Hall," replied Mother.

"Crunchem Hall?" Pancake asked, trying to place the name.

"It's a specialized facility that houses a handful of juvenile offenders," he replied. "She'll get one-on-one attention, counseling, and a first-rate education."

"Are we placing her in detention or sending her to summer camp?" asked the prosecutor. "The taxpayers aren't footing the bill for that."

"All the fees will be paid by a private foundation," Mother said, waving a sheet of paper from his briefcase. "I have the documentation right here. Sara Martinez will no longer cost the taxpayers a penny."

Sara didn't know what to think when she saw the "documentation." It was a takeout menu from a nearby deli. According to the watch, he was down to twenty-six seconds.

"It sounds too good to be true," said the judge. "Which undoubtedly means it is. We don't reward criminal behavior with luxury accommodations. Ms. Martinez broke the law, and she will be going into a supervised group home when we're done here."

Ten seconds.

"You might want to rethink that," said Mother. "She either goes to Crunchem Hall or we change our plea to 'not guilty' and move on to a trial that I can guarantee both of you will regret."

"Why is that?" asked the judge.

Mother paused.

His time was up, and he looked at Sara. She was torn. She didn't know where this was going, but it seemed to being going . . . *somewhere.* He had a fake name, no legal training, and his key piece of evidence was a list of twenty-seven different sandwiches. He also told lies with alarming ease. Yet, despite all of this, he seemed totally pleased with how events were unfolding. She handed him back the watch, and he smiled.

"This is about to get fun," he whispered to her confidently.

Mother turned to the judge. "If we go to trial, the first thing I'll do is insist you remove yourself from the case."

"On what grounds?" he protested.

"On the grounds that you're prejudiced against my client because when she hacked the juvenile justice portal, she came across personal e-mails of yours that are embarrassing in nature."

Sara had no idea what he was talking about. She hadn't gotten near any e-mails.

"The e-mail server wasn't compromised," insisted the judge.

"Then how do I have a copy of this note you sent two weeks ago?" Mother said, and began to read from a piece of paper. "'Yesterday I had dinner with the mayor, and let me tell you that man is an absolute—'"

The judge slammed his gavel repeatedly to keep Mother from reading any further.

"Why don't I just put that one down for a second?" Mother said as he laid it on the defense table. "There are also e-mails from various attorneys, such as this one," he said as he began to read from another. "'How can you take a man seriously when his name is Judge Pancake? Where'd he go to law school? Hash Brown University?'"

"Objection!" the prosecutor exclaimed as soon as she recognized it as an e-mail she'd written to a friend.

"He should object, not you," said Mother. "It's his name you're making fun of."

"Your Honor, he's trying to blackmail us."

Mother laughed. "No, that's not blackmail. But this next one's pretty close." He picked up another paper and started to read. "'About the legal conference last week in Atlantic City, please don't tell my wife any of . . .'"

"Order in the court!" the judge bellowed, pounding his gavel. "Order in the court!"

Sara looked up at Mother, and he shot her a wink.

He turned back to the judge. "There are dozens of such e-mails, and I will make sure that every one is read aloud and placed into the public record, which I can only imagine will be embarrassing for both of you. Or . . ." He stopped speaking for a moment to give the judge a chance to consider his options.

"Tell me more about Crunchem Hall," said the judge. "Who's in charge there?"

"Trunchbull," said Mother. "Very tough."

"Right, Warden Trunchbull," the judge said. "Tough . . . but fair, if I remember correctly. Tell me more."

Four hours later Sara Maria Martinez was released from custody into the care of a man claiming to be Gerald Anderson, attorney-at-law. He signed a few papers, and they exited the courthouse through a revolving door into a sunny Brooklyn afternoon.

Sara took a deep breath of fresh air and asked, "So do you want to explain what happened in there?"

"We won," said Mother. "Bit of a drubbing, if I'm being honest."

"I'm not so sure we can call that a victory," she replied. "You got me sentenced to six years in custody."

"True, but they're to be served at a fictional facility, so it shouldn't be too difficult."

Sara gave him a look. "What are you talking about?"

"Crunchem Hall is the school in *Matilda*," he

explained. "Miss Trunchbull is the evil headmistress. They only exist in a children's book." He paused for a moment and added, "Unless you count the movie and the musical, both of which I quite enjoyed."

"Are you insane?"

"I only had ninety seconds, and I needed to come up with something," he said. "The trick was using names that were vaguely recognizable. That way they were more likely to think it was real."

"But what if they remembered the book?"

"The prosecutor seemed too young to have kids, and the judge is old enough that it's been decades since he read any bedtime stories, so I thought we were probably safe."

"Again with the 'probably.'"

"Life is filled with 'probablies,' Sara. You're going to have to get comfortable with them."

"If it's a fictional place, then why did you insist on me being sentenced until I was eighteen?"

"Because you're no longer the concern of the juvenile courts," he said. "You've been sent away until you're an adult. No one's going to come looking for you. No social worker's going to follow up and knock on your door. You've fallen through the cracks of the American judicial system." He smiled proudly. "So cheers for that."

"You're saying I'm free?"

"In every way."

"Then what happens now?"

"Now, it gets interesting," he said. "You've got some massive decisions to make. But first I'd like you to come for a ride." He motioned toward a limousine waiting nearby. "I want to show you something."

"In a limo?"

"I figured you came here handcuffed in the back of a panda car; the least we can do is leave in style."

"Panda car?"

"A police car," he explained. "It's black and white, like a panda."

As she followed him, she asked, "So what made you think of *Matilda*?"

"It was written by Roald Dahl," he said. "He's my favorite author."

"You must really like kids' books."

"I do, but that's not why he's my favorite," said Mother. "He's my favorite because in addition to being a writer, he was a spy." Mother stopped, turned back to face her, and said, "Just like me."

Sara laughed.

"I'm not joking," he said. "I'm an agent with the British Secret Intelligence Service, also known as MI6. That's why I have the passports. That's how I have copies of their e-mails. I command an elite team that is only sent out on high-priority missions."

"And one of those *high-priority* missions was keeping me out of juvenile detention?" she replied suspiciously.

"This wasn't a mission so much as it was a recruitment. An emergency one, at that."

"What do you mean?"

"We're about to go into the field for a critical operation," he said. "And we just discovered that we need one more person on our team. We thought we'd come over and see if that person might be you."

"We?" asked Sara.

Mother opened the rear door of the limo, and Sara saw a familiar face looking back at her from inside.

"Emily?" she said, recognizing her "cell sister."

"Actually, the name's Sydney," she replied with an Australian accent. "Glad he was able to bust you out."

Brooklyn

RATHER THAN A PRISONER TRANSPORT bus, Sara left the courthouse in a limousine with two people who claimed to be spies. Surprisingly, she had no doubt that that's exactly what they were. She just wasn't sure how she fit into their plans.

"Let me get this straight," she said as they took Atlantic Avenue deeper into Brooklyn. "You two are a team?"

"Part of one," answered Sydney.

"And you came here to see if I was a good fit for that team?"

"That's right," said Mother.

"Am I?"

"So far, it's quite promising," he said, "but we can't be certain until we conduct some more tests."

"What do you mean, *more* tests?" she said. "I haven't taken any."

"Actually, you've taken two so far," he answered. "First when I asked you to hack into the juvenile justice portal and make me your attorney. That's performance under pressure. An essential skill." He turned to Sydney. "She did it in under two minutes."

"Impressive," said Sydney.

"The second was trusting me in the courtroom," he continued. "That demonstrated your ability to adapt to rapidly changing situations. Also essential."

"I wish I could've been there to see it," said Sydney.

"It's too bad," joked Mother. "I was sensational."

Sydney rolled her eyes and shared a look with Sara. "By the way, I did some shopping earlier." Sydney handed her two department store bags. "I tried to guess your sizes and what you might like."

Sara looked in the bags. "You bought me clothes?"

"Just to hold you over until we can get you a proper wardrobe," she replied.

"Although, most days you'll wear your school uniform," added Mother.

Sara gave him a curious look. "My school doesn't have a uniform."

"About that. You're going to be enrolled in a new school called Kinloch Abbey."

"Sounds about as fake as Crunchem Hall," she said. "Let me guess. It's from *James and the Giant Peach*."

"No, this one's not in a book," Mother said. "It's in Scotland."

Sara waited for him to laugh, but he didn't. She waited some more, but there was still no laugh.

"You're serious?"

"It's a bit posh," said Sydney. "After all, part of it's in a castle. But once you get over that, you'll like it."

"We're going to Scotland?!"

Instead of answering, Mother leaned toward the driver and asked, "Can you please turn left and take us to house number 197?"

"We're pressed for time," Sydney reminded him. "If we miss this flight, we'll lose an entire day."

"I know, I know," he reassured her. "It's just a quick detour for context. Besides, I really want to see it."

"I'm sorry," Sara interrupted, "but can we get back to the whole Scotland thing?"

"Shortly," Mother assured her as the limo parked in front of a three-story redbrick town house. "First, tell me what you know about Winston Churchill."

"Absolutely nothing," she said blankly. "The name sounds . . . kind of familiar, but that's it."

"Jaw-dropping," he said disapprovingly. "Kinloch will take care of that in a tick. But, for now, just know that as prime minister during World War Two, Churchill saved Britain and quite possibly the world from annihilation. He's a personal hero of mine and did more for the British Secret Intelligence Service than anyone else."

"Okay," she said. "So why are you telling me this?"

"Because his mother was born in this house." He gestured out the window. "Think about that. The mother of the man who saved Britain wasn't from London or Oxford or some grand estate out in Surrey. She was from Brooklyn, just like you. So it follows that we'd come full circle back here to find you. Brooklyn's imprinted on our DNA." He turned his attention back to the driver. "Okay, we can move along now."

The limo started again.

"That's interesting and all," said Sara. "But it really doesn't answer my question. Are you seriously taking me to Scotland? Because I don't even have a passport."

He popped open his briefcase and handed her two British passports, each with her picture and a phony name. "Pick the one you like better."

"Of course," she replied, shaking her head. "You have all the passports you want. How'd you get this picture of me?"

"That bit about us being spies?" he said. "We're exceptionally good at getting things. As to your first question, yes, we're taking you to Scotland. Whether you stay there or not, however, will be entirely up to you."

"How do you mean?" she asked.

"Soon you'll start classes at Kinloch. It's one of the top boarding schools in the UK. You'll get a first-rate education. And if you're happy there, you can continue until you graduate and leave for university. That's option one."

"And if I don't like it?" she asked.

"Option two," he answered. "If, at the end of the school year, you decide Kinloch's not right for you or that you miss living in the States too much, we'll find you a proper home back here in America. It won't be like the ones you've been stuck in before. We'll get you a good family. I'll see to that. Although, we might want to avoid metropolitan New York because of the whole business about them believing that you're in detention somewhere."

"Good point," she said. "But what does any of that have to do with spies and MI6?"

"Not a thing." He leaned in conspiratorially and added, "Option three is the one that involves the Secret Intelligence Service."

She looked at both of them before saying, "Then option three is the one I want to hear about."

"You attend Kinloch not as a boarder but as a day student," said Sydney. "And you live at the farm with Monty, me, and the rest of the team."

"Monty?" asked Sara. "Who's that?"

"Dr. Alexandra Montgomery," said Mother. "She's a biophysicist-slash-cryptologist who loves to bake. Think of her as part Marie Curie and part Mary Poppins."

"She's brilliant," said Sydney. "You're going to love her."

"And the rest of the team?" asked Sara.

"Kids like you and me who Mother's found around the globe," said Sydney. "They're amazing." She rethought this for a moment. "I mean, the boys totally drive me bonkers and I usually want to strangle them, but other than that they're amazing."

"How many are there?"

"Two boys and another girl," she said. "Paris, Rio, and Kat. When you join the team, you have to create an entirely new identity. It's hard to keep track of all the aliases and fake names, so we just call each other by where we're from. That way we still have a small connection to our past."

"There's a city called Kat?" asked Sara.

"Kathmandu," answered Mother. "It's in Nepal but that's rather a mouthful, so we just go with Kat."

"That means I'd be Brooklyn," Sara said, liking the sound of it.

"*If* you decide to join," stressed Mother.

"What does *joining* even mean?" she asked.

"It means that in addition to your studies at Kinloch," he said, "you'll receive instruction in espionage, counterintelligence, self-defense, code-breaking, and other assorted goodies."

"My favorite assorted goody is explosives," said Sydney. "I like making things go boom."

"So we're talking spy school?"

"Yes," said Mother. "But not just school. We go on real missions. We face genuine danger."

"And you said that there's a mission coming up that you want me to go on," Sara replied.

Mother sighed. "Normally, you receive extensive training before you go into the field, but we're in a pinch at the moment. There's an operation in three weeks, and we find ourselves one person down."

"And if that person's me?"

"Then I would limit your role as much as possible, but you would have to go into the field with us."

"Cool," she said with a grin. "Sounds more fun than juvenile detention."

Sara would've asked more about the upcoming mission, but she was distracted when the limo turned down a familiar street. It was her neighborhood and just the sight of it made her wince. Everything here was the opposite of boarding schools and castles. There were chain-link fences with razor wire, iron bars on windows, and graffiti covering the wall of an abandoned warehouse.

"Why are we here?" she asked.

"We're about to cross an ocean," he answered. "I thought you might like to stop by home before we left."

"This isn't my *home*," she corrected. "It's a *house* where I lived. There's a huge difference."

"Duly noted," he said. "But either way, you won't be returning. If there's anything of sentimental value in there, now's the time."

"There's a shoebox with some things that are special to me," she said. "But I can't get it."

"Why not?" he asked.

"The Clarks are home," she said. "Considering I just tried to have them arrested, I doubt they'll hand it over."

"Then let's not tell them," he replied.

"You want me to break in?"

"In the spy trade we call it a 'black bag job,'" he said. "We'll make this your first alpha test."

This brought a smile to Sydney's face. "I like it."

"What's an alpha test?"

"Every mission has a team leader, called an *alpha*, who comes up with the plan and runs the operation," he explained. "To prepare for that, we run alpha tests as practice."

"Except, I haven't had any training," Sara replied. "I don't know how to plan a mission."

"Don't sell yourself short," Sydney said firmly. "You already have the intel."

Sara gave her a confused look.

"The intelligence," Sydney explained. "You know the inner workings of the house. All you have to do is break down the variables and devise a scheme. For example, who's inside right now?"

Sara checked her watch. "It should just be the Clarks," she said. "The kids are all either at day care or after-school programs for another forty-five minutes."

"Excellent, so we only have two people to deal with," said Mother. "Where's the shoebox?"

"On the top shelf of my bedroom closet . . . which is on the third floor."

"That's not ideal," said Mother.

"And the only way to get there is to go through the living room, where I'm sure Leonard is sitting in his recliner watching television and drinking a beer."

"Also less than ideal," he said. "But it's still clear-cut. You just need some sort of bait that will get them out of the way."

"That's called the nugget," said Sydney.

"The nugget?" Sara asked.

"Something to distract them," answered Sydney. "To lure them from the living room."

"What do they find . . . *irresistible*?" asked Mother.

"Beer . . . pizza . . ." Sara continued thinking as she studied the house. For her it was filled with memories of sadness and disappointment. She looked up at the roof where she and Gabriel had been locked out for an entire night. And that's when the brainstorm hit. ". . . and money!" she said. "They love money."

"I don't think we have enough cash for a bribe," said Mother.

"That's okay," Sara replied. "Just the idea of money should be enough to get them. Can you pass yourself off as an FBI agent?"

"I'd need a wardrobe change," Mother said.

He opened his briefcase and pulled out a black tie, which he swapped with the stylish patterned one he was wearing. Then he took out his pocket square and put on a pair of dark sunglasses.

"Wardrobe change complete," he said. "What's the plan?"

The Alpha Test

PERHAPS BECAUSE OF THEIR OWN dishonesty and criminal inclinations, Leonard and Deborah Clark viewed the United States government with deep-seated paranoia. Leonard was always on the lookout for the "surveillance drones" he claimed flew nightly missions over Brooklyn. "They're spying on us," he'd say angrily. "Our own government is spying on us."

It was this suspicion, combined with the Clarks' unbridled greed, that formed the basis of Sara's plan. She needed them out of the way long enough to slip up to her old room and come back down without being noticed. To do that, Mother had to lure them away with what he and Sydney had called the nugget.

The limo driver parked around the corner, and the girls hid across the street behind a car, while Mother went up the stoop and rang the bell. As he always did, Leonard Clark peered through a side window to see who was there. After eyeing Mother suspiciously, he cracked the door slightly open and said, "What?"

"Are you Leonard Clark?" Mother asked, using a Texas drawl and doing his best to project FBI cool and calm.

"Who wants to know?"

"The Federal Bureau of Investigation." Mother flashed an official-looking badge. "I'm Special Agent Marlborough of the cybercrimes division."

Leonard shifted uneasily but said nothing.

"I'm here because of your daughter," Mother continued. "Sara Martinez."

"That girl's not my daughter," Clark replied, wagging an angry finger. "She's a criminal who belongs in jail."

"Be that as it may," said Mother, "it has come to our attention that she recently hacked into a bank and made a substantial withdrawal."

Clark's eyes opened wide. "Did she take money out of my account? Because if she did . . ."

"No, sir," Mother replied. "The money was procured from the bank's currency reserves. We have reason to believe she hid the cash here on the premises."

Suddenly the mention of cash hidden in his home put a smile on Clark's face. "How much are we talking?"

"I'm not at liberty to share that information," responded Mother.

"But you said it was 'a substantial withdrawal.'"

"Please, sir. If I could just come in."

Leonard began to formulate a strategy fueled entirely by greed. "Why do you want to come into my house?"

"Obviously, I need to retrieve the money."

"You got a search warrant?" asked Leonard.

"No, sir, I don't," Mother replied. "But I don't actually need to search your property. I just need access to your roof."

"So that's where she hid it," said Clark. "Up on the roof. Clever girl. Devious, but clever."

"Please, sir," said Mother. "It will only take a moment."

"Sorry, buddy. No warrant, no entry. I know my rights."

Mother played the part beautifully as he feigned

frustration and pretended to call a superior. "The homeowner is noncompliant," he said into his phone. "Activate drone retrieval."

"What?!" bellowed Clark. "You're not coming at my house with them drones."

"You've given me no alternative," said Mother. "They should be here any minute." He looked to the sky as if waiting for a squadron of drones to swoop into action.

Clark slammed the door shut, and Mother heard the sound of the bolt locking. He leaned over to the side window and pleaded, "Perhaps we can work out some sort of finder's fee for you and your wife."

Leonard flashed a grin and yanked the curtains closed. Mother waited a moment before motioning the girls over from their hiding place.

"How'd it go?" Sara asked as she dug in her pocket for her house key.

"Just like you said it would," answered Mother.

She pressed her ear up to the window and listened until she heard the sound of the door to the roof slam shut.

"They're on the roof," she said. "They'll tear it apart looking for that money."

She unlocked the door and quietly raced up the stairs to the third floor with Sydney following close behind.

They entered a room where three beds had been fit together like a jigsaw puzzle.

"Look at that," Sara said, pointing at a bare mattress and empty nightstand. "They've already gotten rid of my stuff."

"Think they tossed your shoebox?" asked Sydney.

"No way," she said. "I hid it too well."

Sara stood on her tiptoes so she could reach the top shelf of the closet and groped around until she felt what she was looking for.

"Got it," she said as she carefully pulled down a pale blue box, its color faded with age. She held it tightly, making sure not to spill its contents. "Let's get out of here."

Back in the hall they heard the commotion on the roof as the Clarks frantically searched for the non-existent money. The plan had worked perfectly, and she and Sydney had an easy getaway . . . until Sara froze.

She stood motionless and thought about the cruelty she'd witnessed from the Clarks. She looked at the closet where they'd locked Gabriel and thought about how scared he'd been that night on the roof.

"Hurry up," said Sydney. "We've got what we came for."

Sara looked at Sydney for a moment and then at the door to the roof, her anger building as she remembered the sound of Gabriel's sobbing.

"Sara!" Sydney said urgently. "Believe me when I say we don't want them to catch us in this house. It could ruin everything."

Sara ignored her and went up the final flight to the roof access.

"What are you doing?"

"Letting them know how it feels." Sara reached for the door and turned the lock, trapping them on the roof. "That's for Gabriel."

Sydney sighed. "Okay, I like that. But can we go now?"

"You bet we can," Sara said. "I don't ever want to see this dump again."

They rushed down the stairs and burst out the front door. Just as they reached the sidewalk, they could hear Deborah Clark call to her husband.

"The door, Lenny! It's locked!"

The limo pulled up, stopping just long enough for them to hop in. They were still laughing as they pulled away down the street.

"I missed something," Mother said, looking at the two of them. "What's so funny?"

"I locked them on the roof," Sara said, satisfied. "Just like they did to Gabriel and me."

"That wasn't part of the plan," said Mother.

"No," she countered. "But you said I was the alpha."

"Right."

"And you said that the alpha is in charge of the mission once it's operational."

"Also true," he admitted.

"So, I made it part of the plan," she said defiantly. "Did I pass the test? Am I three for three?"

"Yes," answered Mother. "You passed. And, while I see the appeal of locking them on the roof, it probably wasn't the best thing to do."

"Life is filled with 'probablies,'" she said, repeating his line back to him. "I guess we're both going to have to get used to them."

A smile slowly formed on his face, and he chuckled.

"What?" asked Sydney.

"I'm wondering what I've gotten us into," he said.

Sara grinned. She spun around in her seat and looked back toward the house as it disappeared in the distance.

"They'll be stuck up there until the kids get home," she said. "I wonder what they'll tell them."

"Nothing," replied Mother. "The kids aren't coming home."

A panicked Sara turned back to face him and asked, "Why not? What happened to them?"

"Everything's fine," he assured her. "At MI6 we have friends in American law enforcement. We passed along the files you hacked as well as some others we found and asked them to dig a bit deeper. Right now, a senior social worker is meeting with the children and seeing to it that all of them are assigned to better homes. Meanwhile, the New York Office of Children and Family Services is taking a closer look at the Clarks and their history as foster parents. The roof is only the beginning of their problems."

Sara was stunned. "You did that?"

"No, Sara, you did," he said. "I just made a few phone calls. You did the difficult work. I know you're not familiar with it, but this is what justice feels like. This is what we're all about."

As Sara considered this, she reflexively hugged the shoebox against her chest. Her defiant attitude melted away and tears began to stream down her face. She didn't try to stop them. For the first time in her life she didn't mind someone seeing her cry.

The others were quiet for a moment until Sydney placed a gentle hand on her knee. "Are you okay?"

Sara wiped away some of the tears and nodded. "Better than okay," she said. "I just don't understand how all of this happened. This morning I woke up in jail, and now I'm about to fly to Scotland for spy training. It's just so . . . overwhelming."

"I know exactly what you mean," said Sydney. "I felt the same way."

"It's a lot to take in," said Mother. "I'm sure you have some questions."

"Only a few thousand," joked Sara. "I don't even know where to start."

"How about we start at the beginning?" He looked down at the scars on his hand. "Why don't I tell you about the fire?"

The limo glided into traffic heading toward JFK Airport.

"Five years ago, I went to Paris on a top-secret mission called Operation Gumdrop. . . ."

Operation Gumdrop

Paris, France—Five Years Earlier

DESPITE ITS PLAYFUL NAME, OPERATION Gumdrop was deadly serious. Mother had spent more than a year trying to infiltrate Umbra, a global crime syndicate made up of mercenaries, terrorists, and former intelligence agents. Its leader was a shadowy figure known simply as *Le Fantôme*, which was French for "the Ghost."

Little was known about him, although it was believed that, in addition to being a master criminal, he was also an avid art collector. This was why Mother went to

Paris posing as a black-market dealer with three priceless Monets. MI6 didn't think Le Fantôme would trust an underling to judge whether they were forgeries. If Mother could arrange a face-to-face meeting, he might be able to arrest him.

A key to this plan was setting up shop in an abandoned factory on the outskirts of the city. The factory had once manufactured candy, which was how Operation Gumdrop got its name.

Mother looked at the building through a rusted chain-link fence. Its royal-blue walls were dull and peeling. Broken windows lined the second floor, and the parking lot was overrun with weeds and wildflowers.

"Beautiful," he said, taking it all in. "Absolutely beautiful."

With bolt cutters for the chain on the fence and a lockpick for the main door, he was inside in less than ninety seconds. Skeletal remains of old machinery filled the factory floor and reminded him of the dinosaur exhibits at the Museum of Natural History. A wall was lined with giant sacks of sugar long since devoured by rats.

This was where he planned to set his trap. Just as rodents had been lured into the building by the sweet scent of sugar, Mother hoped Le Fantôme would be unable to resist the temptation of three stolen Monets, which were in fact masterful forgeries confiscated by Scotland Yard.

On the second floor Mother found a row of offices that had once housed *Confiserie Royale S.A.*—or the Royal Candy Corporation—a grandiose name for a company that manufactured low-quality gummies and lollipops. He looked in each office and found nothing of interest until he reached the final one.

As the beam from his flashlight swept the floor, he spied a blanket and pillow laid out like a bed. Next to them a row of books was neatly lined against the wall. He squatted down and ran his finger along their spines. Some titles were in English and others in French. He smiled when he noticed they'd been alphabetized by author.

He turned on a reading lamp by the pillow, and amber light filled a corner of the room. That's when he heard the rustling behind him. He spun around, rising to his feet, expecting to confront either an attacker or a rodent, but instead saw only a boy cowering behind an overturned desk.

Mother exhaled deeply and, once his pulse calmed, said, "*Bonjour.*"

The boy did not respond.

"Je ne suis pas la police," Mother told him. "I'm not the police."

He carefully placed the flashlight on the floor and held up empty hands to show that he meant no harm. The boy responded by cautiously moving out from behind the desk, keeping his back to the wall and his eyes fixed on the man. He looked to be about ten or eleven years old and wore several layers of clothes to fight the winter cold. He had dark skin and cropped hair, and he looked like he was ready to bolt for the door.

"Please don't run," said Mother. "You speak English, right?" He motioned to the books on the floor. "I say that because some of the books are in English and my French is not very good."

The boy did not answer but nodded.

"I'm not going to hurt you," Mother promised. "Is this your home?"

Another nod.

"Do you live here with the rest of your family?"

The boy spoke for the first time. "No family."

Mother noticed a dingy yellow electrical cord leading to a larger lamp in the corner of the room.

"I'm just going to reach over and turn this on," he said, slowly moving toward the lamp, careful not to scare the boy away. "So we can see better. Is that okay?"

"Yes."

This illuminated the entire room, and now Mother saw that, in addition to the makeshift bed and books, there was a drawer on the floor holding several items of neatly folded clothing. There was also a chess set with the pieces arranged in the middle of a game.

"Who are you playing?" he asked, worried another, possibly larger, person might be hiding nearby.

"I play myself."

Mother was both relieved and saddened. His first instinct was that the boy's accent was from Central Africa. That would mean he was far from home and completely alone. He examined the progress of the match and said, "You're good."

"Do you play?" asked the boy.

"I do."

"Want to play me?" This was accompanied by a hopeful grin.

"I wish I had the time," said Mother. "But unfortunately, I don't." His mind raced as he tried to solve this unexpected wrinkle in his plan. "You live here alone?"

"Yes."

"But the fence was locked. How'd you get in?"

"I have a secret way," said the boy. "So no one can follow me."

"Where is it?"

The boy smiled. "If I told you, it would not be a secret."

"Fair enough," Mother conceded. "Can you tell me your name? Or is that a secret too?"

"They call me *Le Roi du Paris.*"

At first he thought the boy had said "Leroy," as in the name, but then he remembered that in French "*le roi*" meant "the king." He chuckled. "You're the king of Paris?"

"They call me that to make fun of me, but I do not care."

"Well, I'm not going to make fun of you," said Mother. "So which would you rather I call you? Leroy or Paris?"

The boy shrugged. "Paris, I think."

"Okay, Paris, I'd like to make a business arrangement with you. I'd like to rent this building for the next month. I'll pay a generous rate."

"I do not understand."

"It's hard to explain," said Mother. "But I need this building . . . for my work."

"I will share it with you," said Paris. "There is enough room for us both. We can play chess when you are not working."

"I'm afraid that's not possible," he said. "It wouldn't

be safe for you. You need to go someplace else."

According to MI6 protocol, Mother had three options: cancel the operation, move to a different location, or use intimidation to get rid of Paris. But he'd spent a year getting to this point, the building was perfect for his needs, and he couldn't bring himself to threaten a child. So, he came up with a fourth option instead.

They went shopping.

Mother bought Paris new clothes and a winter coat. He arranged for him to stay in an MI6 safe house and fed him better than he'd ever been fed. They even squeezed in time for a few games of chess. Part of the arrangement, though, was that Paris was not allowed to come anywhere near the factory.

This was a rule the boy broke every evening just after sunset when he snuck back to spy on his new friend. Paris watched one night as Mother unloaded wooden crates from the back of a moving truck. Another time, he saw him installing hidden surveillance cameras. He couldn't imagine what the Englishman was planning, but his curiosity was piqued.

Paris didn't see anyone else there for three weeks, until he arrived one night to find two black Mercedes parked in front of the factory. A light snow had fallen, and one

car's engine was idling. He assumed someone was inside using the heater, although the tinted windows made it impossible to tell.

He crept closer and hid behind an abandoned delivery truck. When he heard people coming out of the building, he crawled under the truck to spy on them.

The group consisted of a woman and three men, with no sign of Mother. One man had a gun and constantly scanned the road, looking for possible threats. The other two carried narrow wooden boxes, which they loaded into one of the trunks.

A fourth man got out of the car and began an angry conversation with the others. He was bald with a gray-black beard and wire-framed glasses. Paris couldn't make out the language they spoke, so he crawled closer to hear better. He must have made a noise because two of the men instantly looked his way.

Paris pressed his body against the cold, hard ground and said a silent prayer, hoping they didn't see him. He tried not to move a muscle, but a moment later he heard a bang and the sound of glass exploding. He assumed the guard with the gun had shot at the truck and broken its windshield, but when he opened his eyes, everyone was looking up at the building.

There was more exploding glass, and Paris inched forward so he could look up from beneath the truck. That's when he saw the fire burning inside the factory. The sound had been a second-floor window shattering due to the heat. He waited for the people to react, but they just stood there watching the building burn.

In the same room where he first discovered Paris, Mother was about to die. His hands were tied behind his back, his feet were wrapped together with wire, and a rag had been forced into his mouth so he couldn't scream for help. He writhed on the floor, trying to break free, his face covered in sweat from the heat of the nearby flames. He strained with all his might, but there was nothing he could do to loosen the bindings. Each breath filled his lungs with smoke and brought him closer to death.

He closed his eyes and did his best to accept that this was where his life would come to an end. He tried to figure out where he'd gone wrong. How he'd wound up in this situation. But mostly he thought about the woman who Paris had seen outside the building.

It was Mother's wife, Clementine.

She was also an MI6 agent, yet she'd betrayed him

and their country to join forces with Umbra. How could she have done that? How could the woman he loved leave him to die in a fire?

He pushed those questions away and instead thought about their two children. He wanted their faces to be the last pictures in his mind. He heard the crackling of the wooden floor as the fire closed in on him, but just as he started to fade away, the gag was yanked from his mouth.

Mother hacked out smoke and opened his eyes, expecting to see his wife. But she wasn't his rescuer.

It was Paris.

"Get out of here," Mother said, coughing.

"Quiet," replied the boy. "They are still outside. Do not let them hear you."

The flames dancing along the wall cast eerie shadows on Paris's face as he struggled to free Mother's wrists.

"You need to save yourself," Mother insisted. "Even if you can untie me, we can't escape without them seeing us. They'll hurt you, too."

Finally the knot loosened and came undone. Paris smiled at Mother and said, "Maybe now I will show you my secret way out of the building."

The Welcoming Committee

Edinburgh, Scotland—Present Day

THE SOUNDS OF MORNING COMMUTERS echoed through Waverley station, interrupted every minute or so by a woman announcing arrivals and departures over the public address system. Paris had just gotten off the train from Aberdeen and was in a hurry as he expertly navigated the jumble of passengers and luggage trolleys that filled platform twelve.

It had been five years since he'd saved Mother from the fire, and during that time he'd grown seven inches and added fifty pounds. But his physical transformation was nothing compared to the other changes in his life. The Rwandan refugee who lived alone in an abandoned factory was now part of a family in which he played the role of protective older brother. He'd flourished in his new environment, adapting in every way except one: No matter how hard he tried, he simply could not get used to the weather.

Looking up through the glass-paneled roof, he saw the sky was nothing more than a dismal swirl of black and gray with no hint the sun even existed. "Another lovely day in Scotland," he muttered as he flipped up the collar of his overcoat and braced for the cool, damp air that would greet them outside the station. "Hurry up," he said, turning to the others. "We're on a schedule."

"So's my stomach," replied Rio, who'd stopped in front of a takeaway stall with a display case full of pasties. They'd skipped school in order to be at the airport when Sara arrived. And while Rio didn't mind missing class, he definitely minded missing lunch. "Just give me a minute," he said as he checked his wallet. "And spot me a fiver."

"No and no," Paris answered. "We don't have a minute, and you already owe me twenty quid."

Rio made an exasperated gesture toward Kat, who stood next to him eating an egg sandwich. "How come she has time to eat and I don't?"

"Because this morning, she got up early and packed a lunch," answered Paris.

"Once I checked the train timetables and factored in how long it would take to get to the airport, I knew I wouldn't get a chance to eat otherwise," she said before taking another bite.

"It's called planning ahead," Paris said. "You might try it sometime."

Rio pointed to the other half-sandwich she was carrying, its delicious goodness wrapped in neatly creased wax paper. "I don't suppose you factored sharing into your equation."

Kat tried not to laugh too hard with her mouth full.

"There'll be food at the airport," Paris promised as he headed up the exit ramp. "But right now we've got to move. If we're not there before they land, this whole trip will be a waste."

The three of them were serving as Sara's welcoming party, but with a twist. They weren't actually going to greet her so much as they were going to spy on her. After all, they worked for MI6. Spying was their specialty.

They wouldn't officially meet her until later at the house. But introductions like those were awkward, making it hard to get a good read on someone.

They were just weeks away from an important mission, and if she was going to be part of their team, they wanted their first impressions to be unfiltered. So rather than bringing balloons and a banner that read WELCOME TO THE UK, they headed for the airport with surveillance equipment and hidden transmitters ready for reconnaissance.

"I hope she's nice," Paris said as they exited onto Waverley Bridge. "And plays chess. I'm tired of beating you lot."

"I just want her to stay out of my room," said Kat. "I don't like it when people touch my things."

"Really?" Rio said. "We never would have guessed that from the padlock on your door or that expression you make whenever someone stands close to you."

She shot him a dirty look, and he laughed.

"Just stating facts," he said.

"Besides, it doesn't make sense to add someone right now," Kat continued. "There's not enough time to prepare."

"Well, it makes sense to Mother," said Paris. "And that's all that matters."

They boarded a sky-blue double-decker bus that ran from the train station to the airport, and found the top deck empty. The privacy allowed them to continue their "spy talk" as they sat sideways across the back three rows.

"What about you?" Paris asked Rio. "What do you hope she's like?"

"I'm with Kat," he said. "I don't think we should add anyone so close to a mission. But, if we're going to do it, I just hope she's younger than me. I'm tired of being the youngest."

"Why?" asked Kat. "What's bad about that?"

He gave her an incredulous look. "Every. Single. Thing. I get leftovers. I get hand-me-downs. And most of the time, I get overlooked."

Paris scoffed. "That's rubbish."

"Is it?" asked Rio. "Take today, for example. Why are you the alpha?"

"Because I'm the . . ." Paris thought about the right phrasing before saying, ". . . most experienced."

"That's just another way of saying 'oldest,'" said Rio. "Coming here was my idea, but I bet you never considered letting me plan it."

"I would've," he said defensively. "But it's a tricky mission."

"This isn't a mission," Rio protested. "A mission's nicking files from the Russian embassy without getting caught. Which we both did even though you got most of the credit. This is . . . *sightseeing.* We're just going to follow a girl."

"Hey," Kat said, offended.

"I'm not saying it because she's a girl," he responded. "I'm saying it because she hasn't had any training. We're not even going to come into contact with her. It's easy-peasy. But you still wouldn't let me be the alpha. And it's too bad, because I'd ace it."

Rio liked to joke, but Paris could tell this was different. This was something that had been building up inside him.

"I even solved the problem," Rio added.

"What problem?" asked Paris.

"The one you haven't mentioned because you don't know what to do about it," he answered.

Paris waited for more, but Rio didn't elaborate. "All right, enlighten me. What problem haven't I solved?"

Rio shook his head. "It doesn't matter what I think.

I'm not the alpha. I'm just a helper. I'll do what I'm told and keep my mouth shut. Even when this whole thing goes pear-shaped."

Paris turned to Kat, who rolled her eyes and nodded her approval.

"Okay," said Paris. "*You* can be the alpha."

"Really?"

"I'm handing you the reins, mate. Now, what's the problem?"

"This bus," Rio said, eager to share his thinking. "When she exits the airport, she's either going to take the bus or the tram into the city."

"What's the problem with that?" asked Kat.

"Following her means we need to get on board," he said. "That's fine on the tram because there're seven cars. But if she rides the bus, she'll likely see us. And then she'll recognize us tonight at dinner."

Paris nodded. "You're right. I *was* worried about that. What's your solution?"

"Three positions," Rio said. "First, a lookout right outside International Arrivals. The lookout identifies Sara and describes her to the others. Second, someone in the terminal to see if she takes the bus or the tram."

"And third?" asked Paris.

"Already waiting back in the city," Rio said with a sly grin. "No matter which way she goes, the third person has time to get to the bus stop or the tram station and follow her from there."

"That's clever," said Paris.

Rio grinned and kept going. "The key position is going to be the lookout. Mother always makes us split up as soon as we get through passport control. That means she'll be by herself when she comes through the door. The lookout has to pick her out of the crowd."

"Got it," said Kat.

Rio stopped and looked at her. "What do you mean, *got it*?"

"I mean I'll have no problem spotting her," she said, as if it were obvious.

"What makes you think you're the lookout?" asked Rio.

"Common sense, past experience," she replied. "The fact that I'm better at it than either of you."

Paris went to protest, but Kat held up a hand to stop him. "Just stating facts."

"Well, I'm sorry you feel that way, but you're wrong," replied Rio. "It's the hardest job. It's the most important job. And since I'm the alpha, I'm the lookout."

"But I'm . . ."

"No buts," Rio said, cutting her off. "There's no way I'm changing my mind."

"I'll give you the other half of my sandwich," she said, holding it up.

"Deal," he said without hesitation as he snatched it from her hand. "Kat's the lookout."

"Oh, you're some alpha," said Paris.

"You bet I am," Rio said as he unwrapped the sandwich and took a huge bite. "I was always going to make Kat the lookout. I was just hungry."

"That's okay," she replied. "I was always going to give you the sandwich."

"Where do I fit in this plan?" asked Paris.

"You're in the terminal," Rio said with a swallow. "I'm going to ride back to the city center and wait for her there."

Paris smiled. "Which gives you just enough time to run back to the pasty shop and get a pie."

"Traditional Cornish steak with beef, potatoes, and onions in a golden-brown crust," Rio replied, savoring the thought of it. "Like I said, it's the perfect plan. At least it is if you spot me the five quid."

The bus reached the airport, and the passengers started to get off. Paris reluctantly handed Rio a five-pound note and said, "That makes twenty-five you owe me now."

"I know," he said. "I'm good for it."

"Okay, is that everything?" Kat asked.

"Yes," answered Rio.

"Then say it," she told him. "It's the alpha's job, and we can't start without it."

Rio grinned from ear to ear. "This operation is hot. We are a go."

Chaos Theory

MOTHER LIKED TO MAKE UP LITTLE sayings, called Motherisms, to help his team remember key principles of spycraft. One of his favorites was *You can't look out if you stand out.* This was a reminder that an essential element of surveillance was disappearing into the background.

Kat often found this challenging in Scotland, where it seemed like everyone was fair-skinned. She was Nepali and had a dark complexion that most people mistook for Indian or Pakistani but was impossible to confuse with Scottish. Luckily, with travelers from around the world, the airport gave her plenty of places to blend in.

She found a perfect spot in the coffee shop near customs and immigration. Rather than solid walls, it had angled wooden slats designed to let in plenty of light. This gave her an ideal vantage point where she could hide from view but still see everyone passing through the International Arrivals gate.

Kat was an excellent lookout because she saw the world differently. The complex math that continuously ran through her head tended to make her socially awkward, but also let her identify patterns where everyone else saw chaos.

"I still don't understand how you do it," said Rio, talking to her through the tiny earpiece she was wearing. "What's the trick?"

"You think everything's a trick," she whispered into the microphone hidden in her coat's lapel. "But it's not. It's just maths."

Even though Rio had ridden the bus back to Edinburgh, and Paris was waiting in another part of the terminal, they were able to talk to each other using a custom-made communication app on their phones.

"How many passengers are on an international flight?" asked Rio.

"At least two hundred fifty," Paris answered, joining in the conversation.

"And how many have landed in the last half hour?"

Paris checked the arrivals monitor and answered, "Four: Bangkok, Amsterdam, Istanbul, and New York."

"That means there are at least one thousand people coming through Passport Control," said Rio. "How is finding one person out of a thousand not a trick?"

"Your first mistake is thinking of it as one thousand people," Kat answered. "It's easier to calculate as four groups of two hundred fifty. Each group acts as a single unit. They get off the plane together. They get their baggage together. They go through customs together. And you can instantly eliminate three of the groups."

"How?"

"Bangkok, Amsterdam, Istanbul, and New York have different ethnicities and styles of dress," she explained. "My only concern is the group that's predominantly American."

"That makes sense," said Paris. "But it still leaves you with two hundred fifty people."

"No, it leaves me with a single *group* made up of two

hundred fifty people," she replied. "And one person in that group won't fit in with the other two hundred forty-nine. That's your one in a thousand."

"I still don't get it," said Rio.

"I'd love to explain it in more detail," she replied. "But I just spotted Sara, so we should probably start following her."

"How confident are you that it's her?" asked Rio.

"I didn't say *I think* I spotted her," replied Kat. "I said I spotted her. That means I'm one-hundred-percent confident. She looks about twelve years old. Latina. Brown hair pulled back in a ponytail. Jeans and a blue sweatshirt with white trainers. I'm sending a picture."

Kat pretended to text someone but actually snapped a photo of Sara and sent it to the others.

"How can you be positive it's her?" pressed Rio.

"I could go through the maths again," she replied. "Or you could just look at the picture and see that she's carrying Sydney's purple rucksack."

The key to spotting Sara had been simple. The pattern she didn't fit was that she was a twelve-year-old girl by herself instead of with her parents. Kat knew to look for that because Mother always insisted they separate in an airport. He said the combination of queues and cameras made it the easiest place for a spy to be photographed and identified.

Between airport security, government surveillance, and tourists taking vacation snaps, you were bound to have your picture taken multiple times. And, with the advances in facial recognition software, there was always a danger he could be identified, which is why he didn't want any of the kids on the team to risk having their picture taken with him.

Mother also saw this as a chance for Sara's RV test. He gave her detailed instructions to an RV, or rendezvous point, in the city. They were stored in a new mobile phone along with an emergency number in case she got lost. Sara was determined not to use the number. She wanted to ace her tests. Her first instruction was to find the sign marked AIRLINK BUS.

"Paris, she's moving toward you," said Kat.

"I got her," he replied.

"Roger that," Kat answered as she left the coffee shop and disappeared into the crowd. She needed to make sure Mother and Sydney didn't spot her when they came through the gate.

Paris stood by a Visit Scotland kiosk trying to blend in with a group of students on a school trip. As Sara walked toward him, he got a good look at her face. He noticed her eyes were darting side to side, trying to take everything in.

"She looks nervous," he said to the others.

"That's understandable," said Kat. "I was terrified when I arrived."

"Not me," Rio said confidently.

"Really?" Paris retorted. "Because I could've sworn that was you crying yourself to sleep the first few nights at the farm."

There was silence on the other end, and Paris felt bad for bringing it up.

Sara checked the directions on her phone right before she passed Paris. He gave her about ten feet before he started following. Once they exited the terminal, he closed the gap enough to eavesdrop on her conversation with the attendant at the Airlink ticket window.

"Is this the bus to Waverley Bridge?" she asked.

"Yes," answered the man. "It's four and a half pounds."

She gave him a confused look. "Four and a half pounds of what?"

"That's the price of the fare."

It took a moment, and then Sara flashed an embarrassed smile. "Right. Because here pounds are money and not how much something weighs." She handed him one of the five-pound notes Mother had given her and boarded the bus.

Paris chuckled to himself and kept walking. "I can already tell that I like her," he said to the others. "She just got on the one hundred bus and should be there in twenty minutes, Rio. Kat and I will take the tram and catch up with you."

"Roger that," mumbled Rio, his mouth full of Cornish beef pasty.

"Sounds like you've already spent my money," said Paris. "How's the pie?"

"Delicious," Rio answered, contorting his body so no gravy dripped on his shirt. "Absolutely delicious."

The pie was an appropriate reward for what had been a good morning. Not only had Rio stood up for himself but also now his plan was working perfectly. This was the first time he'd been an alpha for anything other than practice. Although Mother wouldn't know about it, at least Paris and Kat would see what he could do.

His problem wasn't just that he was the youngest. He felt like he was overlooked because he wasn't as good a student as the others. School was a struggle, and this was a chance to show that his street smarts more than made up for it.

He finished the pasty and took a position on Waverley Bridge, which connected the old part of the city and its medieval streets to the new, modern section. He spotted Sara as she got off the bus and walked toward New Town.

"I've got her," he told the others. "She's heading toward Princes Street."

"It'll take another fifteen minutes for the tram to get there," Paris responded. "So you're on your own until then."

"I can handle it," he answered cockily. "Like I told you, easy-peasy."

Princes Street was the city's main shopping avenue. One side was lined with stores and boutiques while the other ran beside a mile-long park that provided postcard-perfect views of Edinburgh Castle. Sara stopped several times to make sure she was following the directions properly, once making a U-turn only to spin around and head back in the original direction a few feet later.

"There's no way she'll be ready for a mission in three weeks," Rio said to the others. "She's totally lost."

"It's a new city," Paris said, defending her.

"We go to a lot of new cities and can't afford to stop and ask directions," Rio replied.

He followed her into Jenners, a large department store that filled an entire city block. It had operated out of the same location since 1838, and its three-story atrium was ideal for spy work. Rio would've looked out of place following Sara through women's fashions on the middle level but was able to watch her from the balcony of home furnishings one floor above.

"We're in Jenners," he said. "This may be the RV location."

"Careful," said Paris. "Mother and Sydney could be nearby."

"Yes, I know that," answered Rio.

"Keep your distance, and make sure they don't see you," Paris continued.

"I know that, too," Rio replied, exasperated.

"We're off the tram and headed your way," said Paris. "As soon as we get there, we can take turns tailing her."

Rio tried to ignore the fact that Paris was giving instructions like he was the alpha. "Roger that."

"Think it's the RV?" asked Kat.

"Don't know," said Rio. "Right now, she's looking at watches."

"Any sign of Mother or Sydney?" asked Paris.

"Don't you think I would've mentioned that when Kat asked me if I thought this was the RV?" Rio replied. "Letting me be the alpha means not treating me like I'm a total plank."

"Sorry, mate," Paris said. "Old habits."

Rio watched intently as Sara tried on several watches. The salesperson helping her was distracted when another customer asked a question. When she looked away, Sara slyly slid one of the jewelry boxes off the counter and into her backpack.

Rio was so stunned, it took him a moment to react. "I don't believe it!" he exclaimed. "I don't believe it!"

"What?" asked Paris.

"She just nicked a watch."

The salesperson turned her attention back to Sara, who was once again admiring the watch she had on. The woman obviously had no idea that one of the boxes was missing.

"What do you mean?" asked Paris.

"I mean she nicked a watch," said Rio. "It was on the counter, and she slipped it into her backpack when the saleswoman looked away."

Sara handed the watch she was trying on back to the

woman and left the counter. Once she was about fifteen feet away, she picked up her pace.

"That doesn't make sense," said Kat. "Why would she do that?"

"I'll make sure to ask her," Rio replied as he tried to keep up. "But right now she's doing a runner."

Rio bumped into a couple looking at living room furniture, and by the time he got around them, Sara had disappeared into the crowd. He sprinted to the stairs and tried to close the gap, but when he reached the ground floor, there was no sign of her.

He couldn't believe it. He took a deep breath before admitting to the others, "She's gone. I lost her. I *am* a total plank."

Moments later Paris and Kat arrived to find Rio standing on his tiptoes looking for Sara among the people on the sidewalk. He was frustrated and embarrassed. He'd blown his first chance as an alpha. The others were more concerned with the idea that Sara was a thief.

They crossed the street and sat on a park bench next to the statue of David Livingstone, a famous Scottish explorer.

"What are we going to do?" asked Paris.

Rio gave him a look. "If we tell Mother, then we have

to admit we skipped school and spied on her. He'll be brassed off."

"But we know she's a thief," he replied. "We can't just let her join the team with this mission coming up. How many different ways can that go wrong?"

"You're right," said Rio. "We've got to tell him, even if it means getting in trouble."

Haystacks

MOTHER AND SYDNEY WERE ON THE upper level of the Scottish National Gallery admiring a painting of haystacks when Sara came up behind them.

"Found you," she said with an easy smile.

Mother checked his watch and raised an eyebrow. "You were supposed to *find us* twelve minutes ago."

She cringed. "Does that mean I failed?"

"No . . . you passed . . . but only just," he said. "Remember: *Bad guys never wait, so good guys can't be late.*"

"Catchy," said Sara.

"*Motherisms*," said Sydney. "You get used to them."

"Let me guess," Sara said, pointing at the painting. "You picked haystacks because finding a rendezvous point's like finding a needle in a haystack?"

He laughed. "No, but I wish I had. You're very clever, Sara."

"Not everybody likes that about me," she said sheepishly. "In some of the houses where I've lived, being clever was considered a bad thing."

"Fear not," he replied. "We're quite fond of cleverness on the farm. Now let's get you there so you can see for yourself."

Sara walked toward the exit, but changed direction when she noticed Mother and Sydney going the opposite way. As she hurried to catch up, she asked, "We don't actually live on a farm, do we?"

"That's just what we call it," answered Sydney. "You'll understand when we get there."

Mother led them down a hallway of offices before stopping at an elevator marked STAFF ONLY. He pressed the down button.

"Is this another test?" asked Sara. "Because I don't think we're supposed to use this elevator."

The door opened with a ding, and Mother and Sydney got in. He turned and asked, "Why not?"

"Because it's only for employees."

He pointed at an ID badge clipped to his belt. "I am an employee."

Sara couldn't believe it. She stepped in and asked, "How many fake IDs do you have?"

"I've not counted, but it's quite a lot," Mother said with a chuckle. He pushed a button, and the elevator lurched into motion. "Although this one's legit. I really work here."

Sara studied his expression. "I don't know how to tell if you're joking or not."

"I'm not," he said. "I'm a consultant specializing in art of the late-nineteenth and early-twentieth centuries. You know that Monet painting of the haystacks?"

"What about it?"

"I helped the museum acquire it last year. I'm quite proud of that."

Downstairs they exited the building into a small employee parking lot and headed straight for a sports car that looked like it belonged in a James Bond movie. It was sleek, with tinted windows and a matte black paint job. As she walked toward it, Sara wondered if it came fully loaded with secret weapons and an ejector seat. She was just about to run her fingers along the body when Mother called her.

"Sorry, but that's not ours," he said.

She turned to see that he and Sydney had stopped at an oldish Volvo station wagon that looked more *mom* than *Bond*.

"Contrary to what you've seen at the cinema, spies have practical cars that don't attract attention," he said. "Driving that would spoil the whole *secret* part of 'secret agent.' Besides, we've got too many people. We need more seating."

"And room for groceries," added Sydney.

"Excellent point," said Mother. "The boys are voracious eaters."

"You can have the front seat," Sydney said, holding open the passenger door. "You'll get a better view."

Before they drove off, Mother leaned over conspiratorially and whispered, "There is, however, one special feature, if you'd like to press that button."

He pointed at a button on the dashboard.

"Really?" Sara said.

"Just make sure everyone's got their seat belts on."

She clicked her seat belt, checked the others, and then

cautiously reached for the button. When she pressed it . . . the engine started, and Mother let out a cackle.

"Okay," Sara said, grinning but a bit embarrassed. "You got me."

"Forget the movies," he said. "The life of a spy is nothing like 007."

They pulled out of the gravel car park and drove north out of the city.

"So in addition to being a spy you're also a museum consultant," she said. "Any other jobs I should know about?"

"I'm caretaker of a small airfield," he said. "It's a little grass runway next to the farm. During World War II it was an RAF base, and now it's open a few days a week for use by private planes."

"And MI6 is okay with all these side jobs?"

"They can't really complain," he answered. "As far as they're concerned, I'm dead."

Sara gave him a curious look. "It just gets stranger and stranger with you."

"And you've only scratched the surface," Sydney chimed in from the backseat.

"Officially speaking, I died in that fire," Mother explained. "I was double-crossed by our own agents, none of whom know Paris rescued me. So when I contacted my superior and told her what happened, my instructions were to lie low and disappear. Meanwhile, she convinced French police to report that the body of an unidentified man had been found in the factory. Internally at MI6, it was understood that I was that body."

"That way any agents passing information to Umbra told their handlers that Mother was no longer a worry," Sydney added.

"The thinking is that a dead agent can accomplish more than a living one," said Mother. "That's why they hid me in the middle-of-nowhere Scotland. There are only a handful of people inside the Service who know I'm alive, which means they can't pay me without attracting attention. The museum and airfield jobs let me earn a salary without anything leading back to MI6."

"Do you even know anything about the art of the late-nineteenth and early-twentieth centuries?"

"I have an MA in art history from the University of St. Andrews," he said proudly. "My cover as an agent was posing as a black-market art dealer."

"But what if you cross paths with someone from the art world who recognizes you?" asked Sara. "Won't they find out you're alive?"

"Paris saved me from the fire," he said. "But I was badly burned and needed surgery. When they operated, they altered my appearance."

"How much?" asked Sara.

"If she were alive today, my own mother wouldn't recognize me," he said. "And sometimes I'm still a bit surprised when I look in the mirror and see who's there."

They drove north along the coast through farms and fishing villages like nothing Sara had ever seen. She especially liked looking out at the dark storm clouds forming over the North Sea. Finally, she asked the question that had nagged at her since Mother told her about the fire.

"What about your wife?" she asked cautiously. "She was one of the agents who double-crossed you, right?"

"Clementine," he answered. "We worked together for fifteen years and were married for twelve. I have no idea how Umbra corrupted her, but they flipped her to their side and she helped set me up."

He said this without emotion, but Sara knew it had to be devastating.

"What happened to her?"

"After the fire, she disappeared with Annie and Robert."

"Are they other agents?"

"No." He paused for a moment. "They're my children. Our children, I mean. Mine and Clemmie's."

"You have kids?!" She said it more as an exclamation than a question.

"Yes," he said. "Annie's fourteen and Robert's eleven."

"And you don't know where they are?"

He shook his head. "No. At MI6, Clementine's specialty was *vanishing* assets."

"What's that?" asked Sara.

"Say a Russian spy flipped sides and joined forces with the British, she would erase all trace of his previous existence and create an entirely new identity. There's no one better at scrubbing a trail than Clemmie. She's certainly done a good job hiding Robert and Annie. I know, because I've been looking." He paused for a moment. "But no one knows her methods better than I do. I will find them."

Soon they reached a sign reading WEATHER STATION and AIRFIELD. An arrow pointed them down a dirt road to a squat air traffic control tower next to a grass landing strip. RAF AISLING was painted in faded letters on the side of the tower along with the blue, white, and red roundel that symbolized the Royal Air Force.

"This is where you work?" asked Sara.

"And where I live," he said. "I've got a little flat—an apartment—in the tower."

"Luckily, our home's a bit more grand," Sydney added with a laugh.

Sara laughed too when she saw what Sydney was talking about.

Just beyond the airfield was a sprawling three-story stone house overlooking the sea. It had a turret on one side, and Sara wondered if it might technically be a castle.

Curiously, the roof and surrounding yard were filled with scientific equipment. There was a radar tower, wind turbine, antennae, and various other weather instruments. Mother parked the station wagon in front of the house, and Sara noticed a sign that said THE FOUNDATION FOR ATMOSPHERIC RESEARCH AND MONITORING.

Mother turned to her and smiled. "Welcome to FARM."

FARM

THE FIRST THING THAT GREETED THEM inside the house was a portrait of a large, jowly man with a pencil-thin mustache and thick glasses. In the painting he was standing next to a globe and holding an anemometer, a device for measuring wind speed.

"Who's this?" Sara asked.

"The twenty-fourth baron of Aisling," answered Sydney. "But we just call him Big Bill."

"It was thought that the twenty-third baron had no surviving relatives," said Mother. "But, right before he passed away, a successful industrialist and distant cousin named William Maxwell was discovered living in Los Angeles. As the only heir, he inherited all of this."

"If he inherited it, why are we here?" asked Sara.

"He didn't want to leave sunny California for gloomy Scotland," said Sydney. "And since he was already rich, he decided to use his inheritance to create the Foundation for Atmospheric Research and Monitoring. That's how an old Scottish manor house become a state-of-the-art weather station and research center."

"You'll have to memorize all this for the tours," said Mother.

"Tours?"

"Weather Weirdos," Sydney said, shaking her head. "They knock on the door at all hours and ask to look around."

"I prefer the term 'meteorology enthusiasts,'" said Mother. "And we're happy to welcome them. It's all part of our mission as defined by the baron. He thought the study of ocean and weather patterns was vitally important. The fact that this house overlooks the North Sea made it an ideal location to do both."

"So he turned it into a weather station, but he stayed in California?" asked Sara.

"He made one visit," Mother said. "During which he posed for this portrait and cut the ribbon at the grand-opening ceremony. He also gave a rousing speech about the importance of climate research long before it was fashionable."

"A shame nobody heard it," said Sydney.

"Why not?"

"Because the grand opening was held on the second of June, 1953," said Mother. "The same day as Queen Elizabeth's coronation."

"Not surprisingly, most people chose to watch their new queen receive her crown rather than listen to some crackpot millionaire talk about the weather," said Sydney.

"I prefer the term 'eccentric philanthropist,'" said Mother. "But, otherwise, yes."

"Why didn't he just reschedule it?" Sara asked. "He had to know no one would come."

"That was the intent," answered Mother. "Fewer attendees meant fewer questions and fewer chances to blow his cover. You see, the twenty-third baron of Aisling really didn't have any surviving relatives. Big Bill wasn't a successful industrialist; rather he was a small-time Hollywood actor who specialized in portraying successful industrialists. He was hired by MI6 to play a role because in addition to studying the ocean, this house was perfectly situated to study the Soviet Union."

Sara's eyes opened wide. "I wondered how MI6 figured into this."

"This is the part we don't mention on the tours," said Mother. "FARM was a covert listening station throughout the Cold War. All the equipment that studied the climate was specially designed to also eavesdrop on our Russian counterparts. The upstairs was turned into a dormitory able to house up to eight spies."

"Spies who posed as scientists working at the weather station?"

"Exactly," he said. "Although it wasn't just posturing. They spied *and* conducted scientific research. FARM continues to be a working weather station to this day. That's the key to its cover and the reason why *meteorology enthusiasts*"—he shot a look at Sydney—"come knocking on the door. But with advancing technologies and changing politics, the eavesdropping component went away. That's when MI6 converted it into a cryptography center."

"But if its cover's still as a weather station," said Sara, "how do a bunch of kids living here not ruin it?"

"We're part of the FARM Fellows Program, which

engages talented but disadvantaged youth from around the world and helps us become the next generation of climate scientists," Sydney said, as if reciting from a brochure. "That's also part of the tour."

"FARM Fellows?" Sara asked.

"Just flows off the tongue, doesn't it?" said Sydney. "At Kinloch they call us the *farmers*, and they don't mean it as a compliment."

"You may be farmers," said a voice with a pleasant Scottish accent, "but they're just *farmadach*."

Sara turned to see a woman in her midthirties with dark red hair down to her shoulders. She wore black jeans, a thick sweater, and a pair of boots known as "Wellies."

"Farmadach?" asked Sydney.

"It's Scottish for jealous," replied the woman. "They're envious because they're stuck in that fussy old school and you get to live here with me."

"You must be Ms. Montgomery," said Sara.

"Call me Monty." She shook Sara's hand. "It's lovely to meet you."

"We were telling Sara all about Big Bill and FARM," said Mother. "I was just going to explain how—"

"Sounds riveting, but I'm sure it can wait," Monty

interrupted. "This poor girl's had an arduous forty-eight hours. The least we can do is let her catch her breath." She turned to Sara. "You must be knackered."

Sara gave her a confused look.

"Exhausted," explained Monty.

"I hadn't really thought about it, but yeah," she answered. "I'm . . . *knackered.*"

"Why don't I show you to your room," said Monty. "You can relax. Maybe even take a short nap. I'd recommend that, actually. It helps fight the jet lag."

"Sounds good," said Sara.

"But I haven't even gotten to the part where MI6 sent Paris and me to live here," Mother said.

"You mean the day the circus came to town," Monty replied with a playful laugh. "As I said, it can wait."

Just beyond the portrait of Big Bill was a grand staircase, and Sara followed Monty up to the second floor. "Who's my roommate? Sydney or Kat?"

"Neither," answered Monty. "Everyone has a room to themselves."

"Really?"

"It's not very big, but it's all yours," she said.

Upstairs was a long hallway with four rooms on each end. Monty pointed to the right and said, "The boys live over there, which explains the assortment of odors." She headed the other way. "You're down here with Kat and Syd. The three of you have your own loo, which you're all responsible for keeping clean."

"Got it," said Sara.

"You also have some chores," she added. "Nothing drastic; laundry, Hoovering, that sort of thing. It's a secret facility, so we can't exactly hire staff to clean up."

"Of course." Sara pointed at a padlocked door. "What's with that?"

"Kat's still working on some sharing issues," Monty said. "She's rather protective of her privacy."

"I'll make sure to remember that," said Sara.

As they reached the end of the hall, Monty said, "And here we are."

Sara opened the door and couldn't believe her eyes. In spite of Monty's warning about its size, the room seemed huge to her. There was a bed along one wall, a desk and chair next to the window, and a tall dresser with a mirror. Best of all was the view of the sea. It was spectacular.

"This is mine?" she asked, stunned.

"Yes."

"I've never had a room of my own."

"You can do it up however you'd like," said Monty.

"I know Sydney got you some clothes in New York, and this morning I picked up some more. Just a few basics to hold you over." She motioned to the closet where the clothes hung neatly. "Soon as we get a chance, you and I can go into Edinburgh and start filling out your wardrobe. The shops there are stellar."

"That sounds amazing."

"Now, you take a wee nap," Monty told her. "I'll call you for dinner in a few hours. Tonight's my night to cook, so I'm making roast beef. It's my specialty."

"Yum."

"Everyone will be home by then, so we can do some proper introductions and Mother can tell you even more about Big Bill and FARM."

Monty went to leave, but Sara took hold of her arm. "Thank you," she said softly. "Thank you so much."

"It's my pleasure. We're delighted to have you."

Monty left the room, closing the door behind her, and for the first time in as long as Sara could remember, she enjoyed a feeling of total peace and privacy. It felt like . . . *home.*

She opened the window, and a blast of cool salt air filled the room. The view was unlike any she'd ever seen. The overcast sky blended into the dark choppy water, so there was no way to tell where one ended and the other began.

"It's perfect," she said to herself.

Sitting at the foot of her bed, she unzipped her back-pack and pulled out the shoebox she'd saved from her old house. The box contained photographs, a few small objects, and a snow globe from the Coney Island light-house.

The globe no longer held water, and its plastic shell had been broken and pieced back together with tape now yellowed with age. It had been a present from her *abuela*, who passed away when Sara was seven, and it was Sara's most prized possession. She momentarily lifted it out of the box, as if to show it their new home, then carefully put it back before placing the box on the top shelf of the closet.

Next, she sat at the desk and looked through the drawers. In one there was a small pad of paper and a stray computer flash drive. In another she found a pencil, along with some paper clips, rubber bands, and a tube of strawberry-scented lip gloss. She took the paper and pencil and wrote a note. When she finished, she folded it twice and laid it on the desk.

Content, she sucked in another lungful of sea air and moved over to the bed, where she lay down and fell into a deep and wonderful sleep.

The Dinner

DINNER WAS DOOMED BEFORE THE ROAST beef even made it out of the oven.

While Sara slept in her new room, Paris, Kat, and Rio were on the train from Edinburgh plotting ways to keep her off the team.

"First thing we do when we walk in the door is tell Mother the truth," said Rio. "We can't go on a mission with someone we can't trust."

"What if he wants to give her a second chance?" asked Paris.

"Coming here *was* her second chance," Rio replied. "I heard Mother tell Sydney they had to get her out of jail. Who knows what kind of trouble she was in back in the States. She's a thief, not a spy."

When they reached the FARM, Sydney was looking at a Stevenson screen, a wooden box with slats that sat on a pole like an oversize birdhouse and held weather instruments. She was recording data in a notebook when she saw them.

"I thought you were going to take these readings for me while I was gone," she said, glaring at Rio.

He mumbled some excuse, and Sydney let it drop.

Paris noticed the car was gone. "Where's Mother?"

"He went to see a cobbler," she answered.

This caught the others off guard.

"Why?" asked Rio.

"Paperwork for Sara," she said. "The new girl from New York."

"Already?"

"The mission's in a few weeks," replied Sydney. "There's no time to wait."

Cobblers were spies who specialized in making false documents, like birth certificates and passports, necessary to create a cover identity. If Mother was having those made, that meant he already considered Sara part of the team.

"Did she go with him?" asked Paris.

"No," said Sydney. "She's taking a nap."

"She's in the dormitory *by herself*?" Rio asked, dismayed.

"That's generally how people sleep," said Sydney.

"Good thing I padlocked my door," Kat said under her breath.

"What's that supposed to mean?" snapped Sydney.

"Nothing," Kat said. "Just a joke."

They'd already decided not to say anything to Sydney or Monty until they'd spoken to Mother. Unfortunately, he still hadn't returned by the time they were helping with dinner. That's when Sara came into the kitchen, still a bit groggy and wearing a dark blue hoodie that Monty had bought for her.

"That smells incredible," she said.

"Ah, Sara," said Sydney. "I was just about to come get you."

Sydney handled some quick introductions, and when Sara asked what she could do to help, Monty told her, "You can help tomorrow, but tonight you're the guest of honor. Just go have a seat at the table."

The dining room was large, and Sara assumed the paintings on the wall were portraits of the various barons and baronesses of Aisling. Thirty seconds after she sat down, Kat entered the room to set out plates.

"You're in my chair," she said.

"I didn't realize certain chairs belonged to specific people," said Sara.

"They do," said Kat. "And that one's mine."

"Sorry." She pointed at the seat next to her. "How about here?"

"No," said Kat. "That's Rio's."

Living in six different foster homes had taught Sara the importance of standing up for herself, but also the significance of not making waves on the first day. "What about there?" she asked, pointing at the seat directly across the table from her.

"That'd be fine if you were Sydney, but you're not Sydney, so no," said Kat.

Sara's patience was running out. "Fine. Then where should I sit?"

Reluctantly Kat pointed at the seat next to Sydney's. "That'll do, I guess."

Sara got up and moved to the new seat. "Nice to meet you too," she said, her snark totally lost on Kat.

From here, things only got worse.

Mother got home just before the food reached the table, so Paris never got a chance to talk to him alone. He didn't know what to do. It wasn't like he could say, *Please pass the mushy peas, and oh, by the way, Sara's a thief.* So he and the others just sat quietly and waited.

"Sunday roast on a Friday, what a treat this is," Mother said as he went to take a bite. "I don't know about you, but I'm Hank Marvin."

Sara had a perplexed look and turned to Monty. "Who's Hank Marvin?" she whispered.

"It's not a 'who,'" said Monty. "It just means he's hungry."

Sara looked even more confused until Mother explained. "Rhyming slang," he said. "Hank Marvin rhymes with starvin', so it means 'hungry.'"

"How is it we speak the same language, yet I don't understand about a third of what anyone's saying?" asked Sara.

There were some snickers across the table, and Sara instantly felt self-conscious. An awkward silence was filled with the sounds of forks and knives clinking on plates, so Monty tried to break the ice. "Sara, why don't you tell us a little bit about yourself?"

"Um, okay," she said as she gave her chin a nervous wipe with her napkin. "I was born in Puerto Rico but spent most of my life in Brooklyn. I enjoy reading and play a little soccer, but my true love is computers."

"Football," Rio said curtly.

"What's that?" asked Sara.

"It's another one of those words you don't seem to know," he said. "Its proper name is football, not soccer."

There was a meanness to his tone that caught Mother off guard. He shot Rio an angry look, and Monty tried to salvage the conversation.

"I love computers too," she said. "That's why I joined the SIS. They have all the best ones."

"They do?" asked Sara.

"After university I went straight to work as a crypto math researcher at the Doughnut," she said. "That's a building in Cheltenham that looks like a massive doughnut and houses the Government Communications Headquarters. The computers there were mind-blowing."

"Then why'd you leave?" asked Sara.

"I loved the work but hated the boys' club."

"What do you mean by that?"

"GCHQ is mostly staffed by men," said Mother. "And

a lot of them are intimidated by women who are significantly smarter than they are."

"And Monty's pretty much smarter than everybody on the planet," said Sydney.

Monty ignored the compliment and continued. "When MI6 converted this into a cryptography station, I jumped at the chance to run it. I grew up in Edinburgh, so it was close to home and far from office politics. The best of both worlds."

There was another lull in the conversation, and at this point Mother had had enough. He looked at Kat, Rio, and Paris all on one side of the table. "Is there something going on that I should know about?"

Paris shook his head. "No."

"I find that hard to believe," said Mother. "Because we've got a new team member who just flew across an ocean, and you're treating her like day-old fish."

Kat and Rio both looked at Paris, who nodded reluctantly. "Okay, there is something."

Everyone waited, but he stopped there.

"We're on pins and needles, mate," said Mother.

"Go ahead," Paris said as he nudged Rio. "Tell them."

"Why me?"

"You're the one who told us," he replied.

"I really want to apologize," Mother said to Sara, trying to keep his temper. "This behavior defies expectation. It's like aliens have taken over their bodies."

"She's a thief!" Rio blurted out.

"What?" asked Mother.

"Sara nicked a watch today in Edinburgh," answered Rio. "From the jewelry counter at Jenners."

"That's not possible!" exclaimed Sydney. "She was with us."

"Was she?" asked Paris. "You saying she didn't leave the airport by herself and meet you at an RV?"

"Well, yes," said Sydney. "But she wasn't alone long enough to go to Jenners and steal a watch."

"Yes, she was," said Rio.

"What makes you say that?" asked Mother.

"I saw her do it," he said.

"Some trick," said Monty. "Considering you were at school."

There was a pause before Rio answered, "Paris, Kat, and I skipped school and went to Edinburgh so we could get our own first impressions."

"Okay," Monty said. "The three of you just earned a significant addition to your chores list. But we'll deal with that later."

"Why would you do that?" asked Mother. "Why would you go into Edinburgh to spy on her?"

"Because dinners like this are so awkward," Rio said. "We wanted to have an unfiltered view of her, and we got one. I saw her try on watches and then when the saleswoman looked the other way, she put one in her backpack." He looked directly at Sara. "Go ahead. Tell them I'm lying."

"Do it," said Sydney. "Tell them it's all rubbish."

Sara looked across the table at them and took a deep breath. Then she looked at Mother, and it seemed like she was on the verge of tears.

"Sara?" he asked, not wanting to believe it.

She dug into the kangaroo pocket of her hoodie and pulled out the box from Jenners, which she placed on the table in front of Mother.

"Here," she said. "I wanted to get you a present. For helping me so much."

Mother was dumbfounded. "I'm sorry. I don't understand."

"Open it," she replied. "I think you'll like it."

That's when he remembered the watch in the courtroom. They'd talked about him getting a new one, a posh one. "Sara, you have seriously misinterpreted what we're all about," he said. "You shouldn't have stolen a watch for me. We don't break the law like that."

She closed her eyes for a second and said, "Please, just open it."

Everyone was quiet as Mother picked up the box and opened it. Instead of a watch, he found a folded piece of paper.

"Read the note," Sara said. "Out loud, to everyone."

Utterly confused, Mother unfolded the paper and began reading. "'I'm sorry to have done this, but I had to prove to the others that I was up to the challenge. No matter what you and Sydney told them, they would've had their doubts about me. I needed to show them without your help what I could do. This is the reason I was twelve minutes late. By the way, you still need a new watch.'"

He looked up at her. "I'm sorry, but I'm baffled."

Monty started to laugh. "That's bloody brilliant," she said. "I love it!"

Her reaction only confused the others more.

"Where's the watch?" asked Rio. "What'd you do with it?"

"I didn't steal a watch," Sara answered, flashing him a look. "I'm no thief."

"I saw it with my own eyes," he said.

"No," she said. "You saw what I wanted you to see. You saw me steal an empty box."

Now Mother started to smile. "That's impressive," he said, piecing it together, his voice barely able to contain his glee.

"What's impressive?" asked Paris.

"You fell for the nugget," Mother said. "In the middle of an RV test, fresh off the plane with absolutely no training, she set out a nugget, and you fell for it. Go ahead, Sara, tell them."

"Okay, at first I just thought they were part of the test," she said. "I thought they were there to make sure I didn't mess up." She looked right at Paris. "Sydney showed me some pictures of you all when we were on the plane, so I recognized you when I saw you at the airport. You were trying to blend in with that school group, except they all had matching sweatshirts and you didn't."

"What?" he asked.

"Let me show you."

She pulled out her phone and showed everyone a picture she'd snapped of Paris when she was pretending to read directions. "Look at their sweatshirts," she said.

"They're blue with that logo, but you're in an overcoat. That's how I first noticed you. Then you followed me out toward the bus."

"You let her take your picture?" Rio said in disbelief.

"I got yours, too," she said. She flipped through the images on her phone. "Here you are on Princes Street. I spotted you in the reflection of the shop window." She flipped to another picture. "And here you are in Jenners."

Rio slumped in his chair.

"That's when I had the idea about shoplifting. I knew you couldn't follow me into the women's department without standing out, so I went there to buy myself a little time. When I saw the jewelry display case, I knew what I had to do. I told the saleswoman that I needed a box to wrap my mother's birthday present. I even offered to pay for it, because, despite what you think, I don't steal things. She said she had plenty and gave me one. I put it in my backpack when she was looking the other way so you'd think I'd stolen it."

Kat looked at Rio and then Paris, shaking her head with disappointment. "I would like to point out that I'm the only one she didn't get a picture of."

"No," said Sara. "But I saw you in the coffee shop in the airport."

"You lot are pathetic," Sydney said to them. "First you're pathetic because you spied on her. Then you're pathetic because she *saw* you spy on her. Who was the alpha of this little catastrophe?"

Kat and Paris both looked at Rio, who reluctantly raised a finger.

"Me."

"Should've guessed," Sydney said. "You're always asking, 'How come I never get to call the shots?' Well, here's your answer. Good thing Sara's not Umbra or the three of you'd be dead."

There was quiet around the table as everyone considered what had happened. Paris and Kat looked embarrassed, but Rio was devastated. He knew that he'd take the brunt of the blame because he'd been in charge.

"I wasn't trying to embarrass anyone," Sara said. "I was just trying to prove something."

"What was that?" asked Mother.

"That I can do this," she said. "There's a mission coming up in three weeks. I don't know what it is, but I know I want to be a part of it. I want to fill in for Charlotte."

This caught everyone by surprise.

"You told her about Charlotte?" Rio asked Sydney.

"On a plane where someone could overhear you?"

"I know better than that," said Sydney. "I didn't say a word."

"Nobody told me anything," said Sara. "I figured it out."

"How could you?" asked Mother.

Sara reached into her pocket again and pulled out two items: the lip gloss and the flash drive. "I found these in my room," she said. "The lip gloss is new, so it seems like a solid guess that a girl's been living there recently."

Mother and Monty shared a look, impressed by her reasoning.

"Before I came down here, I checked our bathroom—sorry, I mean *loo*," Sara continued, with a glance at Rio. "And there were three different shampoos on the shelf, which seemed odd considering there were only two different girls using that bathroom. Someone had used a marker to label one of the shampoos 'C-H-A-R-period.' That could be short for Charlene, but that doesn't make sense because everyone takes a city as their name, and to my knowledge there is no city called Charlene. There is, however, a city in the United States called Charlotte."

By now, she had the rapt attention of everyone at the table.

"Which brings me to this." She held up the drive. "It looks like a normal flash drive, but it's not. It's actually a nasty little device called a *keylogger.* It copies everything someone types on a computer. It's basic gear for a hacker."

She put it back on the table.

"So this is what I know. Very recently an American girl who's a hacker was living here, while you were planning a big mission that's taking place in three weeks. But now she's gone, and you came and got me, an American girl who's also a hacker. I figure you planned the mission with her in mind, and, now that she's out of the picture, you need me to take her place."

Sara looked at the others, trying to read their expressions.

"Or am I wrong?"

"No," said Mother. "You're not wrong . . . not at all."

Sara smiled. "And if there are only three weeks left, that doesn't leave me a lot of time to get up to speed. So, I did all this to show you that I *can* do all this. I can learn fast. I can be a valuable part of the team."

"Wow," said Paris. "That's stunning."

"Isn't it?" said Monty.

Mother looked at her, his mind at work figuring out

his next step. "You really know how to make a first impression, Sara."

"Thank you," she said. "But, if you don't mind, I think I'd like it better if everyone started calling me Brooklyn."

11. Sydney

Sydney, Australia—Three Years Earlier

COUNTING THE LAYOVER IN HONG KONG, it took Mother twenty-three hours to fly from London to Sydney. And, as if the jet lag wasn't disorienting enough, in crossing the equator he'd gone from winter to summer. So it wasn't surprising that he was off his game when he arrived at the Wallangarra School for Girls.

Wallangarra was the fourteenth different boarding school he'd visited in the three days since he'd landed, and they were all beginning to blur together. To clear his mind, he looked into the rearview mirror of his rental car and recited one of his own Motherisms. "*You don't need any hocus-pocus. All you need to do is focus.*"

That did the trick, and after wiping the sweat from his forehead, he was ready to go.

"Good afternoon," he said with a flawless Australian accent to the receptionist in the main office. "I'd like to speak to . . ." He checked a name in a thin spiral notebook. ". . . Ms. Madeline Cooper. I believe she's the head of the school."

"That's *Dr.* Cooper," the woman corrected with a raised eyebrow. "May I ask what this is in reference to?"

"Police business, I'm afraid." He flashed an Australian Federal Police badge and said, "I'm Detective Sergeant Nicholas Henderson with the AFP."

Her tone changed instantly. "Of course, Detective," she said respectfully. "Please have a seat, and I'll let her know you're here."

Mother had come to Australia on short notice after receiving word that a woman resembling his wife had been photographed at Sydney Airport. She'd arrived on a flight from Kuala Lumpur only to leave seventeen hours later for Manila. She wasn't detained, because the facial recognition software only scored her as a 31 percent match: possible but unlikely.

Mother, however, knew it was her the instant he saw the video. She'd altered her appearance with makeup and possibly surgery, but she couldn't hide her mannerisms. He recognized the way she adjusted her glasses and her tendency to hold each hand in a fist, a habit she developed as a child to keep from biting her nails.

MI6 sent agents to Kuala Lumpur and Manila in hopes of picking up her trail, but Mother focused on her midway destination. She was in Australia too long for it to be a layover, but not long enough to really do anything. *What if that's where she hid the children?* he wondered. *What if she went to Sydney to check on Robert and Annie?*

"Detective Sergeant Henderson, is it?"

Mother looked up and saw an impeccably dressed woman in a dark blue pinstripe suit.

"You must be Dr. Cooper."

She led him to her office, which was impressive though not at all welcoming. There was a formal sitting area with a couch and two stiff-backed chairs around an antique coffee table. The walls were covered with pictures of smiling students in blue-and-yellow blazers with matching boater hats.

"It's a lovely campus."

"We're proud of it," she said. "Wallangarra girls have

been going on to great things ever since Mrs. Hobart founded the school in 1901."

"And I see that you were one of them." He pointed to a picture on the wall. It was Dr. Cooper when she was a teenaged student at the school.

"Very good eye," she said, impressed. "No wonder you're a detective. Now, what brings you here today?"

"Two missing children." He made sure to sound like a hardened police officer and not a desperate father. "We have reason to believe they enrolled in area boarding schools sometime in the past eighteen months and wondered if the girl ended up here."

He handed her a picture of his daughter and son.

"Pretty girl," she said. "But I'm afraid she's not one of ours."

"You're certain? The photo's two years old."

"We have six hundred forty-seven girls at Wallangarra," she replied. "And I know each one."

"Maybe she didn't enroll but visited as a prospective student. Is there someone else she might have spoken to? Someone who might've given her a tour?"

"I insist on meeting all candidates myself," she said. "If she was here, I would've seen her." She handed the picture back to him. "Sorry."

Even though it had been a long shot, Mother's heart still sank at the news. There were only three more schools to check. A once-promising lead looked more and more like a dead end.

"Thank you for your time."

"Always a pleasure to help the AFP," she said. "If you'd like, I can send the picture around to other schools. It would save you the trouble of going to each one."

"No, thank you," he said. "It's sensitive, and we want to control the flow of information."

"Well, good luck, then."

They were interrupted by an explosion that was so unexpected, Mother initially thought his ears were playing tricks on him. Then came the scream, and he knew it was real.

The originator of the scream was a teacher standing in the quad in the middle of campus. She had a stunned expression and held her hand over her mouth when Mother rushed onto the scene with Dr. Cooper.

"Heaven's sake, Alice, what happened?" Dr. Cooper asked anxiously.

"It's Mrs. Hobart!" shrieked the teacher. "Look what they've done to her."

In the center of the quad stood a bronze statue of

the school's founder. Or rather, stood *most* of a bronze statue of the school's founder. The statue's head had apparently been blown off in the explosion and now sat upside down in a nearby flower bed. There was still some residual smoke emanating from Mrs. Hobart's neck.

The aura of effortless perfection that Dr. Cooper had conveyed up until that point began to falter. Her left eye started twitching, and crimson blotches formed on her neck and cheeks. "That girl," she muttered. "That foul, wretched girl!"

She trembled and seemed on the verge of erupting when she was struck by inspiration.

"Wait a moment!" she exclaimed. "This. Is. Perfect." She turned to Mother. "Look at the damage. Someone could've been injured. Someone could've been killed. And you're a witness. This is now a police matter."

"What are you talking about?" he asked, utterly confused.

"You're coming with me," she said to him. Then she turned to the teacher. "Go get her."

"Who?" asked the woman.

"You know who," sneered Dr. Cooper.

They returned to her office, and while Mother tried to figure out what was happening, Dr. Cooper riffled through a filing cabinet, mumbling to herself. She was possessed, but with what, he wasn't sure.

"Look at this," she said, pulling out a thick file. "I've documented everything she's done."

"Who?"

Just then the door flew open, and Mother laid eyes on Sydney for the very first time. Only, she wasn't Sydney yet. At that moment she was still Olivia. She plopped down on the couch, put her feet up on the antique coffee table, and took off her school hat to reveal a short, cropped purple Mohawk.

"Hello, Madeline," she said with a grin. "What seems to be the problem?"

"You know what the problem is," snapped the principal. "You desecrated the statue of Mrs. Hobart, and you're going to pay for it."

"I don't know what you're talking about," the girl said with total innocence.

"Just like you don't know who took my car apart and reassembled it in the library," said the principal. "Or like you don't know who let a swarm of frogs loose in the chapel."

"An *army*," said Olivia.

"What?" asked Dr. Cooper.

"A group of frogs is called an army, not a swarm," Olivia answered with a smug smile. "We learned that in Ms. Helton's biology class."

"Aren't you clever?" the principal said as she swiped Olivia's feet off the table. "Well, this time you were too clever for your own good. You made the mistake of breaking the law with *him* here."

She pointed to Mother.

"And who are you?" Olivia asked.

"He's a detective with the AFP," Cooper answered for him. She turned to Mother. "Go ahead! Show her your badge."

Mother was reluctant to be pulled into the dispute but didn't see a way out, so he showed his badge to Olivia.

"Nice to meet you, Detective Sergeant Nicholas Henderson," she said as she examined it. "How do you fit into this little drama?"

"That's a good question," answered Mother.

"He's going to arrest you," said Cooper.

He was too cool to show it, but this was when Mother began to panic. Posing as a police officer was one thing, but faking an arrest was something totally different. He'd come to Australia on his own without notifying MI6 or local authorities.

"That's not really my area," he said, trying to talk his way out of it.

"Aren't you with the AFP?" she asked.

"Of course," he said cautiously.

"Well, she just exploded a bomb in the middle of a school. How can that not be your area?" She shoved the file into his hands. "Look at this. It documents everything she's done."

"Allegedly," Olivia corrected. "Things that I've allegedly done."

Cooper glared at Mother, who pretended to look through the file while his mind raced, trying to come up with an escape strategy.

"Either you arrest her," she demanded, "or you stay with her until I have the local police come down here. Then you can explain your reluctance to them."

Involving the actual police was the last thing that he wanted. They didn't take kindly to people pretending to be officers of the law.

"No, no, there won't be any need for that," he said. "I'll take her in."

Rather than protest, Olivia smiled. She even held her hands up for him and asked, "Want to cuff me?"

"There won't be any need for that," he said. "I doubt you're a flight risk."

"Don't be so sure," said Cooper.

Mother desperately wanted out of the situation but couldn't figure out how to do it without taking the girl. "Come on," he said reluctantly. "Let's get you down to the station."

The principal gleefully escorted them to the door as Olivia followed Mother to his car.

"You want me in the backseat or front?" Olivia asked.

"Front's fine," he said as he opened the door for her.

No matter how long he tried to stall, inspiration failed to come. A few minutes later he was driving past the guard gate, furious at himself for getting into this situation. He was still trying to think of what to do when Olivia broke the silence.

"Well, DS Henderson, this is quite the pickle," she said as they drove away from campus.

"How do you mean?" asked Mother.

"Me being in your custody," she answered, "and you not actually being a police officer."

Mother gave her a look. "What makes you think I'm not a police officer?"

"First of all, the badge you flashed is out-of-date," she continued. "The AFP switched the crown about three years ago. It's not something Dr. Cooper would notice, but then again she's never been arrested."

"Unlike you, I suppose," said Mother.

"Let's just say, it's not my first time in a police car." She smiled. "Of course, this isn't really a police car." She pointed at a sticker inside the windshield. "It was rented at Sydney Airport. That was giveaway number two."

She let him stew for a moment before continuing. "Don't worry about it, though. I'm not going to blow your cover. Just head for the beach. I know some people who will take me in."

"Your family?" he asked.

"Hardly," she laughed. "Mum's dead and Dad's, well, I have no idea where Dad is, but I know he's not waiting somewhere to welcome me with open arms."

"If you don't have a family, how can you afford to go to a fancy school like that?"

"It was stipulated in my grandmother's will," she said. "She was a Wallangarra girl and hoped I would follow in her footsteps. It's probably best that she's no longer with us or all of this might have killed her."

Despite the situation, Mother couldn't help but like

Olivia. She was fresh and honest. As they drove down Pacific Highway, he said, "I have a question for you. Why?"

"Why what?"

"Dr. Cooper's car in the library? An army of frogs in the chapel? The headless Mrs. Hobart?"

"Oh, you mean my alleged wrongdoings," she said. "There's no way I'm confessing any of that to a copper. Even a pretend one."

"I can't tell anyone without getting myself into much bigger trouble than you," he said. "Besides, we're not talking random mischief here. These were very intentional acts, and I'm guessing they were meant to convey specific messages."

"That's the drawback with being an anonymous vigilante for justice," she admitted. "You don't get to explain your intentions, and sometimes the general public misses your true artistry."

"Explain them to me," he said. "I'm fascinated."

"Well . . . if you're *fascinated*," she said. "Let's start with Ruby Carlisle."

"Who's she?"

"A girl in year eight," she responded. "She's got the voice of an angel, and she auditioned for the school musical. They were doing *The Frog Princess*. She was amazing, a shoo-in for the lead role. But, when the cast was announced, Ruby didn't have the lead, or a supporting role, or even a single solo. She was at the bottom of the list in the chorus. Now, there's nothing wrong with singing in the chorus, but everyone knew she should've been top of the cast. Even the girl who got the part thought it should've gone to Ruby."

"Why didn't she get it?" he asked.

"Dr. Cooper didn't think she 'had the right look' for such a prominent role. She actually said that. Then Cooper makes it worse and tells her, 'Maybe if you had fewer desserts you'd be more princess and less frog.' Un-freaking-believable."

"And your response?"

"I got on the phone and impersonated Ms. Helton," she said.

"She's the biology teacher you mentioned," said Mother.

"Very good," she said, impressed. "I called the company that provides specimens for our lab projects and ordered fifty bumpy spotted frogs. Then I let them loose in the school chapel." She laughed at the memory. "It was like one of the plagues of Egypt in there."

"What about taking her car apart and putting it back together in the library?" he asked.

"That was in response to Dr. Cooper canceling the Robotics and Engineering Club and then using the money to create a school pageant," she said, shaking her head. "A bloody beauty pageant with girls in sportswear answering questions about saving the planet. I was beyond livid. So, I did my little car trick and put a note on the windshield that said, 'Bet you'd like an engineer now, wouldn't you?'"

Mother laughed at this. "And the decapitated Mrs. Hobart?"

"My masterpiece, if I say so myself," she said.

"Inspired by?"

"The school's systematic mistreatment of aboriginal students," she replied. "We've got a handful of girls who come from indigenous tribes. Not that you'd ever see one in a brochure or in a picture on the wall in her office. And every time these girls try to do something that embraces their culture, like sponsor a native dance demonstration or celebrate Harmony Day, Dr. Cooper stops it."

"Why?"

"Because, beloved Mrs. Hobart, founder of the school,

was a notoriously racist cow. Amazingly ironic considering she named the school Wallangarra, which is an aboriginal word."

They drove in silence for a moment while he considered her reasons.

"Out of curiosity," he said, "did you audition for the musical?"

"No. I sing like a duck."

"Were you in the Robotics and Engineering Club?"

"Also no."

"Are you a member of an indigenous tribe?"

"No," she said. "But you don't have to be part of a group to understand that they're being mistreated." She paused before adding, "Justice doesn't require a membership card. Just a sense of right and wrong."

That's when he knew. He'd failed in his search for his children, but he'd unexpectedly found another spy. They rode in silence together, the sound of the tires thumping on the road.

"Now it's your turn," she said. "Why are you pretending to be from the AFP?"

He smiled. "Funny you should ask. First, though, I've got one more question. What do you think of Scotland?"

Basic Training

Aisling, Scotland—Present Day

THE PURPLE MOHAWK WAS LONG GONE, but Sydney still felt like the same person who'd tormented the faculty at Wallangarra. Being a troublemaker had been fun, but she'd never done it for the sake of being difficult. It was always about justice.

At Wallangarra, fighting injustice meant battling Dr. Cooper. But now MI6 let her fight on a much larger scale. Even better, it had given her teammates to fight alongside, and it was time to train a new one.

She shivered from the cold as she climbed out of bed.

That was one of the problems with centuries-old Scottish manor houses. They were designed to repel attacking armies, not to keep you warm and cozy.

After putting on running tights, a long-sleeve T-shirt, gloves, and a hoodie, she crossed the hall to Brooklyn's room and gave the door three hard thwacks with the bottom of her fist. "Wake up, sleepyhead."

When there was no response, she tried again, this time pounding louder.

Thwack, thwack, thwack! "Yo, Brookie the Rookie! Time to get up!"

"All right, all right," Brooklyn called back. "Come in and stop that banging."

Sydney didn't enter the room so much as she invaded it, flinging the door open and flipping on all the lights. Brooklyn used her forearm to shield herself from their bright glare as she sat up and got her bearings.

"It wasn't a dream," Sydney said firmly. "You really are in Scotland learning how to be a spy. Welcome to basic training!"

Brooklyn rubbed her eyes and tried to focus on the clock next to her bed. "It's four fifty in the morning."

"I know," said Sydney. "It's your first day, so I thought I'd let you sleep in."

"Do you realize that back home in New York it's . . ." She tried to do the time-zone math in her head but gave up and said, ". . . *yesterday*?"

"First of all, New York isn't home anymore, so you're going to have to get used to that. Second, you need to ask yourself something. Are you Sara? Or are you Brooklyn? Because Sara can go back to sleep, but Brooklyn needs to be downstairs ready to run in ten minutes."

That woke her up faster than a bucket of cold water.

"I'll be there in five," Brooklyn said, now fully alert.

"Dress warmly," Sydney instructed as she left the room. "The sun doesn't come up for another hour, and it's cold along the water."

The previous night Brooklyn had demonstrated impressive natural spy skills, but if she wanted to be ready for a high-level operation in three weeks, she needed to prepare around the clock. It was decided that she wouldn't enroll at Kinloch until after the mission so she could dedicate herself to getting ready full-time.

Her training schedule was split up with everyone spearheading a different aspect. Sydney took charge of physical conditioning, which is why early Saturday morning the two of them ran on the beach in near total darkness.

"We're going to start every day this way," Sydney said as the first glimmers of daylight began to peek out from the horizon. "We have to build up your stamina. Missions rarely follow a schedule, and you need to stay alert despite limited rest."

The ocean breeze was cold against their faces, and their strides fell into a steady matching rhythm.

"What was that you called me earlier?" Brooklyn asked. "When you were pounding on my door."

"Brookie the Rookie," she said with a laugh. "We came up with that last night when we were planning your day. I don't remember if it was Paris or Rio who thought of it."

"They hate me, don't they?" asked Brooklyn.

"They're embarrassed, but they'll get over it," said Sydney.

"I'm not so sure," said Brooklyn. "I got angry eyes from Rio all through dinner, and as far as Kat goes, you should've seen her when I sat in her chair."

"That's got nothing to do with you," said Sydney. "That's just Kat."

"What do you mean?"

"She's one of a kind," said Sydney. "And I mean that in the best possible way. It's what makes her amazing.

She sees the world in patterns and equations. That's why she's such a stellar code breaker. But, if something's out of order, like a person in the wrong seat, it knocks her for a stagger."

After a few more strides Brooklyn said, "Thanks, by the way."

"For what?"

"You never believed that I'd stolen anything. You totally had my back."

In a day filled with improbable twists and turns, that moment stood out for Brooklyn. It meant more to her than Sydney would ever know because it felt like something a sister would do. Neither of them spoke for a while until Brooklyn asked, "How far are we going to run?"

"I figured we'd go until you threw up. Maybe a little farther than that. This isn't just exercise, we need to get you in spy shape." Sydney laughed and started running faster. Brooklyn took a deep breath and tried to keep up.

Attempting to keep up with her teammates was a recurring theme throughout Brooklyn's day. She got completely lost in the woods when Paris tried to teach her how to navigate with a compass. Though she took it as a good sign that he came back to rescue her. She was fairly certain Rio would've let her wander for hours.

She did her best to keep pace mentally when Kat tried to explain complex theories on patterns and codes using a Scrabble game. Most of it was beyond her grasp, and she couldn't tell how much of that was because it was hard, how much was because Kat didn't like her, and how much was the result of Kat's social awkwardness. Ultimately, she decided it was probably a bit of each.

But the most difficult lesson was the last one. At least from a confrontational standpoint. It was with Rio, who held the biggest grudge from the day before. She tried to lighten the mood with a friendly smile when they sat down at the kitchen table, but there was no smile in return.

"What am I going to learn from you?" she asked.

"I don't know that there's anything I can teach you," he said mockingly. "I thought you already knew it all."

Brooklyn was not in the mood. She let out a deep sigh and asked, "Do you want me to leave?"

"No," he said. "I want you to keep up." He flashed a sly grin. "If you can."

He placed three plastic cups and a red foam ball on the table between them. "I'm going to place the ball under a cup, and then I'm going to shuffle them around. When I stop, tell me where you think it is."

He did the trick three times in a row and each time, when she missed, he made an obnoxious buzzer noise and said, "Wrong!" After the third time, he added, "Maybe cups aren't your thing."

Next, he did a variation of the same trick except with three playing cards. Again, she missed, getting the answer wrong three times in a row.

"Boy, you're not very good at this, are you?" he taunted.

"I'm done," Brooklyn said, starting to get up.

"What's the matter?" asked Rio. "You don't like it when someone makes you look foolish?"

"No," she said. "I don't."

"Then how do you think it made me feel?" he said. "You have any idea how long I've waited for a chance to be the alpha? And you humiliated me."

"No," she said. "You humiliated yourself. I didn't ask you to spy on me. You chose that. Think about it. What do you think would've happened if, instead of spying, you just greeted me at the airport? If you made me feel like you were at least open to giving me a chance? You looked bad because you wanted me to look bad."

They both sat quietly for a moment.

"Now, what's the lesson?" she asked.

"*This* is the lesson," he said, motioning to the cards and cups on the table.

"Magic tricks?"

"They use confidence, deception, and audience manipulation. Just like spycraft," he said. "The CIA even hired one of Harry Houdini's best friends to teach magic to its agents."

"You're making that up," she said.

"It's completely true." Rio pulled out a copy of *The Official C.I.A. Manual of Trickery and Deception* and placed it in front of her. "His name was John Mulholland, and this is the handbook he wrote."

She flipped through some of the pages. "And you learned magic by reading this book?"

"No, I've been doing magic my whole life," he said. "In Brazil I lived on the streets and made a living performing tricks for tourists. After my act, I'd pass around a hat, and they'd put money in it. One day, Mother was in the crowd."

"And instead of putting money in the hat, he asked if you wanted to go to Scotland?" guessed Brooklyn.

"Something like that," he said, looking at the table. There was an awkward pause before he added, "And when I got here, there was no one to welcome me at the airport either."

"That's too bad," said Brooklyn. "It would've been nice." She paused for a bit and added, "And it's too bad how things went down yesterday. I really didn't mean to embarrass you."

He gave a slight nod. "Right."

"So . . . can you teach me some tricks?"

"Yes."

He spent the next hour demonstrating basic skills like palming a playing card or performing the French Drop, a maneuver in which a small object seemingly disappears when passing from one hand to the other. More important, he explained how these tricks translated directly into spy work.

"If you can palm the ace of spades, then you can palm a flash drive or a piece of paper with a secret message on it," he said. "And if you can do the French Drop, you can convince someone that your hands are empty when they're not. These skills can mean the difference between the success or failure of a mission."

The last thing he showed her was the brush pass.

"This is how a spy passes something to another spy

without anyone seeing," he said. "You act like you don't notice each other, avoid all eye contact, and when you brush past, you slip the object into the other person's hand or pocket."

They were practicing the move when Monty came into the kitchen.

"How's it going?" she asked.

"Good," said Rio. "Just working on the brush pass."

"I need to steal Brooklyn," she said. "I want her to meet Ben before the briefing."

"Who's Ben?" asked Brooklyn.

"The last member of the team," answered Monty. "He's down in the priest hole. That's where Mother's going to brief everyone on the mission."

Brooklyn gave her a quizzical look. "What's a priest hole?"

"Follow me and I'll explain."

Monty led Brooklyn down a narrow staircase that connected the kitchen with the basement. "Many of the castles and manor houses across Scotland and England have priest holes," she said. "They're secret rooms where someone can hide."

"And why are they called that?"

"Because a lot of the time, the person hiding was a

priest or a minister," she explained. "Religious conflict has been a common theme throughout this part of the world for centuries. And there have been times where if you were Catholic and your priest was visiting, the last thing you'd want was for the authorities to find him here."

"So he'd hide down below?" asked Brooklyn.

"Exactly."

In the basement they entered a library that had floor-to-ceiling bookcases on each wall.

"And this is it?" asked Brooklyn.

"No," said Monty. "This would be too easy to find."

She reached behind a book, flipped a switch, and pulled on a bookcase, which swiveled out to reveal a steel door with a keypad. "The priest hole's back here," she said as she typed in a combination. "Of course, it used to be rather small, but then MI6 expanded it and added some new features."

This was an understatement.

The door swung open to reveal a room roughly twenty by twenty with high-tech gear everywhere. There were computers, a virtual reality station, and giant touch-screen monitors on two of the walls. Unlike the rest of what she'd seen at the FARM, this actually looked like it belonged in a spy movie. There weren't, however, any people.

"I thought you said we were going to meet someone named Ben," said Brooklyn.

"Not some*one*, some*thing*," answered Monty.

They stepped inside, and Brooklyn's eyes were instantly drawn to a supercomputer running the length of the room behind a wall of glass panels. It was made up of ten silver units standing side by side like a row of refrigerators, each about six feet tall and two feet wide.

"Brooklyn," Monty said as they approached it, "*this* is Ben."

Brooklyn had never seen anything so beautiful in all her life. She pressed her hand up against the glass, which was cool to the touch. "It's very nice to meet you," she said. "I think we're going to become excellent friends."

Operation Willy Wonka

FOR BROOKLYN, IT WAS LOVE AT FIRST sight.

As a student at PS 394, she'd become a skilled hacker despite only having access to some ancient PCs in the school's computer lab. But now, with Ben, the possibilities of what she could do were limitless.

"Mind if I talk Geek for a minute?" asked Monty.

"Are you kidding?" answered Brooklyn, who stood virtually motionless, mesmerized by the machine. "I'd love that."

"Ben started off as a Cray XC40 supercomputer with a two-point-one gigahertz Xeon processor," Monty explained. "As far as the rest of the world knows, that's what FARM had installed to create state-of-the-art weather forecasting models. Luckily for me, the same type of computer that's used for predicting the path of a hurricane is ideal for advanced cryptography. MI6 doubled the number of racks from five to ten, made some modifications to the operating system, and added a few next-generation technology touches so that now it can perform more than five hundred trillion floating-point operations per second. Unofficially, it's the sixteenth-fastest computer in Britain."

"Why unofficially?"

"Because not too many people know it's here," said Monty. "And almost nobody knows about the modifications."

"And it's ours?" Brooklyn asked.

"Technically it belongs to the people of the United Kingdom. But, since they're unaware of its existence, we get to have all the fun."

"Why do you call it Ben? Do the letters stand for something?"

"It's just a name," said Monty. "I thought it was a bit

daunting to always call it 'the supercomputer.' And since it's a weather-forecasting machine that we've hidden in a priest hole, it seemed right to name it after an actual weather-forecasting priest." Monty pointed to a brown-tinted photo on the wall of a man with a hooknose and wire-framed glasses. "That's Father Benito Viñes, a Spanish-born priest who moved to Cuba in 1870. He was the first person to successfully predict the paths of tropical storms, which saved countless lives. He was known throughout the Caribbean as Father Hurricane."

Brooklyn smiled at the man in the picture. *"Buenas tardes, Padre Huracán."*

For her every bit of it was perfect, especially Monty, who was the first woman she'd ever met who had the same level of excitement that she did while discussing technology. They continued their geek talk until the others arrived for the briefing.

Everyone sat around a large oval conference table, and, trying not to upset Kat, Brooklyn waited until the others had taken their seats to make sure she didn't sit in the wrong one.

"What do you think of Ben?" Mother asked her.

"He's amazing," she said, beaming.

"Excellent," he replied. "The good news is you're

going to spend a lot of time with him during the next few weeks."

"Excellent," said Brooklyn. "What's the bad news?"

"Even with Ben working at top capacity, it's going to be hard to be fully prepared for this operation," he replied.

This brought a smile to Sydney's face. "But, if we need to get prepared, that means we have a mission," she said hopefully. "Did we get official approval?"

"Yes," Mother answered, eliciting enthusiastic reactions from around the table. "I just got off the phone with Vauxhall Cross."

Sydney leaned over and whispered to Brooklyn, "That's MI6 headquarters."

"I told them about Brooklyn and our faith in her," continued Mother. "We also discussed our unique position with regard to the current situation, and we were given the all-clear to implement Operation Willy Wonka."

Brooklyn laughed. "You really do love Roald Dahl books, don't you?"

"I really do," replied Mother. "But in this instance I think you'll find the name's particularly appropriate."

He pressed a button on a clicker, and half a dozen pictures filled the wall monitors. Although most of the photos had been taken from a distance, Brooklyn could tell that they were all of the same man. Only one, however, provided a good look at his face. It was a publicity shot that she'd seen in countless tech magazines.

"Stavros Sinclair?" she said.

"You know him?" asked Mother.

"In the computer world he's pretty much a god," answered Brooklyn.

"He's founder and CEO of Sinclair Scientifica, a mammoth multinational technology company that makes everything from microchips to missiles," said Mother. "He's one of the richest men in the world and also one of the most secretive. These are the only known recent photos of him, and they're not really that recent."

"Let me guess," said Brooklyn. "He's Willy Wonka."

"Bang on," answered Mother. "He hasn't made a public appearance in more than four years, but in a few weeks he's scheduled to be part of the Global Youth Summit on the Environment. Have you heard of it?"

"A little," she said. "It's going to be in Paris, right?"

"That's right," he said.

He pressed another button, and the screens filled with images from past summits.

"Nearly fifty thousand young people from around

the world are expected to descend on the city for four days of rallies and a scientific symposium," Monty said, seamlessly taking over the briefing. "As part of our cover story with FARM, we were already planning to be there before Sinclair got involved. I'm on a symposium panel, and Sydney's giving a speech at one of the rallies."

Brooklyn shot a surprised look at Sydney, who flashed a nervous smile.

"But things changed four months ago when Sinclair unexpectedly announced the Stavros Challenge," said Mother.

"What's that?" asked Brooklyn.

"It's a lot of money, is what it is," answered Rio. "One million euros!" he said, drawing out each word carefully.

"For what?" asked Brooklyn.

"For the team of students who do the best job solving an environmental problem," answered Paris. "Sinclair thinks young people are better at coming up with fresh ideas because they're more open and idealistic. He plans to pick a different issue every year and give away a million euros each time."

"And we're trying to win the money?" asked Brooklyn.

"No," said Monty. "We're aiming for a nice finish between sixth and tenth."

"That's pretty specific," Brooklyn said. "Why between sixth and tenth?"

"First place receives one million euros, with half going to their school or institution and the other half being split up among the five team members for their education," said Monty. "The teams that finish second to fifth will each receive one hundred thousand euros. These students will all have their pictures splashed across media and will undoubtedly be scrutinized."

"Undercover agents hate media and despise scrutiny," said Mother.

"However, very little attention will be given to the teams that don't win anything," said Monty. "Thirty teams were chosen for the competition, but only ten will reach the final stage. We expect those to be the only people who will actually get significant face-to-face time with Stavros."

"So making the top ten is like finding the golden ticket?" said Brooklyn.

"Exactly," said Mother.

"Here's a silly question," said Brooklyn. "Why do we care? I know he's rich and all, but why do we want to work so hard just to be in a room with Stavros Sinclair?"

"To protect him," said Mother. "He's what's known as a national-level asset, which means countries can't let him fall into the wrong hands. He only comes out in the open once every few years, so there will be representatives from every spy agency in the world there. Some will be keeping an eye on him, and others might be looking to snatch him."

"But we'll be the only ones up close," Sydney said proudly. "No one will expect us."

"Including the Purple Thumb," said Paris.

Brooklyn gave him a confused look. "The what?"

"So far there've been three Global Youth Summits on the Environment," Mother answered. "The first was in Stockholm, Sweden, and on the final night, there was a break-in at the headquarters of a recycling technology firm that hosted the main rally." He pressed a button, and the monitors showed images from the crime scene. "Damage was minimal, and the police decided that it was just a prank. The only significant evidence was a purple thumbprint found in the middle of the CEO's computer screen."

"Then came summit two in Tokyo," said Monty. "It was sponsored by a group of renewable energy companies, including the Fūjin Corporation, which makes turbines for wind energy." She walked over to the touchscreen and swiped on pictures from the Japanese crime scene. These showed shattered computers and broken furniture strewn across the room. "This was their headquarters the morning after the summit ended. This time the damage was more substantial, and, of course, there was another purple thumbprint."

"The Swedes only ran their thumbprint through their national database. It didn't match anything, so they stopped pursuing it," said Mother. "But when the Japanese found a second one, they shared the print with Interpol and the FBI, who found a match." He tapped the screen, and a mug shot appeared. "Meet Leyland Carmichael, an environmental extremist who attacked multiple tech companies in the US and Canada."

"Did the Americans arrest him?" asked Brooklyn.

"No, they didn't," he said. "You see, there was a slight problem—he'd been dead for nearly three years."

Brooklyn's eyes opened wide. "That's more than a *slight* problem."

"They even dug up his grave to make sure he was really buried in it," he continued. "They found his body, but you know what they didn't find."

"His thumb?" guessed Brooklyn.

"Correct," he answered. "He was missing his right thumb."

"Yet, somehow, the same thumbprint turned up at one of the hosting companies for summit three in San Francisco," said Monty.

"Is that the one when they had the big protest?" said Brooklyn. "When people locked arms and blocked the street?"

"Yes," answered Monty. "And since so much media attention was paid to that, few people heard about this." She swiped the screen so that the images changed to a different crime scene. "The *Fulgora Storm Three*, a lithium ion battery prototype being developed for a next generation electric car, was stolen, and a purple thumbprint was left at the scene."

"Each time, these people have made a bigger splash," said Mother. "And the worry is that they're going to try to up their game again in Paris."

"Which companies are sponsoring the Paris summit?" asked Brooklyn.

"None," said Mother. "The expenses are being paid by a single individual."

He clicked the button, and once again the screen showed the publicity photo of Stavros Sinclair.

"Which is why we're going to be close to him to make sure they don't do anything," said Sydney.

"So we've got to make it into the top ten," Brooklyn said. "What's the challenge?"

"Rainmaking," answered Monty. "Sinclair Scientifica wants creative approaches to making artificial rainfall. They believe it can be used to counteract drought and famine across the globe."

"And do we have any idea how to make rain?" asked Brooklyn.

"We do," said Monty. "More important, we have access to years of research. MI6 experimented with making artificial rain for nearly a decade. They gave up on the project, but we tweaked their data, made some new models with Ben, and created a proposal."

"For a contest that's supposed to be for students, it sounds like we cheated," Brooklyn said, only half joking. "I mean, it's already kind of unfair that we have a supercomputer, which I'm guessing most teams don't. But to have nearly ten years of secret government research doesn't seem fair at all."

"It would be cheating if we were trying to win," said Mother. "But we're only shooting for sixth place. Besides, we had to ensure that we made the top thirty."

"And did we?" asked Brooklyn.

"Yes," he replied. "We received word two weeks ago

and were told to keep it secret until the official list was announced. That was made public earlier today. There are teams representing leading research institutions and schools from around the world. Including one that's surprising."

He pressed the button, and the names of the thirty finalists appeared on the screen.

Brooklyn smiled instantly when she recognized one of them. "MIST!"

"What?" asked Paris.

"The Metropolitan Institute of Science and Technology," she said. "It's a school in New York. Actually, it's the school I wanted to attend." She looked around the table at the others. "You know, before I found out about teenage spies and castles with hidden rooms."

"Here's a *clanger*," Sydney said, noticing an obvious mistake. "They have us representing FARM." She motioned to the list. "But they also have us listed as Kinloch Abbey."

"That's not a mistake," said Mother. "You're the team from FARM. There's another team of students from Kinloch who made the final thirty."

"How's that even possible?" asked Rio. "Who do they have who knows anything about rainmaking and computer weather models?"

And that's when it hit them.

"Charlotte," said Kat. "They've got Charlotte."

"You mean the girl who used to live in my room?" asked Brooklyn.

"No way," said Sydney. "That can't be." Then she looked at Mother and saw it in his expression. "Can it?"

"Yes," said Mother. "Charlotte is the captain of the team from Kinloch. I just got off the phone with the headmaster. The school's very excited."

"It doesn't make sense," said Sydney. "Why would she quit our team, only to form another one?"

"I can tell you one million reasons why," said Rio. "Because we're going to finish sixth, and she wants the money."

"We can't let her do that," Sydney said to Mother. "It's not fair. We have to get them disqualified."

"We'll do no such thing," said Mother. "It would raise alarms at the school and might make Charlotte retaliate. As far as FARM is concerned, we're thrilled that Kinloch is sending a team, and in the spirit of scientific cooperation, we're going to help them."

"How?" asked Rio.

"We're letting them use Ben to prepare their weather models," said Monty.

"That's bonkers!" exclaimed Paris. "We can't let them down here."

"It will only be Charlotte," said Monty. "She's their computer specialist, and she already knows everything about us."

"And we know everything about her," said Sydney. "Like the fact that she quit on us. Why are we helping them? So they can win a million euros?"

Perhaps because she didn't know Charlotte and this betrayal wasn't personal, Brooklyn was the first one to see Mother and Monty's plan. "No. We're helping them to make sure they *don't* win a million euros."

"Yes," said Mother. "If they win, then Charlotte will get all the media and scrutiny we're working so hard to avoid. Any light that shines on her has the chance to spill over on us. So we need to make sure they don't win anything."

"How do we do that?" asked Kat.

"We use me," Brooklyn said. "If we work side by side, then I can hack her and stop them."

"*You* are going to hack *Charlotte*?" Rio asked, disbelieving. "No offense, but that's easier said than done."

"He's right," said Paris. "She's a computer virtuoso."

Brooklyn looked at them defiantly. "What makes you think I'm not?"

"It's nothing personal," said Rio. "It's just . . . One time we were down here, and Charlotte said she could hack anyone on the planet. Anyone. So we dared her to hack the prime minister."

"And?" asked Brooklyn.

"An hour later we were reading his private schedule," he answered.

"So she failed," Brooklyn said.

"What are you talking about?" asked Rio.

"Instead of the prime minister, it sounds like she hacked some appointments secretary," answered Brooklyn. "That's a fail."

Mother and Monty both smiled at this.

"You think you could do better?" asked Kat.

"I don't see why not," said Brooklyn. "I hacked Serena Ochoa."

The others shared a look for a moment, unsure if this was a name they should recognize.

"I'm sorry," said Sydney. "Who's Serena Ochoa?"

"A hero of mine," Brooklyn answered. "She's a professor of advanced computing and mathematical sciences at Cal Tech. I hacked into her laptop so that it gave her a special greeting on her birthday."

Rio was thoroughly unimpressed. "Not exactly the prime minister now, is it, mate?"

"You didn't let me finish," Brooklyn said. "At the time, Dr. Ochoa was an astronaut on board the International Space Station. In order to reach her laptop, I had to hack into NASA, the Department of Defense, and Roscosmos."

"What's Roscosmos?" asked Sydney.

"That's the Russian space federation," she answered. "And, unlike Charlotte, I wasn't using a supercomputer capable of performing over five hundred trillion floating-point operations per second."

For a moment, there was stunned silence around the table.

"Just out of curiosity," Monty said, "what were you using?"

"An eight-year-old PC in my middle school computer lab," Brooklyn answered.

More silence until Rio uttered a single word. "Wow."

"Yeah," replied Brooklyn in full swagger. "Wow."

"Well, then," Mother said, barely stifling a laugh. "I guess that settles that."

Charlotte

SHE WORE THE KINLOCH ABBEY UNIFORM of burgundy blazer and tartan skirt as she rode in Coach A, seat 22B on the train to Aisling. Her dark brown eyes and full, round cheeks perpetually looked like they were on the verge of a smile. Her chestnut hair was cropped just above the shoulders and swayed ever so slightly due to the motion of the train. And her horn-rimmed glasses managed to look hip, bookish, and nerdy all at once. She was the picture-perfect schoolgirl. No one would have guessed that unlike other passengers who killed time checking social media or playing mindless video games, she was busy hacking into the laptops and smartphones of everybody seated in first class.

You know, just for kicks.

Her name was Charlotte Sloane. That was it. There was a time when that was one of many aliases she had. But she no longer spied for MI6, so now one name was all she got. Of course, in some corners of the dark web, she was better known as UKFlamethrower1999 or DundeeDeathMonger707, but mostly she was just Char, as the girls in the boarding house called her.

In this instance, her hacking was more mischievous than malicious. She wasn't stealing passwords or scamming bank records like she sometimes did. She was just keeping her skills sharp. "The greatest basketball players in the world are great because they practice shooting and dribbling so much it becomes as natural as breathing," she once told Sydney. "This is my practice. This is my breathing."

Coach A, seat 22B wasn't just some random ticket assignment. She'd ridden the train often enough to identify it as the best location for this sort of practice. She even called it "the throne," just as she called herself the "queen of hacks."

There were three things about the throne that made it better than all the other seats on the ScotRail train. First, it was located just two rows behind the plastic barrier that marked first class. This meant it was a cheap ticket but still close enough to the router for her to steal the free Wi-Fi that came with expensive fares. Plastic barriers may stop passengers, but they do nothing to slow down radio waves.

Second, it came with a table and electrical outlet. This allowed her to spread out with her laptop while she charged her other devices. Finally, it had an unobstructed view of six of the nine seats in first class. This let her see most of the people she was hacking, which made it so much more fun.

For example, on this trip, she was able to see that the tall blonde with the movie-star sunglasses sitting in 3F was holding hands with her half-sleeping boyfriend in 4F at the exact same time she was sending flirty text messages to the man across the aisle in 1B. It also let her see that the car salesman in 8A looked nothing like the photo he'd just posted on a dating app.

Everybody lies, she told herself. *Everybody's running a scam.*

"Ticket, please," said the conductor.

"Here you go," she said as she handed him the orange-and-white round-trip ticket. "I bet you enjoyed the Celtic game this week."

His eyes lit up. "You bet I did. Two-nil over Rangers in the Old Firm derby." He stopped for a moment. "How'd you know I was a supporter?"

"I take this train a lot," she said. "I've heard you talk about it before."

This was a total lie. She did recognize him from previous trips, but she only knew he liked Celtic because of an app on his phone. His had been the first one she hacked.

"We're going to win the cup again this year," he said proudly before he continued down the aisle. "Mark my words."

Unlike the hackers in movies who always scurried about in the shadows, Charlotte liked to engage people in conversation. She wanted to be seen precisely because it made people less suspicious. The conductor would remember her fondly as the schoolgirl who talked football. There's no way she could be up to any mischief.

The final hack was the hardest. It was a laptop belonging to an accountant from Edinburgh sitting in 4B who had the latest firewall installed. But Charlotte still managed to breach it just as the train reached the platform at Aisling.

She checked her watch. The trip had taken twenty-three minutes, and during that time she'd hacked nine passengers and the conductor. Solid if not spectacular. *This is my practice. This is my breathing.*

If there was any awkwardness about coming back to the FARM for the first time since she'd left, it was offset by the sense of familiarity that greeted her as she followed the footpath from the station. She knew every inch of it by heart: the curve of the stone fence that lined the road, the vibrant yellow of the rapeseed flowers blanketing the field next to the airstrip. This made it all the more startling when a total stranger answered the door.

"Who are you?"

"Brooklyn," mumbled the girl through a mouthful of chocolate chip cookie. "You must be Charlotte."

Charlotte couldn't believe it. Was it possible that they'd already replaced her?

Brooklyn swallowed her cookie and smiled. "Come on in," she said, like they were long-lost friends. "We've been expecting you."

Ever since learning that Charlotte had a team going

to the competition, Brooklyn had been carefully planning for this interaction. She needed to hack a hacker in order to make sure that Kinloch didn't win the Stavros Challenge. To do that, she had three targets she needed to hit. If she missed any of them, her plan would implode.

The first was to take advantage of the fact Charlotte didn't know she existed. That was why she'd wanted to greet her at the door. It put Charlotte on her heels from the very beginning. Brooklyn had watched as she approached the house and timed it down to the last second, taking a bite of cookie right before answering the door to make it seem like she was goofy and friendly rather than cool and calculating.

Before Charlotte could react, Monty stepped out from the kitchen. "I see you two have met. The kids are at school and Mother's in Edinburgh, so it's just us girls. I'm making lunch right now, so why don't you get to work and I'll bring it down when it's done."

"Sounds good," Brooklyn said as she took another bite of cookie and headed for the basement.

Charlotte's head was still spinning as she and Brooklyn went down the stairs toward the priest hole. "I'm sorry," she said, trying to piece it all together. "Who are you?"

"I'm the new you," answered Brooklyn. Then, with as

much New York City attitude as she could muster, she added, "They call me Charlotte 2.0."

"I beg your pardon."

"'Cause I'm the new-and-improved American," she answered. "You know, like when they come out with a computer upgrade, they call it 2.0?" she said.

"Yes, I'm quite familiar with . . ."

"No offense to you," said Brooklyn. "I mean, they say you're really good at computers. Personally, I don't know anything about them. That's not my specialty."

"No?" she said. "Then what is?"

"Breaking in and out of buildings," said Brooklyn. "Stealing things."

"Well, then, you're quite an upgrade," Charlotte replied snootily.

Charlotte's reaction told Brooklyn that she'd hit a nerve. This was the second part of her plan. She was taking advantage of Charlotte's one great weakness.

She thinks she's better than us, Sydney told Brooklyn the night before. *She's never come out and said it, but I know she thinks she's better than all of us.*

This led to a discussion among the others, and even though none of them had ever talked about it before, they all agreed that it was true. Kat, Paris, Rio, and

Sydney had all survived difficult childhoods filled with poverty and heartbreak. But that wasn't true of Charlotte.

She wasn't poor, Rio had said. *She had a good family.*

Charlotte had grown up in Chapel Hill, North Carolina, where her parents were college professors. Her mother taught computer science and her dad mathematics. Everything about her life was perfect until she was ten years old and her parents were killed in an auto accident. Because of this, said the others, she acted like she was better than they were. They were born into their sadness, but hers was the result of an accident. It was almost as if they deserved it and she didn't.

"So are you excited about going to Paris?" asked Brooklyn.

"It's always exciting to see Paris," Charlotte answered, like she'd been there a thousand times. "It's my favorite city."

"I can't wait," said Brooklyn. "I've never been. Of course, I've never been anywhere. Except New Jersey . . . and now Scotland."

Charlotte gave her a superior look, and Brooklyn knew that the second step of her plan was complete. The third, and most crucial, was to conceal any hint that she was a hacker too. If Charlotte got even a whiff that Brooklyn knew her way around a computer, she'd be suspicious.

Once they got to the priest hole, Charlotte put her backpack on the table and pulled out her laptop.

"Wait a second. I thought you were going to use Beny," said Brooklyn.

"I beg your pardon?" said Charlotte.

"Why do you have your laptop if you're going to use Beny?"

"Who's Beny?" asked Charlotte.

"The big computer," Brooklyn answered, pointing at it.

"First of all, it's not a *big* computer, it's a *super*-computer," said Charlotte. "I'm going to access it with my laptop, which contains the data I need for my weather models. Also, his name is *Ben*."

"I know," Brooklyn said, taking a suddenly serious tone. "But it shouldn't be. 'Ben' is short for Benjamin or Benedict. It's an Anglo name. But this computer is named after Benito Viñes. That's a Spanish name. And the nickname for Benito is *Beny*. Spelled with one *n*, not two." She smiled and added, "I may not know anything about supercomputers. But I know a lot about Spanish."

Brooklyn had Charlotte right where she wanted her, all distracted and discombobulated. She was not her normal, sharp self. And in the middle of all this, Brooklyn saw her opportunity.

She reached into her pocket and pulled out the key-logger that she'd found in her desk the first day. The one that Charlotte had accidentally left behind. She hid it in the palm of her hand just like Rio had taught her and slipped it unnoticed into Charlotte's backpack.

Charlotte was too good to hack head-on, so this was going to be Brooklyn's backdoor. She was counting on Charlotte to find it in her backpack and assume that it had always been there, overlooked somehow. If she checked it, she would see that it was hers. She would see that it had her files on it. What she wouldn't see, however, was the tiny program that Brooklyn installed.

How do you hack a hacker? You don't. You let them hack themselves.

XUHET

THE P4 JEAN MÉRIEUX-INSERM LABORATORY in Lyon, France, was one of the most advanced biological research centers in the world. The scientists inside the highly secure facility had to wear futuristic-looking BSL-4–positive pressure "spacesuits," because they worked exclusively with the deadliest viruses on the planet. Even the slightest exposure to them could prove fatal.

Inside the lab's most secure room, two scientists prepared a vial of virus identified only as XUHET to be transported to their research colleagues at the Pasteur Institute in Paris. This vial was placed in a specially designed metal case the size of a thick book. The case was airtight, strong enough to withstand a blast of dynamite, and could be opened only with a randomly changing fifteen-digit computer-generated code. Even if it somehow fell into the wrong hands, there was no way for an outsider to open it without destroying its contents.

Soon after the scientists were done, a red-and-white armored truck pulled away from the building and got onto the A6 highway leading to Paris. It was closely followed by a chase car with two agents from the DGSI, the French intelligence agency in charge of counterterrorism.

The highly trained agents were ready to use lethal force to protect the cargo. But even they didn't know that the truck was a decoy.

The actual case was tucked inside a backpack carried by another agent, who along with his partner was boarding a train for Paris. This was an old-school intelligence trick. If anyone had learned the specimen was being transported, they'd be focused on the armored truck. No one would suspect the pair with long hair and scruffy beards who blended in with all of the other college students backpacking through Europe. The two certainly didn't look like the assassins that they were.

The train from Lyon to Paris took two hours, and the pair was expected to reach the Pasteur Institute just after noon. When they hadn't arrived by one thirty, the agent in charge of the operation began to worry. By five o'clock an extensive search was underway at all locations along the agents' route.

It was two days until their bodies were discovered floating in the Seine. There was no sign of the backpack or the case, though there was one unmistakable clue that hadn't been washed away by the water.

On each agent's forehead was a distinctive purple thumbprint.

16. The Slater Loan Co.

BROOKLYN STARED AT HER CLOSET AND had absolutely no idea what to do. For the first time in her life she was packing. There'd been six previous occasions when all her possessions were dumped into cardboard boxes and dropped off at a new foster home. But that was moving. Never before had she put clothes into a suitcase with the idea that she would return. This was the latest in a whirlwind of first-time-evers that included flying over an ocean, signing the United Kingdom Official Secrets oath, eating baked beans for breakfast, and learning how to use a bobby pin to pick the lock on a pair of military-grade North Korean leg shackles.

Not only that but it was also the first time she had clothes to choose from. Monty had taken her shopping in Edinburgh, and together with the clothes Sydney bought for her in New York, she actually had a wardrobe. It was mostly jeans, shorts, and graphic tees, but it was still hard to choose. In the end, she decided to take everything. That way she would have plenty of options when she got to Paris.

"What are you doing?" asked Sydney, who walked in to find Brooklyn sprawled across the overstuffed suitcase, using her body weight to hold it closed while she zipped it.

"Packing," Brooklyn answered sheepishly.

"Packing what?" she asked.

Brooklyn gave her a look like it may be some sort of trick question. "My suitcase."

"Bad news, mate," Sydney said with a laugh. "That's *our* suitcase."

Brooklyn sat up and sighed. "Yours and mine?"

"Yours and mine *and* Kat's," Sydney answered. "We're travel triplets. That means we share a room and we share a suitcase. We also only get to bring along one of those little shampoo bottles, so get ready to argue over whose we take."

"Okay then," said Brooklyn. "How much am I supposed to bring?"

"*The only one who travels right is the one who travels light*," said Sydney.

"Wow, there's a Motherism for everything."

"Forget all that tuxedo-and-evening-gown nonsense you see in spy movies," said Sydney. "When you're on a real mission, you've got to be able to pick up and go in an instant. You can't do that if you're lugging around a bunch of suitcases. But we can fix this," Sydney offered as she dumped the clothes onto the bed. "We just have to start over."

As they started packing the appropriate amount, Brooklyn said, "Kat's going to hate being a travel triplet with me."

"What makes you think that?" asked Sydney.

Brooklyn gave her an incredulous look. "I'm pretty sure she despises me."

"Nah," said Sydney. "You got that wrong."

"Really, because she never says more than two words to me," replied Brooklyn. "Unless it's 'Get out of my seat' or 'That's not supposed to go there.'"

“That’s just Kat being Kat,” said Sydney. “I told you, she sees the world differently. Sometimes she’ll say something rude, but she doesn’t mean it that way. And sometimes she’ll do something you think is totally mad only to find out later it’s really quite lovely. Like her caper with the chocolate bars.”

“Her what?”

“For one week last year, she was obsessed with Cadbury Crunchie chocolate bars,” said Sydney.

“Never heard of them,” said Brooklyn.

“You’ve been deprived,” Sydney replied. “You’re going to love the chocolate here. So much better than in the States. Anyway, without warning or explanation, Kat started buying Crunchies like mad. One day, she’d buy ten in a single store. The next day, she’d buy one each from ten different stores.”

“Does she have that much of a sweet tooth?” asked Brooklyn.

“She’d only eat one a day,” Sydney answered. “And for the rest, she’d just open the wrapper and offer the chocolate to us. At first we loved it. I mean, who doesn’t love a free Crunchie? But by the end of the week we’d had so many, even Rio was turning her down. And Rio never turns down food.”

"Did you ask her why she was doing it?"

"All she'd say was that it was a 'project for school,'" Brooklyn answered. "We didn't get the full story for a couple weeks. Turns out, the chocolate company was running a sweepstakes to give away five thousand pounds. Kat was comparing the serial numbers on the outside of the wrappers with the game pieces on the inside. She wanted to see if she could crack the code."

"How is that a project for school?" asked Sydney.

"Because when she did crack the code and won the five thousand pounds, she donated it all to her old school back in Nepal."

"That's amazing," said Brooklyn.

"It is," said Sydney. "And so is she. Kat is absolutely amazing. And if the cost of that is a little social awkwardness, then the price is well worth it." She paused for a moment before adding, "Besides, I think she's scared of you."

Brooklyn couldn't believe it. "In what way am I scary?"

"Not scared like that," said Sydney. "She's scared you'll be like Charlotte. It's difficult for Kat to make friends, but the two of them were thick as thieves. It really helped her come out of her shell. Then one day . . . Char was gone."

"Why?" asked Brooklyn.

"That's the question, isn't it?" said Sydney. "Two and a half years together and she just leaves. No warning. No good-bye. The rest of us went to school one day, but she stayed home. Said she was sick. When we got back, there was no sign of her. Mother had to tell us what happened."

"She didn't give a reason?" said Brooklyn.

"None," said Sydney. "She hasn't even said a word to me at school."

They talked some more about Charlotte until an urgent voice interrupted them. "You do realize that we're wheels-up in less than two hours?"

Monty stood at the door, her face the picture of impatience.

"Is there a reason you're not getting ready?" she continued. "Is it because you're trying to drive me crazy? Or is that just a bonus on top of some other goal?"

"We *are* getting ready," Sydney said defensively. "We're packing."

"Really? Because it sounds like you're gossiping," said Monty. "Besides, when does it take two of you to pack for one person?"

"Um . . . that's my fault," Brooklyn said, a bit embarrassed. "I was having trouble figuring out the whole how-much-you're-supposed-to-bring-on-a-spy-mission thing. I went overboard, and Sydney's helping me get it back under control."

Monty noticed the pile of clothes on the bed and softened her tone. "I see. Well, now you know, so hang those up and let's get a move on. Vauxhall Cross has us under the microscope, and I will not let us fall behind schedule before the mission's even started."

If Monty was uncharacteristically gruff, it was because the team found itself facing unprecedented scrutiny. Everything changed the moment the French secret agents were murdered. Once their bodies were discovered with purple thumbprints on their foreheads, Operation Willy Wonka became an MI6 top priority.

It was so important that the team was about to board a small unmarked plane and fly to a top-secret facility outside of London for a week of mission-specific training alongside British Special Forces.

Before that, however, Brooklyn needed to speak to Mother. She wanted to talk to him in private while they were still at the FARM, so once she was packed, she left the house and crossed the lawn to the airstrip. She found him in the flight tower getting the radar and communication equipment ready for the plane to arrive.

"Well, hello. What brings you up here?" he asked.

This was her first time inside the tower, and her train of thought was derailed when she saw the furnishings. "You live here?" she asked incredulously, looking around at the sparse furnishings. Other than the air traffic control equipment, there was little more than a metal cot, an electric teakettle, and a bookcase filled with old paperbacks.

"Well, I'm the caretaker of the airfield," he said. "And living in the tower comes with the job. Like the old lighthouse keepers."

"When you said you lived in an apartment in the tower, I assumed it was an actual, you know, *apartment*," she said.

"The flat's one floor below," he said. "I use it as an office. To be honest, I prefer sleeping up here. The furniture's not much, but the view's magnificent."

Brooklyn couldn't disagree. Windows wrapped around the entire room, giving it a 360-degree panoramic vista that stretched from the North Sea in the east to the sun setting over the highlands in the west.

"A cuppa, a good book, and this view is the best relaxation I know," he said. "However, I doubt you came here to talk about my accommodations, so . . . ?"

"Right . . . yeah," she said as she tried to refocus.

She wasn't sure how to broach this subject, so she just dived right in. "Have you ever heard of the Slater Loan Company?"

"No," he answered without hesitation.

She stared at him and shook her head. "It's amazing how good you are at lying," she said. "If I didn't know better, I'd believe you."

He paused for a moment and said, "Tell me what you know."

"I've been spending a lot of time with Ben. Or Beny, as I like to call him," she said. "And I've been digging around trash cans."

"You've been doing what?" he asked.

"It's an old hacker's trick," she said. "If you put something in the computer's trash can, it looks like it's been erased, but it hasn't. All you've got to do is pluck it out again. It's the perfect place to hide a file you don't want anyone to see."

"But you saw something?"

She pulled a piece of paper from her pocket, unfolded it, and handed it to him.

"The Slater Loan Company," he said, reading it. "Alton H. Slater, CEO." He looked up at her. "This is the company you think I know something about?"

"Don't even try to deny it," she said. "Now, there's nothing particularly suspicious about this. *Except* that it was hidden. I mean, why go to all the trouble to scrub and hide that in a trash can unless there *is* something suspicious about it."

Now she was getting excited. "So I started looking around. Remember, I was able to hack into a bank using an old PC in my school computer lab. With Beny, the sky's the limit, so I found out everything there is to know about the Slater Loan Company."

Mother was torn. He didn't want her to discover what she'd learned, but he was amazed at how good she was at this. "So what is there to find out?"

"Not much," she said. "Even though it's a loan company, it's never made any loans. Not one. It just borrows money from one bank and pays it back to another. That's all it does. Borrow and pay back."

"So that tells me that Alton Slater's a substandard businessman," he replied. "But it doesn't mean he's a villain."

"That's what I thought too, until I was playing Scrabble with Kat," she said. "You know Scrabble, the word game."

"Quite well," he answered. "Kat's been known to

crush my soul playing it. Which is hard to take, considering English is my native tongue and she spent the first ten years of her life speaking Nepali."

"That's good to hear," said Brooklyn. "I thought she just enjoyed humiliating me. Anyway, she's been using the game to teach me code-breaking, and she said the most amazing thing. She told me that the world champions of Scrabble are never writers or English teachers like you'd think. They're always mathematicians. It's because writers and teachers are obsessed with words but mathematicians just figure out the points. She said the trick was not thinking of the tiles as letters, but as symbols."

Brooklyn reached into her pocket and pulled out a handful of Scrabble tiles, which she spread out on the table. "So I decided to do that with the Slater Loan Company. This is how it's spelled on the document, 'Company' abbreviated as 'Co.'"

She arranged the tiles so they spelled:

THE SLATER LOAN CO

"Now, look at this," she said. She rearranged them so they spelled:

ALTON H SLATER CEO

"They're the exact same letters," she said. "That can't be a coincidence."

"So, what does that tell you?" asked Mother.

"That the Slater Loan Company and Alton H. Slater, CEO, are fake," she said. "They're anagrams. Someone's playing a word game, but they're playing it with real banks and real money. The question we need to ask ourselves is who's playing the game."

She rearranged the letters again so that they now spelled:

CHARLOTTE SLOANE

Mother let out a deep sigh. "And what does that tell you?"

Brooklyn looked up and locked eyes with Mother. "I think Charlotte created a fake company so she could build online relationships with banks and access them without them knowing. I think she either stole or was about to steal a lot of money. *That's* what it tells me."

Mother sat there for a moment and shook his head. "Yes," he said with a heavy sigh. "That's exactly what happened. And it wasn't the first time. She'd done something similar in the States."

"What?" she exclaimed.

"Charlotte was understandably angry at the world when her parents died," he replied. "She expressed that anger with behavior that became more and more criminal. First she hacked some businesses, and then she moved on to banks. It took quite a negotiation with the FBI to get her released into my custody."

"Why'd you go to all that trouble?" Brooklyn asked.

"For one thing, I know exactly what it's like to suddenly lose your entire family," he said. "I thought I understood her. I thought if we put her in a supportive and caring environment, she'd do better." He looked up at Brooklyn. "I was wrong. And, when I realized that, I told her she could no longer be part of the team."

"You kicked her off," said Brooklyn.

"Yes."

"Then why did you tell everyone she quit?"

"To protect her," he said. "And to protect the team. Monty and I caught her before she actually stole any money, thank goodness. That could've destroyed everything. And she really is a good person. She has so many wonderful traits. But she couldn't be part of all this. And, when I let her go, I thought we'd have to cancel this mission. The contest requires five people per team. But then fate delivered us a solution."

"Me?" said Brooklyn.

"You," he said. "I came across the file of a twelve-year-old girl who'd hacked into a government agency, and why? To bring justice." He shook his head in amazement thinking about it. "There were these two astonishing girls who both did the same thing, but for very different reasons."

"So, if you hadn't been one person short for the competition, I'd be in some supervised group home right now?" she asked, slightly wounded.

"I knew the moment I saw your file that you belonged with us," he said. "Nothing would've kept me from being in that courtroom that day."

"How'd you happen to find it?" she asked. "The file with my case?"

"The same way I found Charlotte's," he answered. "I was looking for Annie. My daughter's quite the computer whiz, so I always keep an eye out for any young female hackers who get in trouble."

Brooklyn weighed this for a moment.

"Do you want me to keep this secret from everyone?" she asked. "The part about you kicking Charlotte off the team?"

"I won't ask you to lie to them," he said. "But I'm not sure it does anybody any good if they find out."

"Me neither," she said. "We'll just keep it between us."

"Thank you," he answered. "Now we have to get moving."

Ninety minutes later a twin-engine turbo-prop Beechcraft King Air B200 with no flight markings landed in total darkness on the grass airstrip that was once RAF Aisling. It was on the ground for less than ten minutes as seven passengers boarded. The last one on was Mother, who pulled up the stairs, locked the hatch, and signaled the pilot that they were ready to go.

The interior of the plane was small enough that Brooklyn could almost reach from side to side. There were a total of eight seats, and she took one in the back row, staring out the window as the plane took off and soared into the moonless night.

When they encountered turbulence above the North Sea, she clutched her armrest and told herself not to panic. She took a deep breath and counted to ten. But the nervousness didn't fade.

She had no idea what to expect, but she was positive that the whirlwind of first-time-evers was just beginning.

17. Goldfinger Avenue

THE BANK ROBBERY TAKING PLACE twenty miles west of central London was nothing like the cyberattacks committed by Brooklyn and Charlotte. This was an old-fashioned heist, complete with bad guys who carried guns and wore ski masks to hide their faces.

The fact that Brooklyn and the rest of the team witnessed it in person was just a case of being in the wrong place at the right time. They were on their way to training but the street had been blocked off, so all they could do was stand a safe distance away and watch the drama unfold from behind a line of wooden barricades.

"I can't believe we're actually seeing this," Brooklyn said to Monty. "How's it even possible?"

Before them four police cars were fanned out in a semicircle in front of the bank entrance. The officers had taken cover behind their vehicles, and everything was at a standstill until one of the robbers leaned out the front door holding a hostage.

He shouted something at the cops, but Brooklyn couldn't make it out. She noticed a police sniper crawling into position on a rooftop across the street and pointed it out to Sydney and Kat who nodded silently, as if speaking aloud might alert the criminals.

"Give up now! Before somebody gets hurt!" an officer called over a bullhorn.

The robbers responded to this demand with a hail of bullets, and soon shots were fired from both sides. Even at this distance, Brooklyn reflexively stepped back to avoid getting hit by any stray gunfire.

Suddenly the shooting stopped as a silver Jaguar convertible came racing down the street. The driver slammed on the brakes, and the rear of the sports car fishtailed all the way around until it slid to a screeching halt against the curb.

Out stepped the driver, dressed in a slick black suit and tie. He deftly pulled a pistol from his shoulder holster, pointed it right at the door to the bank, and . . . *froze.* He just stood there for what seemed like an eternity until he finally put his gun back in the holster, turned in the opposite direction, and asked, "What's my line again?"

"Cut!" yelled the director as an entire film crew let out a groan of exasperation. This was their third try, and there was no reason to think he'd get it right on the fourth.

"'I'm here for queen and country, and I've come to make a withdrawal!'" the director said into his bullhorn.

"That's it, that's it!" said the actor. "I'll get it this time. I promise."

"We'll pick it up on the reverse angle when we come back," the director said, seething with frustration. "That's lunch!"

A bell sounded, and crewmembers suddenly materialized from everywhere. Brooklyn was amazed at how many people were involved in shooting a movie. It was jarring in a humorous way to watch the men who moments before were playing bank robbers take off their masks and make small talk with the cops who'd just been pointing guns at them.

The woman showing the team around the film studio turned to Mother and shook her head. "You'd think he'd be able to remember one bloody sentence," she said, incredulous. "The name of the movie is *Queen and Country*. That's half the line."

Their guide was unlike anyone Brooklyn had ever met. Nearly six feet tall, she had a shock of silver hair, was missing her left pinkie, and walked with a slight limp. Her name was Gertrude Shepherd, but to everyone at Vauxhall Cross she was known simply as Tru. A legendary MI6 operative, she'd served as a field agent for more than twenty-five years, and rumor had it the missing finger and limp were the results of a back-alley knife fight in Bangkok. In reality she lost the finger gardening and the limp was an old skiing injury, but she never let the truth get in the way of her own mythology. Besides, she really had been in a Bangkok knife fight but walked out of that alley unscathed, although the same couldn't be said of the Chinese spy who'd lured her there.

Tru was now a command officer, and among other duties she was Mother's direct supervisor. She was also the technical advisor for the upcoming spy thriller *Queen and Country*, which is why the team was at Pinewood Studios just outside of London in the town of Iver Heath.

"Is that Jonny Lott?" Paris asked excitedly when the forgetful movie star walked past them, headed for his trailer.

"Tragically, yes," said Tru.

"Who's Jonny Lott?" asked Brooklyn.

"One of the best footballers in the world," said Rio. "He's the star of Man U. He's a star on the national team too."

"And unfortunately, he's the star of this cinematic masterpiece," said Tru. "That's what you get when you try to turn a footballer into an action hero. Wonderful to look at. Thick as a post. I imagine you'd have the same level of success if you took the lead from some West End play and put him in goal for Arsenal." She turned to address the whole group. "Back to the buggies."

They climbed into a pair of golf carts and, with Tru driving one and Mother the other, resumed their caravan across the studio lot.

Ever since the 1930s, Pinewood had been home to movies ranging from early Alfred Hitchcock mysteries to massive *Star Wars* blockbusters. But the series most associated with the studio was evidenced by the fact they drove along 007 Drive before turning onto Goldfinger Avenue.

"Every James Bond movie has filmed on the lot going back to *Dr. No* in 1962," Tru said while she drove. "So Pinewood holds a special meaning for creaky old bird-watchers like me. As a goodwill gesture, MI6 makes a senior agent available to offer technical expertise on any films that feature the Secret Intelligence Service."

Sitting next to her, Brooklyn was awestruck as they passed the different soundstages. Each had a sign on its door with the name of the movie that was shooting inside. Tru listed off the stars of the films like they were old friends. She parked the buggy by the entrance to Soundstage D next to the props building in the middle of the lot.

"*City of Light*," Brooklyn said, reading the name of the production off the door. "Who's starring in that?"

"You are, dear," said Tru.

"What?" asked Brooklyn.

"I'll show you," she responded.

Tru led them through a green door into a cavernous room 165 feet long by 110 feet wide. There were four large sets on the stage, but it was impossible to tell what they were from behind. All the team could see were the backs of fake walls spray-painted with the words PROPERTY DEPARTMENT—PINEWOOD STUDIOS.

"Welcome to Stage D," said Tru. "Countless films have been shot in this room. If you lift up the floor, you can see the water tank that was turned into the Miami Beach swimming pool for *Goldfinger.* This is where they built the entrance stairs to Hogwarts and King's Cross station for one of the Harry Potter movies. And, for the next seven days, it's where you'll conduct your training."

"Let me get this straight," said Mother, disbelieving. "After years of admonishing me to maintain a low profile and take every possible precaution to mask my identity as a spy, you're training my team on Goldfinger Avenue in a soundstage where they literally make James Bond films."

Tru flashed a wide grin, revealing a gap between her middle teeth. "Ingenious, isn't it?" she said. "Come now, I'll show you."

She motioned them to follow her around to the other side of the sets and continued talking as they walked.

"The set designers have re-created key locations you'll encounter in Paris, and you're going to spend the next week learning every inch of them," she said. "Now, if we wanted to do this somewhere else, say, an empty warehouse in Milton Keynes, we would've had to haul everything over there in lorries, which would've taken time and attracted attention. Then we'd have a group of children going into the warehouse every day alongside hulking Special Forces commandos, which also would've attracted attention. But here on the lot, the props were all next door, and anyone walking by will just think you're making a film. And, to be blunt, since none of you are famous, no one's going to give you a second look."

"That works for anyone walking by," said Brooklyn. "But what about the people at MI6, with the studio, and whoever's working on the soundstage? Won't they find out who we are? Aren't we supposed to be a secret?"

"There are exactly four people at MI6 who know about this team," said Tru. "And only two of us know Mother's actual identity. Everyone else at Vauxhall Cross thinks we're making an educational film to be shown in schools across the UK. As for the commandos, they think you're training for a reality television series called *The Spy's the Limit.*" She glanced at Mother. "I came up with that one myself." She turned back to Brooklyn and said, "Trust me when I say that your anonymity is secure."

Monty marveled at the cleverness of it all. "That's bloody brilliant."

"*Anyone can hide under darkness of night, but the cunning one hides out in plain sight*," recited Tru.

"Ooh," said Paris. "Is that another Motherism?"

"Motherism?" Tru turned to Mother. "Have you been taking credit for my sayings?" She laughed and turned to the others. "That's a Truism!"

Tru showed them three separate sets: a small auditorium, a laboratory, and a ballroom, each of which was a meticulous copy of a room in the Paris headquarters of Sinclair Scientifica.

"These are the rooms where Stavros Sinclair is scheduled to make appearances during the summit," said Tru. "If you advance through the competition, you'll be with him each of those times. That means you'll be our eyes and ears in these rooms, and I can't emphasize enough how vital that will be."

"What happens if the Purple Thumb attacks?" asked Paris. "Are we supposed to stop them?"

"No," Mother interjected. "You're to alert us to anything that's going on so that we can come crashing in. They've already killed two agents. We're not putting you in harm's way for Stavros Sinclair."

"But you are our first line of defense," Tru said, sounding much less protective than Mother. "This week we'll run through a wide variety of simulations, and you'll see there are scenarios where we think you can protect Stavros without putting yourselves in too much danger."

Mother and Tru shared a look but neither said anything, and the phrase "too much danger" hung in the air for a moment.

"The auditorium is where Sinclair will deliver his address opening the summit," said Sydney. "And the lab's where we'll be working on the weather models, but what's happening in the ballroom?"

"On the final night of the summit, the ballroom's where the top ten teams will assemble so he can announce the winner of the Stavros Challenge," said Tru.

"That explains these three rooms," said Paris. "But what's that one?"

He pointed to the fourth set, which they hadn't yet entered.

"Let's have a look," said Tru. "Now, you have to understand that Stavros Sinclair is extraordinarily secretive," she said as they walked. "It took endless arm-twisting to get the French authorities to release the blueprints to make these sets. And while we believe they are exact, we don't know for certain what's in here."

They entered the set, which was made up as a computer server room.

"Why don't you know?" asked Paris.

"Because the blueprints only show its structure, not what's inside," said Tru.

"Then what makes you think it's a server room?" asked Brooklyn.

"Air-conditioning," she said. "There's an excessive number of vents coming into the room, as well as a pair of emergency air-conditioners directly above it on the roof. Sinclair Scientifica uses massive computers that constantly need to be cooled, so a server room makes the most sense."

"Either that or they've got a penguin habitat," joked Monty.

"Penguins are cute," said Brooklyn, "but I'm hoping it's computers." She turned to Tru. "What's our mission in here?"

"Not ours, pet, just yours," she answered. "We want you to break in, hack into the mainframe, and insert a program our top coders are concocting as we speak."

"That's barmy!" said Mother. "This was never part of the plan."

"It is now," said Tru. "In fact, it may be the most important part."

"So now MI6 spies on companies?" said Mother.

"This one, yes," said Tru. "We're quite concerned about some of the people Sinclair Scientifica has been doing business with. We think they've been working alongside Umbra in some instances. If we can get inside the mainframe, then we'll know more about these people and be able to do our job better. As secretive as the company is, this might be our best chance."

"Brooklyn's only been here a few weeks," Mother said. "She doesn't have the training for something like this."

"I seem to remember a phone call during which you told me she was a true natural like you'd never seen," said Tru. "I believe the phrase was 'already better than the other four.'"

This stung the others and put Mother on the defensive, which was exactly what Tru wanted. She wasn't concerned with niceties, only the mission.

"Perhaps we can discuss this in private," said Mother.

"Why? Because you're worried about their feelings?" asked Mother. "Stop treating them like children."

"They are children," he replied.

"No, they're agents," she said curtly. "As are you. I'm your superior officer, and this is your new directive."

"It's okay," Brooklyn said, trying to calm the situation. "I should be able to do this, no worries."

Tru smiled. "Excellent. Although, I assume the difficulty won't be hacking the computer so much as it will be getting into the room."

"Why's that?" asked Brooklyn.

"Because, in order reach it, you'll need to climb up two stories on the outside of the building."

Brooklyn tried to mask her reaction to this development. She hated heights. Especially after the night she'd spent locked on the roof of her foster home. At one point she'd decided to climb to the ground, but when she saw the view over the edge, she instantly got dizzy and backed away.

That same feeling of vertigo was in full force two days later as she dangled in a climbing harness from the ceiling of the soundstage. The set designers had painstakingly re-created a portion of the exterior wall of the Sinclair Scientifica building and Brooklyn was trying to make it from one spot to another using nothing more than the mortar joints between bricks, a rain gutter, and some windowsills.

In all, she had to cover a distance of twenty-two feet, but after two twelve-hour days the farthest she'd made it was nine.

"I'm sorry," she said as her hand slipped and she fell for the umpteenth time.

"That's enough for today," said her climbing coach, a female commando from the Special Air Service. "We'll pick up again first thing tomorrow."

Brooklyn hung in the air with sweat dripping down her face and pain radiating from every fingertip. Her body was happy for the break, but her heart and mind understood some harsh realities. She had only five more days to get ready, and when she made the actual climb, she'd be outside in the dark without a harness.

Two hours later, she came back to practice by herself. Or at least she thought she was alone. She was about five feet off the ground when a noise from behind startled her, causing her to slip and slam her face against the wall.

"Owww!" she wailed as she reached up to hold her quickly swelling lip. She twisted around in the harness to see Rio.

"Oh, that's just perfect. Of course it's you."

"What does that mean?" he asked.

"Let me guess," she said, her frustration rising. "You're here to gloat. To make fun of the American who can't get anything right. Well, go ahead. Hit me with your best shot." She spread open her arms and swayed in the air.

"That's not why I'm here," he said defensively.

"No? Then why?"

"I came here to help you. You shouldn't climb by yourself. You can get hurt."

"Right," she said. "Because that's what you like to do, help me," she scoffed. "The only thing you want to help me do is look foolish so you can get your revenge."

"It's not like that," he said. "You've got me all wrong."

"Really?" she replied. "Have you done one nice thing for me since I arrived? Have you done anything to make me feel welcome?"

"Yes," he said.

"What?"

"I came here tonight," he answered. "Right now. This is me helping you. Welcoming you."

"I don't believe you," she said. "And frankly, I don't have any time to waste. I've got to practice this. So, why don't you do one of your little magic tricks and make yourself disappear?"

Rio stormed out of the room, while Brooklyn turned back to face the wall and started all over again. As she did, a fleeting thought occurred to her. *What if he* had *been trying to help?*

Le Fantôme

THERE WERE MANY IN THE INTERNATIONAL law enforcement and intelligence communities who were convinced Le Fantôme was not a real person. They believed he was a creation of Umbra designed to distract anyone trying to unravel the intricate layers of the criminal organization.

They believed this because they'd failed so miserably to capture him. In fact, he was very real, and unlike the evil masterminds in spy movies who lived in island fortresses protected by giant death rays, he spent most of his time in an apartment located in the Montmartre neighborhood of Paris.

He had other residences around the globe but considered this one home. He'd chosen it not for any strategic value but because it once belonged to Pierre-Auguste Renoir, his favorite artist. An original Renoir portrait of a young girl in a dark blue coat now hung in the study above his desk. The painting was worth more than twenty million dollars, but its value to Le Fantôme was sentimental, not financial. The girl in the picture reminded him of his twin sister, who'd passed away when they were only eleven years old.

Amazingly, the Renoir wasn't the most expensive item in the apartment. That honor belonged to a silver case that held a deadly virus with no known antidote.

French authorities believed it was impossible for someone to steal the case and open it without destroying the contents. But that's because they hadn't considered the possibility that the person who stole it might also own the company that manufactured it.

Opening the case was easy for Le Fantôme, just as it had been simple to disable its hidden tracking mechanism. Once he confirmed that the virus was inside, he placed everything in a wall safe that had also been manufactured by one of his many companies.

Despite the fact that he'd spent years planning for this very day, there was no urgency as he spread butter and jam on a fresh baguette he'd purchased from the corner bakery. His most ambitious plot was hours from being set into motion. Still he approached the day as he would any other.

He sat by an open window, sipping his coffee, and imagined how Rue Cortot had looked when Monsieur Renoir ate his breakfast here more than a century before. He took a bite and started to read *Le Parisien*. The front page had multiple stories about the Global Youth Summit on the Environment. One article mentioned that fifty thousand young people from around the world were coming to Paris with the belief that in three days' time they could change the world.

Le Fantôme took another bite. *They have no idea how much the world is going to change in the next three days,* he thought to himself. *No idea at all.*

The Eurostar

BROOKLYN STARED OUT THE WINDOW AT a landscape of green, yellow, and brown as the Eurostar raced through the French countryside, going nearly 190 miles per hour. But her mind wasn't on the beauty of the scenery or the impressiveness of the sleek train moving through it.

She simply could not stop thinking about the wall.

During a week of training, she had only made it to the top twice. There were, however, countless times she found herself dangling in the safety harness, forearms aching, fingertips throbbing, after yet another failed attempt. What were the odds she'd be able to complete the climb with everything on the line?

Additionally, there'd been extra pressure ever since Tru said Mother had labeled her "a true natural . . . already better than the other four." They never talked about it, but she saw the resentment in their eyes and felt their contempt every time she failed to live up to that standard.

Directly across from her and riding backward, Sydney was in a similar funk as she worked on the speech she was giving at the summit's closing rally. In the past three weeks she'd written eleven different versions and hated each one. She had a yellow legal pad in her lap, and, as she took a crack at attempt number twelve, she mumbled variations of the first line to herself trying to find the perfect words.

It is time for us to act. . . . The time has come for us to act. . . . We must act now before it is too late. . . . The world is in danger, and we must come together and act. She thought each one was worse than the last, and she punctuated this sentiment with a growl of frustration as she took her pen and crossed through them all.

The two of them were so distracted, neither noticed

Mother take the seat next to Sydney. As he watched them, he was equally concerned and entertained. He was also a bit dismayed. Despite their extensive training, they seemed completely unaware he was there. To remedy this, he opened a small red canister of Pringles, took out a potato chip, and crunched it as loudly as he could.

This startled them both.

"How long have you been sitting there?" asked Sydney.

He finished chewing and swallowed before answering, "Long enough to know that something's troubling you." He looked across the table at Brooklyn. "Both of you."

"The only thing troubling me is that my speech is total rubbish," said Sydney. "Oh, and the fact that I have to deliver it at the base of the Eiffel Tower in front of tens of thousands of people."

"That's a reasonable cause for concern." He turned to Brooklyn. "What about you?"

"Nothing's bothering me," she said defensively.

"Really?" he chuckled. "Then what were you thinking about as you stared out the window?"

"Um . . . just what I read in this book." She held up a biography of Stavros Sinclair that she had bought in a bookstore at the train station before they left London.

"I thought it might help to know more about him."

"Which is why you've made it all the way to . . ." He took the book from her and opened it at the bookmark. ". . . page seven. We've been on the train for almost two hours, and you've read seven pages. Must be riveting. Which part has you deep in thought? The table of contents?"

She gave him a guilty shrug.

"I know you're worried about the climb," he said. "That's also reasonable. But, lucky for both of you, I'm quite skilled at problem-solving." He popped another chip in his mouth and chomped on it.

"How can you fix my speech?" wondered Sydney.

"I thought you'd never ask." He pulled a folded piece of paper out of his pocket and handed it to her. "Read this."

Sydney opened it and began to read aloud. "'Some problems are so big they can't be solved by adults,'" she said. "'Luckily, there are young people like us who are ready to face the challenge.'" She looked up at him. "This is good. Did you write this?"

He laughed. "No. You did. That's version three from two and a half weeks ago. It was good then, and it's good now. Your problem isn't your speech. You just need to have faith in yourself."

Sydney continued to read the speech, and Mother turned his attention back to Brooklyn. "And now you."

"I have plenty of faith in myself," said Brooklyn. "I have total faith that I will fall off the side of that building and let everyone down."

"You'll do no such thing," said Mother.

"What makes you so sure?" she asked.

"The fact that I'm calling off the climb," he said. "The mission's busy enough. We don't need it."

"You can't just call it off," Brooklyn protested.

"I just did," he said.

"What about Tru?" she asked. "She gave you an order. Actually, she called it a *directive*, which sounds even more official than an order."

"Yes, but once we're in the field, I'm the alpha, and that means I decide what is and what isn't part of the mission," Mother said. "Besides, I can handle Tru."

"Would you be *handling* her if it was Sydney and not me?" asked Brooklyn. "It only took her a couple tries to get to the top."

"Yes, but that's because I spent years sneaking out of and back into the Wallangarra School for Girls," said Sydney. "I got so good at climbing, some of my friends started calling me the Tree Frog."

"Besides, it doesn't matter," said Mother. "Sydney doesn't have your computer skills, so she can't hack into the mainframe."

"Exactly," said Brooklyn. "Only I can do that. Which means my inability to climb the wall is the reason an important part of the mission is in jeopardy."

"You're putting too much pressure on yourself," said Mother.

"It's true," said Sydney. "We wouldn't have been able to go on this mission if it wasn't for you."

Brooklyn appreciated the sentiment but still felt like she was letting down the team. Mother was offering her a "get out of jail free" card, and, as tempting as that was, it seemed like cheating.

Just then, Kat slid into the seat next to Brooklyn and said, "I've discovered a fascinating anomaly."

"There's a sentence you don't hear every day," said Mother. "What is it?"

As Kat spoke, she looked directly at Mother and Sydney, almost as if Brooklyn wasn't there. "Since this mission is about protecting Stavros Sinclair from the Purple Thumb, I thought I'd look for patterns in their past crime scenes."

"The police have been doing that for years," said Mother. "And they've gotten nowhere."

"That's because they're looking for similarities in the crimes," Kat replied. "They think that will help them figure out who's committing them."

"And what did you do?" asked Mother.

"I looked for patterns in the victims."

He leaned forward, intrigued by this approach. "Go on."

"Okay, you've got three of them. Victims, that is. Each is a sponsor of the summit, and each was attacked during the final rally," Kat said. "Other than that, they have almost no commonalities. Fenix is a small Swedish software firm that writes programs to help recycling companies. Fūjin is one of the leading manufacturers of wind energy turbines in Japan. And Fulgora is a Silicon Valley tech startup that develops batteries for electric cars."

"And the pattern is?" asked Mother.

"Their names," said Kat.

"Fenix, Fūjin, and Fulgora," offered Brooklyn. "They all start with *F*."

"Yes, but that's an insignificant coincidence," Kat said, dismissing the observation. "The key is the *meaning* of their names. Fenix is the Swedish name for the mythological firebird that rises from the ashes. Fūjin is the Japanese god of wind. And Fulgora is the Roman goddess of lightning."

"So you think the Purple Thumb is . . . *anti-mythology*?" Sydney asked, totally confused.

"No, ignore the Purple Thumb and focus on the victims," said Kat. "I think Fenix, Fūjin, and Fulgora are all separate parts of the same company. One that likes to name things after gods and other mythological creatures. I think the three victims are actually one victim."

Mother considered this for a moment. "That would mean instead of random vandalism, the Purple Thumb is targeting a single company," he said. "Interesting if it's true, but that's a pretty big leap to take just based on their names."

"It's no leap at all," said Kat. She opened a picture on her computer tablet and handed it across the table to Mother and Sydney. Brooklyn leaned across to get a look. "This is from the crime scene in Stockholm."

"It's the purple thumbprint on the CEO's computer monitor," said Sydney. "We've looked at it a hundred times."

"True, but we never considered the Asset Inventory Code," said Kat.

"How silly of us," Mother joked. "What's the Asset Inventory Code?"

"It's the way companies keep track of the things they own, like computers, furniture, and office equipment," Kat explained.

Mother laughed. "And you know this because . . . ?"

"Because she's Kat," said Sydney. "She knows everything about codes."

Kat smiled, a bit embarrassed, and said, "It's the key to everything. Look at the sticker."

The computer had a sticker on which was printed:

FENIX

SS2K FE13 A3C2 D1PK

"Okay," Mother said, still not getting it. "What qualifies that as intriguing?"

"It's sixteen characters long," said Kat. "Do you know how many different combinations there are in a sixteen-character alphanumeric code?"

"I'm guessing rather a lot," said Mother.

"Slightly less than eight septillion," she said. "That's eight followed by twenty-four zeros." She let this sink in before adding, "But there are fewer than forty employees at Fenix, which makes you wonder: How many different pieces of office furniture do you think they're planning to buy?"

"Right," said Mother. "My interest is officially piqued. What else do you have?"

"I was able to find AIC codes from each of the crime scenes," said Kat. "All three companies use sixteen-character coding systems, and in all three of them the first four characters are identical."

She showed them the police photos and zoomed in so they could see what she was talking about.

"Each one starts off with S-S-2-K," she continued. "There are nearly one million, six hundred eighty thousand different combinations of the first four characters. The chances the same combination would be at each location are astronomical." She paused for a moment. "Unless it's all one company with one coding system. Then it makes total sense."

"Boom!" said Sydney.

"Once I knew that, I started deciphering more of the string," continued Kat. "The second set of characters tells you the location. Everything at Fenix has FE13: *F-E*, the first two letters of 'Fenix,' which was founded in 2013. And no matter where they were, all of the computers have A3C at the start of the third group. That's true of the computers in Tokyo, San Francisco, and Stockholm. It has to be one company."

"I'm beyond convinced," Mother said, marveling at it. "I don't suppose you figured out which company owns them all."

Brooklyn interrupted and said, "Sinclair Scientifica!"

"Correct," Kat replied as if she'd just noticed that Brooklyn was also at the table. "How'd you know that?"

"We've just spent seven days learning everything we possibly could about their headquarters in Paris," said Brooklyn. "A building that's called . . . Olympus."

"Home of the gods," said Sydney.

"Not only that," Brooklyn said, happy to be noticed, "but the first four characters are S-S-2-K. My guess is that stands for Sinclair Scientifica, which was founded on January 1, 2000."

They were all surprised by this revelation, especially Kat. Brooklyn held up the biography and said, "That part's on page three."

Kat studied her for a moment and nodded. "That's sound deductive reasoning."

From Kat, that felt like a five-star review, and Brooklyn beamed. Through the window they could see the outskirts of Paris as they neared the Gare du Nord train station.

"Why would Sinclair Scientifica keep their ownership of these companies a secret?" asked Sydney.

"There are a lot of reasons," said Mother. "Some companies do it to avoid government regulation and others to keep their competitors in the dark. There are endless secrets in the business world."

"Well, somebody knew this one," said Kat.

"What do you mean?" asked Brooklyn.

"The Purple Thumb," she answered. "Whoever's committing these crimes knows they're all part of one company. Maybe that's why they're doing it: to send a message. To let Sinclair know they're onto them."

"That's extraordinary, Kat," said Mother. "I don't know if anyone else could've found that pattern."

"It has a flaw, though," said Brooklyn.

"What flaw?" Kat asked defensively.

"One crime scene doesn't fit," Brooklyn answered. "The two dead agents floating in the Seine. It wasn't an attack on Sinclair, and it wasn't during the summit. Why did the Purple Thumb break their pattern? And what are they going to do with the stolen virus?"

The All-Seeing Reggie

BECAUSE HE WAS TRAVELING UNDER A different cover story, Mother split up from the group at the Gare du Nord. Technically, he wasn't part of FARM, so he wasn't in Paris for the summit. Instead, if anyone got suspicious and checked his travel plans, they'd see he was in the city visiting museums as part of his job with the Scottish National Gallery.

Before separating, though, he gave Brooklyn a pep talk as they walked along the platform next to the train. "Just because you don't see me doesn't mean I'm not nearby watching everything," he reassured her. "And you know what to do if you need to talk directly?"

Brooklyn nodded.

"I want to hear you say it," he said.

"I text you the word 'pancake,'" she responded. "Just 'pancake' and a time."

"That's right," he said. "If someone hacks us, it won't mean a thing to them. But I'll know where and when to meet you."

Anyone intercepting the text would assume it had something to do with breakfast, but it would actually be a reference to the judge from family court. Mother would know to meet Brooklyn in front of the Palais de Justice, which was located in the exact center of the city.

"And remember," he added. "Forget about the wall. You don't have to climb it."

Brooklyn took a few more steps and was about to respond when she looked up and saw that he was gone. She had no idea how he disappeared so quickly, but as she scanned the travelers on the platform, there was no sign of him.

"Come on," Sydney said as she walked up and threw a friendly arm around her shoulders. "You're going to love this city."

Outside the train station they hopped on the number forty-two bus to get to their hotel. The Three Lions Inn was located in the Madeleine neighborhood of Paris where two roads intersected at sharp angles, making the building wedge-shaped like a four-story slice of cake. As with most hotels in the city, the staff worked diligently to maintain its star rating in guidebooks and on travel websites. Except, unlike others who tried to move up the scale, the Three Lions was determined never to earn more than a single star, the lowest score possible.

To achieve this, the staff offered mediocre service; the rooms were kept clean, but not too clean, and the building's lone elevator was almost always out of order. Not surprisingly, though there were only twenty-eight rooms to let, the hotel always had at least a handful of vacancies. Even during the busiest tourist seasons. As one reviewer put it, *"It's amazing the Three Lions is able to stay in business."*

What no reviewer could possibly know was that the Three Lions stayed in business because it was one of several hotels in Paris owned and operated by the British Secret Intelligence Service. Constant vacancies were necessary in case an agent needed emergency lodging. And while the hotel didn't offer luxuries such as plush bedding, gourmet meals, or a day spa, it did have bullet-proof windows, an underground communication center, and three separate hidden exits, one of which led to a tunnel connecting to the British embassy two blocks away.

Of course, none of that was apparent as the team approached the building's rather unimpressive entrance. The paint was fading on the old sign above the doorway, and the *H* was so faint it looked like it said "Tree Lions."

"*This* is where we're staying?" Sydney asked unenthusiastically.

"Trust me," said Monty, who'd kept the hotel's MI6 connection a secret. "There's more to it than you see at first glance."

When they entered the equally uninspiring lobby, Sydney leaned over to Kat and whispered, "Hopefully there's more to it than you see at second glance too."

Before Kat could even laugh, a voice boomed from across the room. "I heard that!"

Sydney looked up and was startled to see a man looking directly at her from behind the check-in counter. She was certain he couldn't have heard her whisper from so far away. At least she was *almost* certain.

"You heard what?" she asked cautiously.

"I heard you disparage this fine establishment," he answered. "The first rule of the Three Lions is that Reggie sees all and hears all."

"I'm so sorry," Sydney replied, suddenly backpedaling. "I-I didn't mean to . . ."

He cut her off with a roar of laughter. "I'm only joking. You should hear how I talk about the place. It's a dump. But it's my dump."

Of all the special features at the hotel, the most special was Reggie, who was seemingly on duty around the clock. He'd been with MI6 for twenty years, and like many great spies, he was of uncertain age and ethnicity. Depending on the lighting and whether his hair and beard were neatly trimmed, he could pass for anything from a thirtysomething Middle Eastern businessman to a midfifties South American beach bum. In reality, he was forty-five and from Liverpool. He'd been an operative in Southeast Asia until a bullet lodged in his right knee and ended his career as a field agent.

Now he put his cloak-and-dagger skills to work at the Three Lions, where a state-of-the-art security system and the hotel's unique triangular shape allowed him to keep a constant eye on anyone approaching the building.

If someone followed you, Reggie knew it. More important, he knew exactly what to do about it.

"Hello, Reg," Monty said warmly as they approached the desk. She'd known him ever since basic training, when he was one of her weapons instructors.

"Lovely to see you, Alexandra," he replied, calling her, as he always did, by her first name. "Welcome back to the Three Lions."

She looked at the old couch in the otherwise empty lobby, the outdated travel posters on the wall, and the rather uninviting bowl of hard candy sitting on the counter. "I love what you haven't done to the place," she said as she handed him everyone's passports to check in.

"We wouldn't want to over-egg the pudding, now would we?" he said with a sly grin. He wrote the names into a ledger and grabbed three keys from a row of cubbies on the wall behind him. "Let me show you to your rooms and make sure everyone's acquainted with all the amenities."

As he came out from behind the counter, he walked with the help of a cane that had the name "Harry" written on its barrel.

"I thought your name was Reggie," said Rio.

"It is," said the man.

"Then who's Harry?" Rio asked, pointing at the name.

"Harry's the cane," Reggie explained.

It took a moment, but Paris was the first to get the joke, and, when he did, he laughed hard. "You named your cane after the footballer?"

"Indeed I did!" Reg shot him a wink and smiled. "We're called the Three Lions for a reason."

The hotel was named after England's national soccer team, which was nicknamed the Three Lions because of the lions on the crest of King Richard the Lionheart, which they wore on their jerseys. Harry Kane had been the captain of the team during the 2018 World Cup and won the Golden Boot as the tournament's highest scorer.

"I put everyone on the ground floor," Reggie said as they reached one of the rooms. "So you don't have to worry about the lift." He unlocked a door to reveal a plain room with three beds, a desk, a chair, and a large stain on the wall.

"This one's for the girls," he said. "I call it the Princess Suite."

He shot a look at Sydney, who simply said, "Lovely."

"I know you don't mean it, but it really is," he replied.

He gave the window two solid whacks with his cane, and rather than shattering the glass, the cane just bounced off. "These are ballistic level-three glass-clad polycarbonate windows, and the bathroom walls are reinforced steel with armor plating. If things go pear-shaped, that's where you hide."

Suddenly the kids were beginning to get the sense that the hotel was not what it seemed.

"This light switch works the lights," he said, demonstrating by flipping it on and off. "But this one activates a radio jammer so no one can use electronic devices to listen in on you."

"Doesn't that mess up Wi-Fi?" asked Brooklyn.

"Yes, but you shouldn't be using Wi-Fi while you're here," he said. "It's too easy to compromise. If you need to go online, just plug this into your laptop." He pulled up a corner of wallpaper to reveal a hidden computer cable. "It puts you on the same network as the embassy and has a fully encrypted firewall."

"Wow," said Brooklyn.

"Now, let me show you how to use your room key," Reggie said.

Sydney laughed but then realized he was serious.

"Wait. Isn't there only one way to use a room key?"

"If all you're worried about is unlocking a door, then yes," he said. "But this is designed for self-defense."

He held up the key chain: a metal lion's head attached to a key ring with superstrong parachute cord. "If you find yourself in trouble, slide this ring between your fingers like this and it becomes a handle, and the lion's head turns into a weapon." He swung it around like a ninja. "Just hold them at bay until Harry and I can come to the rescue." He lifted his cane for emphasis.

"You're going to beat them with your cane?" asked Rio.

"If I have to," he said. "But I'd rather do this."

He held the cane up like a gun, pressed an unseen button, and a feathered dart shot out of it and stuck to the wall.

"Harry's also a tranq gun," he said. "This should knock anyone out until the cavalry arrives."

The team stared first at the dart and then at Reggie, trying to make sense of the scene.

"I told you there's more to this place than meets the eye," said Monty.

"Finally, the linen closet's across the hall," he said. "The odds are good that the staff will fall behind in its housekeeping, so that's where you'll find fresh towels.

More important, it has a false panel behind the shelf that opens onto a tunnel connecting to the embassy. If you run through the tunnel, it triggers an alarm in the embassy; and believe me, they will be ready and waiting once you reach the door.

"The code to unlock the door is 1-9-6-6," he said. "It's a doodle to remember because that's when England won the World Cup."

"This is officially the greatest hotel in the world," said Paris.

Reggie flashed him a grin and said, "I'm chuffed to hear you say that, mate. Just be sure to keep that opinion among ourselves. I wouldn't want an extra star popping up in the Michelin next year."

Once they'd settled into their room, Sydney lay on her bed working on her speech while Brooklyn and Kat huddled around a laptop to test out their latest weather models. They were halfway through them when Monty knocked on the door.

"Who's ready for some sightseeing?" she asked.

"Shouldn't we be preparing for tomorrow?" asked Brooklyn. "It's the first day of the competition, and we want to get off to a good start."

"You've trained nonstop for three weeks," Monty

replied. "And you're about to start an intense few days. I think a little fun might be in order."

She didn't have to ask twice.

For the next few hours, they were tourists, not spies. They posed for goofy pictures in front of the glass pyramid outside of the Louvre, they ate crepes from a sidewalk cart, and Paris even showed them a favorite "secret spot" he knew from when he lived in the city.

"Follow me," he instructed as they entered Printemps department store.

First he took them up an elevator. Then they rode an escalator to the top floor. The others were fairly certain he was pranking them until they stepped out onto the rooftop terrace and were greeted by a stunning view.

"You can see the entire city from here, and it's free," he said as they looked out at the 360-degree panorama. "There's *Sacré-Coeur, la tour Eiffel*, even the top of the Arc de Triomphe. I used to sit on this bench for hours and forget my problems."

"It's lovely," said Monty.

"Almost too lovely," said Brooklyn. "In some ways this city doesn't seem real. Everywhere you look, it feels like . . . you're watching a movie."

"Like we're back at Pinewood," said Sydney.

“All that’s missing is Jonny Lott jumping out of a Jag and forgetting his lines,” joked Rio.

“I’m here for queen and country,” Paris said, mimicking him, “and I’m here to make an . . . umm . . . umm . . . what’s my line again?”

Everybody laughed, and Brooklyn savored the moment. Her worries from earlier had been replaced by a much happier feeling. It was amazing how much her life had changed in less than a month. And, even though she still felt like an outsider, especially around Rio and Kat, she also felt lucky to be a part of whatever this was and to have these people in her life.

“How does this view compare to that one?” Brooklyn asked, pointing at the Eiffel Tower glimmering in the sunset.

“Don’t know,” answered Paris. “I’ve never been up the Eiffel Tower. It costs money to do that, and I never had any.”

There was quiet until Monty said, “I’ve got money.”

Ninety minutes later, they took a glass-paneled elevator past the two lower decks and went straight to the top of the tower. The view was so breathtaking that, for the moment at least, Brooklyn forgot her fear of heights.

"Okay, Brooklyn," Monty said as the elevator climbed. "Here's your question for the day: Is the Eiffel Tower a work of art? Or is it an exhibition of science?"

The others laughed knowingly.

"Careful how you answer," warned Paris. "This is like a crusade for her."

"Right," said Sydney. "Get it wrong and there's a very long tutoring session involving Monty and a slide projector."

"That's enough from you two," Monty admonished. "I want to hear her answer without any commentary."

Everyone was focused on Brooklyn as she said, "It's definitely beautiful, so that would make it art. . . ."

In the corner of her eye she noticed Kat almost imperceptibly shaking her head no.

"But . . ." Brooklyn continued before Monty could respond. "The engineering is impressive, which would make it science."

Monty gave her a stern look. "Does that mean you think art isn't impressive and science isn't beautiful?"

"I think I hear the projector warming up," teased Sydney.

"You're digging a hole for yourself," Paris warned.

"Enough from you two," said Monty. "Come on, Brooklyn, which one is it?"

Just then Brooklyn saw that Kat had her hands crossed and was just barely extending two fingers as a clue. Brooklyn smiled.

"It's both," she said. "It's a work of art that is also an exhibition of science."

"That's very good," said Monty. "Though I think you may have received some help." She shot a suspicious eye at Kat.

As they stepped out onto the observation deck, Brooklyn whispered to Kat, "Thanks for saving me."

"I wasn't saving you," she said. "I was saving myself from having to listen to that lecture again." Then she turned her back and moved away.

Brooklyn shook her head, wondering if Kat would ever warm up to her.

As the group looked out over Paris, Monty continued her mini lecture.

"The tower is so beautiful that when Eiffel completed it, people complained that he was so focused on artistry that he ignored engineering," she explained. "When in fact, the primary concern during its design and construction was dealing with the wind, proving that true science and true beauty are one and the same." She admired the view for a moment before adding. "Of course, that doesn't do anything about the sun."

"What does the sun do?" asked Brooklyn, her dislike of heights rapidly returning.

"Solar radiation heats the wrought iron, making it expand, which causes the tower to move slightly," Monty explained. "Just about seven inches a day."

Brooklyn reflexively reached for the railing and gripped it tightly.

"You think that's scary, consider this," Paris said. "In a few days this whole area will be packed with people." He turned to Sydney and added, "And they'll all be listening to your speech."

"That's not funny," said Sydney.

"Really?" he replied, unable to contain his laughter. "Because to me it's hilarious."

The others joined in laughing, and eventually Sydney did too. The moment was interrupted when Brooklyn's phone pinged. She pulled it out of her pocket, looked at the screen, and smiled.

"What is it?" said Sydney.

"What was the first thing we did when we checked into our room?" she asked.

"Argued about who was going to get the nice bed," answered Sydney.

"After that," said Brooklyn.

"We checked out our weather models on the laptop to make sure we were ready for tomorrow," said Kat.

"That's right," answered Brooklyn. "And that's exactly what Charlotte and the team from Kinloch Abbey just did."

"How do you know that?" asked Rio.

"Because my hack worked," she said. "I set it up to alert me if it was activated, and it just sent me a text." She held up the phone so they could see the screen. "I can now remotely access their computer whenever I want."

And just like that, they were back to being spies.

Olympus

BROOKLYN WAS ANXIOUS THE NEXT morning as they made the short walk from the Three Lions to the headquarters of Sinclair Scientifica. Despite Mother's "get out of jail free" card, she was still determined to climb the wall and hack into the company's mainframe. She didn't know how she'd pull it off, but the first step was convincing herself that it was possible. To help, she relied on a Motherism: *You cannot achieve what you cannot believe.*

She repeated it like a mantra, and it helped until they

reached the headquarters and were escorted through a gated entrance to the building's courtyard. There she saw the actual wall, and the doubts returned in full force. It was almost identical to the one back at the movie studio but with two big differences: It was outside, *and* it started twenty feet off the ground. Suddenly the climb seemed more terrifying than ever.

You cannot achieve what you cannot believe, she told herself again, though this time she was much less convincing.

While she was focused on the wall, everyone else was scanning the faces of the other competitors waiting in the courtyard. The thirty teams selected to compete for the Stavros Prize represented nineteen countries on six continents and spoke twelve different languages. But the group from FARM was focused on one: Kinloch Abbey.

"I see Abir and Catriona," said Sydney. "They look confident."

Paris nodded toward someone and said, "Rachel Henderson's over there."

"And that's Henry Haddix with Charlotte," added Rio.

"I've got to be honest," said Paris. "Those are probably the four smartest students in the entire school."

"And with Charlotte on the computer they'll be difficult to beat," said Kat.

"Luckily, we've got an ace up our sleeve," Sydney said as she gave Brooklyn a friendly nudge. "Isn't that right, Brook?"

At first Brooklyn was still too focused on the wall to respond, but then her mind caught up with the conversation. "Right," she said.

"I mean it," said Sydney. "We can't let them win. The media attention could open up all kinds of trouble for us."

"They're not going to win," Brooklyn said confidently. "I've got it covered."

A young woman in a blue blazer introduced herself as Juliette, their Sinclair ambassador. It was her job to escort them around the building and answer any questions. First, though, they had to pass through security.

Because they were going into the Research and Development section, security was intense and included photographs, retinal imaging, and a full-body scanner. They also had to empty their pockets, take off their shoes, and place all electronics, including phones and computer tablets, into small lockers for the day. The only exception was that each team was permitted one laptop for work on the project, but it had to be handed over to be scanned, debugged, and approved for use.

"It will be waiting for you when you reach the lab," Juliette informed them.

With security this tight, Brooklyn wondered how the Purple Thumb could get close enough to Stavros Sinclair to cause any trouble.

"I'm not sure they need our help protecting him," she whispered to Sydney as they sat on a bench putting their shoes back on.

It took a while for thirty teams and their chaperones to make it through the screening process, so while the team waited, Juliette gave them a brief tour of the ground floor. The architecture was modern with ivory walls and big windows that looked out on the courtyard. The main lobby was impressive, and featured giant black-and-white photos of different Sinclair projects around the world. Brooklyn was drawn to one of African children laughing and splashing each other with water from a newly installed well.

"Welcome to Olympus," Juliette said as they walked through the lobby. "We believe this is the most intelligent office building in the world."

"How can a building be intelligent?" Monty asked, both intrigued and skeptical.

"For one, it keeps track of every person who comes through the door," said Juliette. "There is a magnetic strip in your visitor's badge that allows it to monitor your location. If you walk into an empty space, it turns on the lights. It knows how many people are in any room at any moment and adjusts the temperature accordingly. In the afternoon, when people naturally tire, it directs extra oxygen into rooms to boost energy levels."

To Monty, this sounded an awful lot like Olympus was spying on them, but she decided not to say anything about that. Instead she just replied, "Fascinating."

Once everyone was finished with security, they headed up to "the Workshop" on the second level. A cross between an auditorium and a classroom, the Workshop was designed for lectures and presentations. There was a small stage with a video camera and seating for about two hundred people. It was one of the rooms that had been re-created on the soundstage, and the team was impressed by how well the set designers had duplicated it.

"This looks familiar," Rio whispered as they took seats in the back row.

Stavros Sinclair was scheduled to open the summit with a brief speech broadcast from here to giant video screens inside the Stade de France, a soccer stadium just north of the city where thousands of young people were gathered for a concert and rally.

The different teams from the Stavros Prize were here as part of the summit but also as human props so that Sinclair was actually face-to-face with people.

"All right, team," Monty said. "You know your assignments."

Of the three times Sinclair was scheduled to appear, this was considered the least likely for the Purple Thumb to attack. That's because it was at the start of the summit and he was only going to talk briefly. Still, they'd practiced scenarios at Pinewood and knew what they were supposed to do.

Brooklyn and Sydney kept their eyes on the exits to make sure no one suspicious entered the room. Paris and Rio watched the crowd, looking for any sudden movements. And Kat did her Kat thing, looking to see if there were any patterns that didn't make sense.

At precisely ten o'clock, Stavros Sinclair entered through a door by the stage. He was dressed in his signature look of black jeans, black boots, and a gray T-shirt. Brooklyn had read more of his biography the night before, and it said he dressed this way so he didn't have to waste time every morning deciding what to wear.

He stepped up to the podium, ran his fingers through his stylishly long hair, and as soon as a light on top of the camera turned red, he started speaking. "Hello, my name is Stavros Sinclair, and I'm a scientist," he said with a slight accent that Brooklyn couldn't quite place. "More important, I'm a citizen of this planet who is committed to protecting the environment that all of us share."

He paused for a moment, and there were cheers in the stadium, which they could see on monitors in the room.

"I am personally dedicating the vast resources of Sinclair Scientifica to that fight," he continued.

Sydney and Brooklyn continued to watch the doors in case anyone rushed in while he was talking.

"And now it gives me great pleasure to announce the start of the fourth Global Youth Summit on the Environment," Sinclair said. "May what we do these next few days spread across the globe."

Now there were huge cheers, and he had to wait before adding his closing.

"Green is good! Green is good! Green is good!"

The chant began to spread throughout the stadium and among the people in the Workshop. Sinclair smiled and pumped his fist enthusiastically until the red light went off. The instant it did, he turned and exited through the same door through which he'd entered less than a minute earlier.

The room was silent for a moment, and then people started to get up and leave.

"Is that it?" asked Sydney. "He didn't even talk to us."

"I think that's all we're going to get," said Monty.

Paris turned to Juliette, who was at the end of their aisle. "Is he coming back?"

"Monsieur Sinclair?" she asked. "No. That is it for today. He will talk to you tomorrow in the lab."

Kat leaned over and whispered to Sydney, "Your speech is better than his by a factor of ten."

Brooklyn tried to compare the person in the book with the man she'd just seen. He seemed younger in real life than he did on the page, but he also came across as more cautious. The dynamic pioneer she'd read about took risks, but the real Stavros appeared . . . scripted. He stepped out exactly on cue. He delivered his lines and was gone forty-seven seconds after he'd entered the room. Maybe, like picking out clothes, he couldn't waste time on the mundane things that ordinary people did.

Next, the contestants were broken into two groups of fifteen teams, with each group going to a separate location. Half went to a conference room to present their proposals to a panel of judges, while the others went to a computer lab to test their weather models in different scenarios.

Brooklyn was pleased they were starting in the lab. The nervousness she'd felt earlier in the morning had been replaced by something hard to define. Maybe it was the fact that she was prepared for excitement, and the speech was boring and brief. However, working on a computer the next few hours would help her feel on top of things.

As they walked down the hall toward the lab, they were beside the team from Kinloch. The two groups struck up conversations, but since Brooklyn hadn't started school yet, she dropped back.

"I thought you didn't know anything about computers."

Brooklyn turned to see that Charlotte had come from behind her.

"What?" asked Brooklyn.

"When we met, you said you didn't know anything about computers," said Charlotte. "But now I see you're listed as the team's computer specialist."

"That's funny," Brooklyn said with a smile. "I guess that means I do know something about computers."

They entered the lab, and it looked a lot like the set that had been built at Pinewood, although there were some subtle differences, like the color of the walls and the arrangement of the workstations.

As promised, their laptop was waiting for them, and when she sat down, Brooklyn felt a blast of cool air from a nearby vent. Just as Juliette had told them, the temperature of the room was adjusting to the sudden arrival of people. Olympus was indeed an intelligent building.

The first thing she did was run a few tests of her own to make sure the people from Sinclair Scientifica hadn't planted any software on the laptop to spy on them. That was the problem with being a hacker; you automatically assumed the worst in others. She also checked to make sure they hadn't uncovered the program she'd installed that was tracking Kinloch's computer. She clicked it open, and on her screen she saw exactly what Charlotte saw on hers across the room. She was in total control of both.

"Is everything all right?" asked Juliette.

"Perfect," answered Brooklyn. "Absolutely perfect."

It was then that Brooklyn decided to risk a long shot and asked, "Is there any chance we can visit the server room? I'm fascinated by computers, and I can only imagine that in a building as advanced as this, the servers must be on a whole new level."

"They are," said Juliette. "They're also an entirely different level of security. No one outside of our Information Technology department goes in there."

Brooklyn sighed. "That's what I figured. Still, it can't hurt to ask."

She went back to her screen, but then Juliette added, "Besides, the servers aren't even in this building."

Brooklyn looked at her. "How's that possible? Certainly this much technology needs significant server support."

"A huge amount," answered Juliette. "That's the problem. Space is too limited here. There just wasn't enough room, so they were put in Asgard."

"Asgard?"

"Our sister building on the other side of town," she said. "That's the one drawback of Paris. There are virtually no skyscrapers. So rather than one large headquarters, we have two buildings kilometers apart."

This changed everything. Brooklyn no longer had to worry about climbing the wall. Instead, she had to find the other building *and* figure out how to break into it.

22. The Three Sisters

WHILE THE TEAM WAS AT OLYMPUS competing for the Stavros Prize, Mother was working on his own plan to get closer to Sinclair Scientifica. Through his art contacts in Paris, he'd arranged to tour a few private exhibitions, claiming he was looking for some pieces for an upcoming show at the Scottish National Gallery.

The most prized was the Sinclair Collection, which consisted of art purchased by the company as investments as well as works personally owned by Stavros Sinclair.

It was housed in a highly secure but otherwise unmarked and unremarkable building in the Montmartre neighborhood of the city. The building was so plain, Mother thought he'd come to the wrong place until a slender man in a black suit approached him on the sidewalk.

"Monsieur Archer?" he asked, calling Mother by his cover name.

"You must be Gilles."

Gilles was the collection's curator. He was in his early forties and had a bald spot, which he tried to cover with a comb-over. It didn't work. They shook hands, exchanged pleasantries, and Mother followed him to a doorway with a security camera. Moments later there was a clicking sound, and the door opened.

"Allons-y," said Gilles, using the French term for "Let's go."

The entryway was as plain as the building's exterior, simple white walls in a small square room with a silver elevator door. There was a security guard who looked like he'd recently been a Special Forces soldier. He had a thick, muscular build, carried a pistol in a holster, and gazed at Mother with an unblinking stare.

"Bonjour," Mother said, only to have the guard reply with a grunt.

Two levels down, the elevator opened onto an exquisite gallery. On the first wall alone were paintings by Van Gogh, Monet, and Renoir.

"Amazing, isn't it?" Gilles said upon seeing Mother's stunned reaction.

"More than," Mother said in awe.

Unlike most private collections, which were located in grand homes and centered on a few signature paintings, this seemed more like a secret museum, with multiple galleries and an array of masterpieces.

"Monsieur Sinclair oversees the collection himself," explained Gilles. "He selects the art and negotiates the purchases. He even arranges their placement on the walls."

In other words, Mother thought, *he does everything you're supposed to do as the curator.* Instead of saying that, he smiled and replied, "He has exceptional taste."

"He may be a scientist by training, but he has an artist's eye," answered Gilles. "He favors the Impressionists, especially Renoir."

"One of my favorites as well," said Mother.

They walked through the gallery, discussing the artwork and the possibility of an exhibition in Scotland. Mother noticed there were red dots on many of the identification labels and asked why.

"They signify works from Monsieur Sinclair's personal collection," explained Gilles. "The others are owned by the Sinclair Foundation."

Mother looked back and saw that all the best works had red dots.

"Like I said. He has exceptional taste."

Mother noticed a machine in the corner of the room that monitored humidity levels. It had a sticker with an Asset Inventory Code that was sixteen characters long beginning with SS2K. It fit perfectly with Kat's analysis that all the companies were part of Sinclair Scientifica.

"Is something wrong?" Gilles asked when he noticed Mother looking at it.

"No," he said, shaking it off. "Quite the contrary. Everything's just right."

They entered the final room, and Mother could not believe his eyes. Ahead of him were three paintings side by side on a wall.

"Are those Monets?" he asked.

"Good eye," said the man. "They're not his normal style. He painted them during an earlier period when he was still developing. They're quite remarkable, though. I don't believe they've ever been exhibited. We call them the Three Sisters."

It took everything Mother had not to react. Instead, he coolly approached the paintings and said, "I've never seen anything like them."

This was a lie. Not only had Mother seen them, he once had them in his possession. They were the forgeries that he'd borrowed from Scotland Yard five years earlier in his attempt to lure Le Fantôme. These were the paintings that were in the abandoned factory where he'd been left to die.

Each one had a label with a red dot. The question was, how had they ended up in the possession of Stavros Sinclair?

Asgard

IN THE PRECEDING WEEKS, BROOKLYN had traveled by transatlantic jet, high-speed train, and unmarked spy plane. So it wasn't surprising that she felt more at home riding the Metro to the outskirts of Paris. All she had to do was close her eyes, and it was like she was back in New York on the subway. She was, however, less comfortable with the spur-of-the-moment mission the group was undertaking.

Along with Sydney, Paris, Rio, and Kat, she was on her way to see if they could break into Asgard, Sinclair

Scientifica's secondary headquarters, so she could hack into the company's mainframe. While she was on board with the goal of the mission, it was its spur-of-the-moment quality that concerned her. They'd spent weeks preparing for specific assignments, and now on the first day of the operation, they were already making it up as they went along. Maybe this was how things normally happened. She didn't know.

"Are you sure this is a good idea?" Brooklyn asked.

"It's not like we're actually going to break in," Sydney replied confidently. "We're just collecting intel to see if it's possible."

"But shouldn't we tell Mother or Monty?"

"Mother's doing his National Gallery thing, and Monty's meeting with the scientists on her panel for tomorrow's symposium," she replied. "We don't want to risk blowing their covers. Besides, this *is* part of our original mission."

Brooklyn shot her a skeptical look. "Riding out to some industrial park on the edge of the city is part of our original mission?"

"No," said Sydney. "But hacking into the mainframe is. It's not our fault MI6 doesn't know where it is."

For the moment, Sydney was the alpha, and that

seemed to be good enough for the others. Since no one else was questioning the plan, Brooklyn decided to go along with it too.

"Speaking of MI6," said Paris. "How'd they get this so wrong?"

"I was thinking about that," answered Kat. "Remember when Tru showed us the final room during training? She said it was the one thing they weren't sure about. They just assumed it was the server room."

"Because it had so many vents and air-conditioning," added Sydney. "The server room has to be cooler than any other part of the building."

"Which makes me wonder what's up there," said Rio. "What else needs to be kept that cool?"

"I think it's the climate system Juliette told us about," said Kat. "You know how she said it adjusts temperatures and sends extra oxygen into rooms that need it? It's all part of their 'intelligent building' plan."

The area surrounding the Metro station was more industrial than the parts of Paris they'd already seen. Apparently the presence of Sinclair Scientifica had played an influence, because many of the businesses had tech names and logos.

Paris checked a map on his phone and tried to orient

himself. "According to this, the Asgard campus is this way," he said, pointing down the street.

"Why's it called Asgard?" asked Rio.

"Because, like all things Sinclair Scientifica, it's mythological," said Brooklyn. "Olympus is the home of the gods in Greek mythology, and Asgard is the home of the gods in Norse mythology."

"Oh great," said Rio. "Another mythology geek."

"If you're a fan of mythology, there's an excellent class about it at Kinloch," Paris said enthusiastically. "I'm the teaching assistant."

"Actually," Brooklyn said sheepishly, "I only know that about Asgard because I like Thor movies. I'm more into Marvel than myths."

Everyone laughed at this.

"Well, you're right," said Paris. "Asgard is the home of the Norse gods. According to legend it was protected by an enormous stone wall built by a creature called a rock giant. The wall was impenetrable except for one small weakness."

"What was that?" asked Sydney.

"There was a trickster god named Loki who duped him into not finishing the gate," he said. "So the gods didn't have to pay him for his labor."

"Oh, I like Loki," said Brooklyn. "At least, I like the actor who plays him in the movies."

A few minutes later they reached the building, and Sydney said what everybody else was thinking.

"Unlike Thor, Loki, and all the other Norse gods, I'm pretty sure Stavros Sinclair paid all his bills," she said. "This wall looks pretty solid."

The barrier surrounding the property looked more like something around a prison than an office building. It was sixteen feet tall and topped with razor wire.

"That's some serious security," Rio said, stating the obvious. "What are they keeping in there? Gold?"

Inside the wall a parking lot ringed a modern glass-and-steel building three stories tall. They walked around the entire complex and discovered that there were three openings, two for cars and one for pedestrians. Each had a gate manned by an armed guard.

"Well, the good news is that I don't think we have to worry about the Purple Thumb striking here," Sydney said once they'd completed their lap. "I don't see how they could get over that wall or past those guards. The bad news is that we can't do it either."

"No way," said Paris.

Sydney turned to Brooklyn. "And this is why we don't

bother Mother or Monty until we know there's something actually worth bothering them about. Mother's just going to have to tell Tru that there's no way for us to access the mainframe."

Brooklyn nodded. "Got it."

It wasn't until they were walking back to the Metro station that Paris recognized some familiar buildings and said, "You know, we're not too far from Confiserie Royale."

"What's that?" asked Brooklyn.

"It's an abandoned candy factory," said Paris. "Or at least it was when Mother found me living in it."

"Wait! You mean the warehouse where you rescued him from the fire?" asked Brooklyn.

"That's the one," he said.

"Let's go see it," Sydney said, excited.

"Really?" asked Paris.

"Absolutely," said Sydney. "It's like the birthplace of our team."

Suddenly a disappointing trip had become interesting again. The building was only a half mile away, yet it seemed like it was in a different world. The high-tech industrial park surrounding Asgard gave way to old warehouses and abandoned factories. Confiserie Royale was still empty, although there were indications things were about to change.

A shiny new chain-link fence surrounded the property, and the weeds that once overran the parking lot had been cleared. There was a sign for a demolition company, and the windows had been removed so that only the shell of the building remained.

"Look at that," Sydney said when she saw the fire damage on the exterior wall. The once-blue paint had been charred black by the smoke and flames pouring out of the windows. "That fire must have been horrific."

Paris was overwhelmed by the damage, which was worse than he remembered. "I was hiding over there," he said, pointing to where he'd crawled beneath an old truck. "And the cars and people were there." He motioned to a spot by the entrance and paused as the memory replayed in his mind.

"It was so brave of you to rescue him," said Rio. "Stupid, but brave."

"Stupid-but-brave is my specialty," Paris joked.

"How'd you get in and out?" asked Brooklyn.

This memory made him smile. "My secret entrance," he said. "It's funny if you think about it. The thing that kept him alive was traveling through the City of the Dead."

"The what of the what?" Brooklyn asked, alarmed.

"There are countless tunnels, catacombs, and abandoned mines underneath this part of the city," he said. "They're filled with the bones of dead Parisians. When I lived here, that's how I got around. Mother and I escaped through one of the passageways."

"I can't believe that you used to sneak around tunnels filled with dead people," Rio said with a shiver.

Paris nodded. "Unlike the living, the dead can't hurt you," he said. "I felt safest when I was underground."

Everyone was grossed out but Kat. She was intrigued. "If there are tunnels beneath this part of the city," she said, "does that mean there might be one underneath Asgard?"

The Catacombs

FOR HUNDREDS OF YEARS, MUCH OF Paris was built with limestone mined from nearby quarries to the south. As the city grew and expanded in that direction, the mines were covered over by the construction of new roads and neighborhoods, which created a labyrinth made up of nearly two hundred miles of tunnels.

In the seventeenth and eighteenth centuries, these tunnels were used to store human remains from overcrowded cemeteries. During the French Revolution, royal family members and aristocrats went underground to escape the Reign of Terror. And when the Nazi army occupied Paris, the French Resistance used the catacombs as a base of operations to fight for freedom.

In many places, the tunnels had been reinforced with massive columns to keep the buildings above from collapsing down into them. And, with the exception of a small area open to tourists, it was illegal to venture into them.

Despite this, exploring the catacombs was a popular Parisian pastime.

The team certainly wasn't going to let the threat of a possible fine keep them from searching for a secret passage into Asgard. If they could find that, Sinclair Scientifica's mainframe would be within reach.

Paris explained that the trip would take three to four hours, and because there was no cellular service underground, there'd be no way to communicate with the world above. They decided to split up, with Rio and Kat returning to the hotel to let Monty know what was happening, while Paris led Sydney and Brooklyn down below. Once they'd stopped at a store and picked up some flashlights and bottled water, they were ready to go.

"Welcome to the Gate of Hell," he said as they approached a pair of matching buildings on opposite sides of a public square called *Place Denfert-Rochereau.*

"Wait, what?" Brooklyn asked, stopping in her tracks.

"Hundreds of years ago, Paris was a walled city, and this was the southern entrance," he said. "It was called the *Barrière d'Enfer*, or Gate of Hell, and marks the beginning of the catacombs. This is where we're going underground."

It was the magic hour between day and night when there was just enough light for them to see what they were doing but also enough darkness so they could slip into the shadows. Paris led them down a mossy embankment into an abandoned train tunnel where he found a narrow passageway leading to something he called a "wormhole."

"There's a chamber directly below us," he said. "If you wiggle through this hole, you'll fall through it and down into the catacombs." He smiled, and before the girls could ask any follow-up questions, he crawled down into an opening just wide enough for his shoulders. He wriggled for a moment and disappeared from view. The girls stared at each other.

"This is crazy," said Brooklyn. "We are literally entering an underground city of the dead through a wormhole at the Gate of Hell."

Sydney smiled and replied, "Suddenly climbing a wall doesn't sound so bad, does it?"

Brooklyn was smaller than Paris, but her wriggling skills definitely needed work. She scraped her shoulder against a rock, got stuck for a moment, and when she finally made her way through, slammed face-first into a mound of dirt.

"Unff," she said as the impact knocked the wind out of her.

She was spitting dust out of her mouth when Paris urgently yelled, "Roll to your left! Roll to your left!"

Despite being totally disoriented, Brooklyn managed to spin onto her side and get out of the way just in time as Sydney crashed into the same spot with a splat.

The two girls sat up and tried to wipe the dirt from their faces. When they'd cleared enough to open their eyes, the first thing they saw was a smiling Paris.

"Welcome to my old neighborhood," he said.

"Lovely," said Brooklyn.

"Makes the Three Lions look like the Palace of Versailles," added Sydney.

"We'll use my torch first," Paris said as he turned on his flashlight, illuminating the way down a narrow corridor. "Save your batteries."

It was about fifteen degrees cooler than it had been on the surface, and there was a dampness they could feel in their lungs.

"How well do you remember the way?" Sydney asked as they walked, hunched over so their heads wouldn't hit the stone ceiling.

"Well enough to get us close," he said. "Then we'll have to search around."

Having never been in an ancient catacomb before, neither Sydney nor Brooklyn knew what to expect. Some tunnels were claustrophobic while others opened onto huge stone chambers. There was graffiti on the walls, but people had also painted impressive replicas of masterpieces like the *Mona Lisa*.

They stopped periodically to catch their breath and take a few sips of water. It was just after their third break that they turned a darkened corner and Brooklyn let out a bloodcurdling scream.

Directly ahead of them was a wall, ten feet tall, made entirely of human bones that had been carefully stacked so that a line of skulls was right at eye level. Just the sight of it was every one of Brooklyn's worst nightmares rolled into one.

"Are you okay?" Paris asked. "By the time I remembered, it was too late to warn you."

As Brooklyn tried to keep from hyperventilating, Sydney used her flashlight to see how far the wall stretched and discovered it continued into the darkness well beyond the reach of her beam.

"Crikey," said Sydney. "You told us that there were dead bodies down here, but it's endless."

"How . . . many . . . are . . . there?" Brooklyn asked in between deep breaths.

"I read somewhere that it's six million people," he answered. "Let's keep going."

He started walking, but Brooklyn didn't move a muscle.

"Come on, Brooklyn," he said to her. "It's best we get you away from here."

"I can't," she replied. "I'm sorry."

Paris moved closer so that his face was right in hers.

"Forget the bones," he said. "Just look at me. I'll be in front of you, going where you should go. Point yourself in the right direction and follow your eyes. You are much braver than you realize."

She nodded. "I can do that."

It took them about fifteen minutes to make it past the bones, and Brooklyn spent most of that time focusing on Paris directly in front of her. At one point she stumbled, and when Sydney reached out of the darkness to help her up, she practically jumped out of her skin.

"I like this much better," a relieved Brooklyn said when they reached a wide part of the tunnel where the walls were made of stone and blue signs marked which streets ran directly above them.

"Why are there road signs?" asked Sydney. "No one's supposed to come down here."

"True, but people do, and the city doesn't want them to get lost forever," he explained. "Besides, there is an agency called the *Inspection générale des carrières* that's in charge of catacombs and has to make sure the buildings and roads don't collapse. The signs help them keep track of where they are while they're working. That's also why there are lights along some sections."

After nearly two hours, Paris said they were close to the old candy factory. He even pointed out a little room where he and Mother had slept the night of the fire.

"He was too weak from the smoke to make it out," Paris said. "So we stayed here." He couldn't believe he was back five years later.

Using a map and the compass on his phone, Paris was able to lead them to a spot he thought should be directly beneath Asgard.

"I thought phones didn't work down here," said Brooklyn.

"You can't make a call, but you don't need service for the compass to work," he said. "It uses a magnetic concentrator built into the phone. That's important to remember if you ever get lost somewhere without a cell tower."

"Good to know," she said. "Although, remember what happened when you tried to teach me to use a compass during training."

He laughed. "That's right, you got lost in the woods."

"I think I'll just try to stay close to one of you guys," she replied.

"Good idea," he said.

"Look at this," Sydney said, pointing toward a shaft that led toward the surface. "Let's check it out."

Cast-iron rungs were cemented into the wall, and

since Sydney made the discovery, she went first, followed by Brooklyn and then Paris.

The rungs were hard and cut into their palms as they climbed, but Brooklyn reminded herself it was less painful than climbing the wall at Pinewood. It took about ten minutes to make it to the top, and when they did, they discovered that they hadn't made it to Asgard quite yet.

They'd reached a storm drain directly across the street from one of the guard gates. Luckily, it was dark, and with their flashlights turned off, the guards couldn't see them.

"We're close," said Paris. "Anything about fifty to one hundred meters in that direction should put us right underneath."

The process of climbing down the ladder was slow, and at one point the mud on the bottom of Sydney's shoe caused her to slip and almost fall.

They spent the next thirty minutes searching the area beneath the building until Brooklyn spotted something that looked out of place. Someone had painted a stylized night scene with glowing stars like Van Gogh's *Starry Night*.

"What's wrong?" Sydney asked when she saw Brooklyn studying it.

"The lines on this star don't match up," she said. "Everywhere else they're perfect, but this side's about half an inch higher than that."

"And this matters because?" she asked.

"Because I think there's a door hidden in the wall," replied Brooklyn.

They ran their fingers along the edge, and sure enough, covered by the paint was an old door. It didn't have a handle, but Paris was able to reach under the bottom and pry it loose.

It creaked opened to reveal a spiral stairway, covered with dust and grime. It looked as though no one had used it in decades.

Paris turned to the others and smiled. "Maybe the rock giant did leave a section of the wall incomplete."

They quietly climbed the stairs until they reached a metal security door with a key card sensor. The light on the sensor blinked red, indicating that it was operational.

"Look at that," Brooklyn said, pointing at a sticker on top of the sensor.

"What is it?" asked Paris.

He hadn't been with them on the train when Kat laid out her theories, so he didn't recognize it.

"The Asset Inventory Code," said Sydney.

The first four characters were SS2K, just like in the pictures Kat had shown them.

"This is the door to Asgard," Brooklyn said triumphantly.

Bring It On

IT WAS NEARLY MIDNIGHT WHEN THE trio returned to the Three Lions. The story of their adventure into the catacombs was evident from the dirt encrusted in their clothes and the smiles etched onto their faces. As always, Reggie was on duty at the check-in desk, and when they reached the door, he greeted them with a brusque, "Shoes!"

"What?" asked Paris.

"Take off your shoes," he instructed. "No matter what you think about this hotel, I will not have you trudging all that muck through my lobby into your rooms."

Sydney started to protest. "But what about . . ."

"Socks, too," he said, cutting her off. "Just leave them at the door."

They could tell he was serious, so they stripped off their shoes and socks and left them in a pile. Brooklyn was relieved that she'd packed a second pair for the trip.

"Alexandra's waiting for you in her room," Reggie said as they walked barefoot through the lobby.

It took them a moment to realize that Alexandra was Monty.

"Right," Brooklyn said with a nod. "Thanks."

Monty wasn't alone. Mother, Kat, and Rio were also there, eager to hear what they'd discovered in the catacombs. The three filled them in on everything from the wall of skulls and bones to the secret doorway into Asgard.

"So we still should be able to hack into the mainframe," said Brooklyn. "Just like Tru wanted."

"Of course, we'll need an electronic key to get through the door," added Sydney.

"And I'm sure we'll need one for the server room too," said Paris.

"Oh, and not just any electronic key," said Brooklyn.

"Juliette said that only members of the IT staff can access the server room, so we'll have to get a key from one of them."

Suddenly the hack, once again, seemed nearly impossible. But Brooklyn had completed her first day of actual spying, and it had been thrilling.

"We've got an early start tomorrow," Monty reminded them. "So clean up, and it's lights-out."

Brooklyn would've loved passing out on her bed, but she knew the memory of countless skulls staring at her would make that impossible. Instead, she showered and opened the Stavros Sinclair biography. She wanted to read until she fell asleep from exhaustion. Maybe that would keep the bad dreams at bay.

It must've worked, because the next thing she remembered was Sydney leaning over her and shaking her by the shoulders. "Yo, Brookie the Rookie, time to wake up!"

Brooklyn was still groggy as they walked from their hotel to Olympus, but by the time they'd gone through security, her adrenaline had kicked in and she was alert and ready to go.

"*Bonjour!*" Juliette said, greeting them. "I hope you had a good night's sleep. Follow me to the first station."

Once again everybody was separated into two groups,

although this time Juliette led the team from FARM to the presentation room. Here they would go before a panel of judges who could ask them questions about their rainmaking proposals.

The teams went up in threes, and FARM was in the last group. This was a huge advantage because they heard the questions multiple times before answering. This was especially helpful to Brooklyn. Each team member had to answer one question, and since she was new to the project, she didn't know the science as well as the others. Hearing all of them let her pick the one she knew best.

"I want to answer the question about what makes our proposal special," she whispered to the others as they took the stage.

"What are you going to say?" asked Paris.

"I'm going to talk about the triple blend," Brooklyn answered, referring to the special mix of chemicals used in their proposal.

"Excellent," he said. "You take that one. You'll kill it."

Joining FARM on the stage were Kinloch Abbey and a team from Mumbai, India. The questions unfolded as they had the previous times, and Brooklyn stood back as her teammates gave answers about their proposal's practicality, its environmental impact, how it compared to previous attempts at rainmaking, and the developmental steps that would be necessary before it could be enacted.

Brooklyn stepped forward to answer the final question.

"What makes your concept special?" asked the judge. "What is the inspiration that sets it apart from the others?"

Brooklyn was still a bit tired from the previous night, so she closed her eyes for a moment to focus her thoughts. She wanted to give a concise and complete answer.

"As you know, historically rainmaking has involved seeding clouds with one of three different chemicals: silver iodide, potassium iodide, and solid carbon dioxide. Each of these has advantages and disadvantages, which is why none has truly separated itself from the others. What makes our concept *special*, as you say, is that it uses a unique blend of all three chemicals. Our belief is that this blend maximizes the advantages of each."

The answer was concise, specific, and absolutely everything that Brooklyn wanted to say. The only problem was that she wasn't the one who said it. When she paused to focus her thoughts, Charlotte jumped in and answered for Kinloch Abbey. She knew all about the triple blend from her time working with FARM.

While she was walking up onto the stage, she'd heard Brooklyn tell the others that this was the answer she wanted to give.

"That's excellent," said the judge who asked the question. "It's a very interesting concept."

Brooklyn looked over at Charlotte, who smiled back at her with a devilish grin. She couldn't give the same answer. That would look ridiculous—as if they were copying Kinloch, even though it was the other way around. But no one could come to her rescue. This was the last question, and she was the only one who hadn't answered yet.

Brooklyn's mind raced as one of the students from Mumbai gave an answer that she didn't even hear. It was drowned out by the voices in her head replaying everything she could remember about their project. Mostly she programmed the computer models; she didn't know what made it work. She'd spent the entire last week trying to climb the wall while the rest of the team fine-tuned the proposal.

She was totally lost.

"What about you?" asked the judge.

Brooklyn looked up and saw that the woman was now talking directly to her.

"What?" asked Brooklyn.

"What's special about your proposal?" she asked. "What makes FARM's idea different from all the others?"

Brooklyn wasn't sure how long she stood there not talking, but it felt like forever. Finally, she just spat out the only thing that came to mind.

"Benito Viñes," she said, referring to the priest whose photograph hung above the supercomputer back at the FARM.

It was such a random answer that the entire room fell silent except for Charlotte, who let out a laugh. She'd wanted to stick it to Brooklyn and the rest of the team, but she had no idea she'd be this successful.

"I'm sorry, who?" asked the judge.

"Benito Viñes," Brooklyn answered again.

"I've never heard of him," said the judge. "Is he someone on your team?"

"No," said Brooklyn. "He was a priest who moved to Cuba in 1870. They called him *Padre Huracán*, or Father Hurricane, because he was the first person to successfully predict the path of tropical storms. Up until that point everyone treated the storms the same way, and as a result they acted too late. But Father Hurricane looked at the clouds that preceded the storms, searching for a pattern that no one else had seen. He saved countless lives because he broke the mold."

The more she answered, the more confident she became. Somewhere in the middle of it, she remembered a passage she'd read the night before about Stavros Sinclair's first significant breakthrough.

"It's the same way that Stavros Sinclair approached the difficulty of solving big problems," she said. "Up until that point, companies were trying to squeeze as much data as they could into a small space. But just as Father Hurricane looked to the clouds for information, Stavros Sinclair looked to the computing cloud to help bring together a vast array of computers working together."

She looked out at the eyes of the judges and knew they were eating this up.

"So that's what makes our proposal special," said Brooklyn. "We embrace the spirit of Stavros Sinclair, for whom this prize is named, and that of Benito Viñes, who is such a role model for us that we keep his photograph on the wall of our workspace. We look to the clouds to find our inspiration. And we'll see to it that those clouds will bring the rain."

There was applause from the judges, the other teams

who were watching, and most of all from the team standing behind her. But for Brooklyn, the only reaction that mattered was the angry glare she got from Charlotte.

You want to play hardball, Brooklyn thought as she looked at her rival. *Bring it on.*

The Rainmakers

CHARLOTTE'S DAY WAS GOING FROM BAD to worse. First she'd set Brooklyn up for an epic fail only to see her turn it into a huge victory. And now, something was going wrong with the computer weather models she was using for Kinloch Abbey. She was inputting the different situations given to the team by the judges, but the results weren't turning out like they'd predicted.

"Are you sure you entered it correctly?" one of her teammates asked her.

"Of course I am," snapped Charlotte. "Are *you* sure you read the numbers correctly?"

Across the room, Brooklyn struggled to mask her glee. *She* was the problem with Charlotte's weather model. She'd hacked into the Kinloch computer and every so often would tweak some of its code. She made sure it wasn't so much that it would attract attention, but just enough so that the results came out wrong.

"Five minutes," one of the judges announced. "All work needs to be completed in five minutes."

That was all the time that was left for the teams to vie for the top ten spots and advance to the final day of the competition. FARM didn't need it. They'd already completed the scenarios and submitted their work for final judging. But the tension at the Kinloch table was escalating.

"Look at Abir," Paris said under his breath to the others. "I've never seen him so angry."

"Catriona, too," whispered Sydney. "She looks like she's going to take over the keyboard from Charlotte."

"Normally I wouldn't enjoy this," said Brooklyn, "but after what she did to me, I'm loving every second."

"Let that be a lesson for all of us," Paris said to the others. "Do not mess with Brooklyn."

This brought a laugh even from Kat and Rio, which they had to stifle when Charlotte looked up and glared at them.

A few minutes later a buzzer sounded, and the judges told the teams to stop working and submit their data. Brooklyn cracked a smile as Charlotte angrily clicked her send button.

They broke for lunch in the dining commons, which was more like a nice restaurant then a typical office cafeteria, but they were all too nervous to enjoy the meal. Afterward, all the teams returned to the lab so that Stavros Sinclair could meet them and announce who'd advanced to the final round. This was the second of his three scheduled appearances and the one for which the team had trained the most at Pinewood.

Unlike the previous day, Monty was across town participating in a symposium at the Pasteur Institute. In her absence, Paris was the alpha, a responsibility he took seriously.

"Remember your assignments," he said. "If the Purple Thumb attacks now, it won't be one of the kids on the teams. It'll be an adult. So look at faces for anyone who's out of place."

"We've got it," Rio said.

"Good," he responded. "Because this operation is hot. We are a go."

Once again Stavros Sinclair was wearing his customary black jeans, black boots, and gray T-shirt. As he went from station to station and mingled with the teams, he kept his hands clasped behind his back. This served two purposes. First, it made him lean forward, which gave the impression that he was interested in whatever someone was telling him. More important, it kept anyone from trying to shake his hand. Among his many eccentric traits, Sinclair was a germophobe.

Two large bodyguards followed him on either side, and Brooklyn wondered if this was always the case or a response to the possible threat from the Purple Thumb.

Even during this face-to-face "personal" time, many of Sinclair's comments seemed scripted. There were variations of "Are you having a good time?" and "I think your proposal shows great promise" and "This is a very creative approach."

In fact, one of the only original interactions came when he reached the FARM table and smiled at Brooklyn. "Ah, Father Hurricane!" he said happily. "What did you say his name was again?"

"Benito Viñes," answered Brooklyn.

"What a wonderful story," said Sinclair. "How did you know about my breakthrough with the cloud?"

"I read about it in your biography," she said. "I found it very inspiring."

"Thank you," he replied. "I find you very inspiring too. All of you."

For Brooklyn this was a heady moment. She was actually talking with Stavros Sinclair, someone who she'd read about and admired for years. It didn't hurt that across the lab Charlotte was watching with uncontrolled envy.

After Stavros completed his tour of the workstations, he moved to the front of the room to address everybody. Paris and the rest of the team scanned the faces in the crowd, looking for any possible threats. They were relieved that Sinclair had his bodyguards in tow. It would be difficult for anyone from the Purple Thumb to get past them.

"First of all, I want to congratulate you all on your wonderful projects," Sinclair said, addressing the room. "I'm afraid I came up with this on short notice, which didn't give you much time to prepare. Still, your work has exceeded my expectations, so please, give yourselves a hand."

Polite applause rippled through the lab.

"For centuries the idea of creating artificial rain has been mocked as pseudoscience," he continued. "People say it's hocus-pocus and make-believe. But you've shown that there's much more to it than that. If we can manufacture rain, then we can help solve the problems of drought and famine around the world."

Sinclair continued to talk about the project, and the team kept their eyes moving, looking for anybody out of place. For some reason, Paris found himself focusing on the bodyguards. Who would be in a better position to hurt Sinclair than the people who were supposed to protect him? Of course, they must have passed through extensive background checks to get their positions, but it was still possible.

"Many people assume that nature and technology are working against each other, but nothing could be further from the truth," Sinclair said as he continued his speech. "Right now in Sinclair Scientifica labs, our scientists are studying cloning methods to regrow the Great Barrier Reef. We're developing prosthetic limbs so lifelike, they re-create a person's fingerprints. And now, with your help, we're trying to bring water to areas dying of thirst. At Sinclair Scientifica we are moving forward with our eyes set beyond the horizon."

The speech was inspiring, and the room erupted in applause.

"Ten teams are about to advance to the final phase of the competition. There's a lot of money at stake: a million euros to the winners. But more important, the future of our planet's at stake. Together we must protect it."

Paris flinched and almost sprang into action as someone approached Sinclair, but he held back when he recognized that it was one of the judges bringing him the final results.

"This is very exciting," Sinclair said as he opened the envelope. "Here are the ten teams who will advance."

He read the names, and after each team was announced, there were muffled cheers from the one who'd just received the good news and applause from the others. The top ten came from around the world and included teams from China, India, South Africa, France, and the United States. Despite their difficulty with the computer, Kinloch Abbey had made the cut. He'd listed nine teams, however, without mentioning FARM.

"And last," he said. "The team from Aisling, Scotland, the Foundation for Atmospheric Research and Monitoring."

The team celebrated with high fives and hugs while Sinclair continued on to thank the teams who were not advancing.

"Stay sharp," Paris reminded them. "It's in this chaos when he's most vulnerable."

"Congratulations!" Juliette said when she came over to them. "We will get another day together."

Paris was focused on Sinclair when out of the corner of his eye he saw a man enter the room and head toward the tech guru.

Paris moved forward, pushing Juliette out of the way in the process.

The man was bald with a beard and wire-framed glasses. Something about him triggered an alarm in Paris, who picked up speed. He was about to jump into action when Sinclair acknowledged the man and they had a brief conversation.

Paris stood and stared at them, his heart racing.

"What's wrong?" Sydney asked, coming up behind him.

Sinclair left the room, and just before he followed, the man turned to face the room.

That's when Paris recognized him. That's when everything came together.

"What's wrong?" Sydney repeated.

"That man," Paris said, nodding at him. "I've seen him before."

"Yesterday or today?" she asked.

Paris shook his head. "Five years ago."

"What?"

"Five years ago that man and those two bodyguards were outside the candy factory as it burned," he said, remembering the moment vividly. "I saw them from underneath the truck."

"Wait," said Sydney. "They're the ones who tried to kill Mother?"

"Yes," he said. "Which means that they're part of Umbra."

Palais de Justice

THE TEAM ARRIVED TO FIND MOTHER already waiting in front of the ornate black-and-gold gates of the Palais de Justice. Brooklyn had texted him the code "pancake," and rather than a time, simply wrote, "NOW!" The first thing he noticed was that one team member was missing.

"Where's Kat?" he asked urgently. "Did something happen?"

"She's fine," Paris assured him. "Everyone's fine. She said she had to take care of something and disappeared right after Sinclair announced the ten finalists."

"Did you make it?" Mother asked.

"Of course we did," Sydney said confidently. "But so did Kinloch Abbey."

"That's fine, just make sure neither one of you finishes in the top five," he said. "So, what's the emergency?"

"Let's mix in with the tourists," suggested Paris. "We'll explain it all."

The Palais de Justice was located on the *Île de la Cité*, an island in the middle of the Seine in the heart of the city. It was popular with tourists, and the five of them blended in with the endless stream of visitors.

Paris told him about the men in the computer lab whom he recognized from the scene of the fire. This information brought Mother to a sudden halt.

"It's been five years," he said. "Are you certain it's them?"

"One hundred percent," replied Paris. "It's not something you forget."

"Did you get any pictures?" he asked. "I'd recognize the ones who tied me up."

"No pictures," Sydney said. "They confiscate our phones while we're in the building."

"Well, if you're certain, then I'm certain," Mother said. "So what do we know?"

"We know that at least three members of Umbra have infiltrated the security force at Sinclair Scientifica," said Rio. "And not just any positions. We're talking Stavros Sinclair's personal bodyguards and someone high up—maybe even the head of security."

"What if Umbra *is* the Purple Thumb?" asked Sydney. "And every year they attack Sinclair Scientifica to send a message."

"And now?" asked Paris.

"Now, when they want to send the ultimate message, their own people are responsible for 'protecting' Stavros," she said.

"It's possible," said Mother. "But I learned something I didn't have a chance to tell you yet."

"What?" asked Brooklyn.

"The paintings I used five years ago to lure Le Fantôme . . . the Monets."

"What about them?" asked Sydney.

"I saw them yesterday in Stavros Sinclair's private collection," answered Mother.

"Didn't they burn in the fire?" asked Brooklyn.

"Not necessarily," said Paris. "Two of the men loaded boxes into one of the cars right before the fire started. Those might have held the paintings."

"And now they belong to Stavros Sinclair," said Sydney. "How?"

"Umbra could have sold them to him," said Mother.

"Tru said Umbra and Sinclair were doing business together," said Rio.

"But there's a simpler explanation," Mother said. "One that would also explain why Umbra is providing Sinclair's security."

Brooklyn looked up, amazed when she realized what he was suggesting. "Stavros Sinclair is Le Fantôme."

"If I had to bet," Mother replied, "I'd bet on that."

"Which means Sinclair Scientifica is just a massive corporate cover for Umbra," Sydney reasoned. "They're both giant multinational operations. They can use the legitimate businesses to launder money from the criminal enterprises. And they can use illegal intimidation to eliminate competitors for the business."

"There are a lot of maybes," said Mother, "but the pieces fit."

"What do we do next?" asked Brooklyn.

"I was on my way to revisit Sinclair's private collection when I got your text," he said. "If I hurry, I can still make my appointment. Maybe I can learn something new."

Just then everyone's phones vibrated, signaling the arrival of a group text from Kat. It was a selfie of her in front of an Indian restaurant with the message, If you want to hack into the mainframe, meet me here as fast as you can. AND MAKE SURE TO BRING RIO!!

"Finally, someone recognizes my value," Rio said.

"I'll go with you," Mother said to them.

"No," answered Paris. "You should go to your appointment. Getting you close to Sinclair's collection gets you close to Sinclair, which means getting you close to Le Fantôme. We can handle the hack."

There wasn't time to debate, so Mother just agreed. "Fine," he said. "You go. But text me the instant you get out safely. No matter what time it is. Send a smiley emoji if you're successful and a frowny one if you're not. Either way, I'll meet you at the North Pillar of the Eiffel Tower, and we'll decide what we're going to do tomorrow."

The Hack

YOU CAN'T LOOK OUT IF YOU STAND OUT.

That was the Motherism Kat had recalled while looking for Brooklyn in the Edinburgh Airport, and it was the one running through her head as she waited for the team outside the Kashmir Café.

Like all good spies, Kat tried to blend into the background. Anytime someone noticed you, it meant they might later recognize or remember you. Neither of these was good. The problem was that she was in an area where there were plenty of businesses but no schools or apartments. That meant there were no other kids on the street, just people grabbing a bite on their way to or from work.

If she were walking down the sidewalk, it would've looked like she was taking a shortcut. But she'd been sitting on the café stoop for twenty minutes. She tried burying her face in her phone to keep from making eye contact and hoped people just assumed she was related to the family who ran the café.

"There you are," Paris said as the group approached her.

"Took you long enough," she replied.

Paris gave her an exasperated look. "We literally ran to and from the Metro. We couldn't have gotten here any quicker."

"Well, try to blend in," she said. "We've got one chance at this, and if he notices us, we're doomed."

"One chance at what?" asked Sydney.

"At any moment the key to this mission is going to pass right by this café," said Kat. "And I mean 'key' as in most significant person as well as 'key' as in the *actual* key that will unlock the server room."

"How do you know that?" Sydney asked Kat.

"I spent most of the day observing which keys opened which doors at the Olympus building," she explained.

"Each person's key is their photo ID, which must contain a magnetic stripe."

"Probably the same one that keeps track of which room you're in," offered Paris.

"Exactly," said Kat. "All keys open the main doors. I noticed this when Juliette entered the building through the courtyard and when one of the judges snuck outside to smoke a cigarette. But specific doors can only be opened by people who belong in those rooms. That's why Juliette couldn't open the lab after lunch. She had to wait for someone to let us in."

"So what does this mean?" asked Sydney.

"It means if we can get an ID belonging to someone who works in the server room, it should unlock that door as well as the main door that connects to the catacombs," she said. "You follow me so far?"

Everyone nodded, and Kat smiled.

"The next step was more difficult," she continued. "I had to figure out who belongs in that room. I couldn't just look it up, because Sinclair keeps all employee information confidential."

"Then how'd you do it?" asked Sydney.

"I looked for the pattern," said Kat. "First I found this café. Judging by the number of reviews posted online, it appears to be the most popular lunch spot in the area. Next I had to determine if it's specifically popular with the people who work for Sinclair Scientifica."

"How'd you do that?" asked Rio.

"There's a fishbowl by the cash register where you can put your business card for a chance to win a free lunch. Half the cards are from Sinclair people."

"So it's popular with Sinclair people," said Paris. "How is that helpful?"

"I'll get to that," she said. "Next I looked for the most popular restaurant in Noida, India. Specifically one within a half mile of the Sinclair Scientifica global data center that opened there two years ago. The restaurant's called Mukherjee's, by the way. According to the reviews, the kebabs are outstanding."

"How did you know that Sinclair has a data center in Noida, India?" asked Rio.

"There's a massive black-and-white photograph of it in the lobby," she answered. "I saw it yesterday morning when we had our tour. According to an article I found online, every Sinclair Scientifica IT manager in the world has to go there for two weeks of training each year. Once I knew that, the rest was easy."

"Really?" said Paris. "Because it doesn't seem easy to us mere mortals."

"Yeah," said Sydney. "What's the pattern?"

"The restaurants," she answered. "Kashmir Café and Mukherjee's are the pattern. I looked to see if anyone posted reviews of both restaurants, because the only person likely to be in both places would be someone who works here but had to go there for training."

"That's brilliant!" exclaimed Brooklyn, earning a slight smile from Kat. "Breathtakingly brilliant."

"Did it work?" asked Rio.

"François Fournier," she said, holding up her phone to show his picture. "He's active on social media, which is where I found this photo. It was taken a few weeks ago, so he should look the same."

"What makes you think he's going to walk past here any minute?" asked Brooklyn.

"He posts reviews for most of the restaurants he visits," she said. "The lunch places are around here, and the dinner ones are in a neighborhood called Belleville. My guess is that he lives there, and if he does, he'll be taking Metro lines four and eleven to get home. That means when he leaves work, he should walk right by here to catch the Metro."

"You're amazing, Kat," Paris said. "Absolutely amazing."

"*Maths* is amazing," Kat said. "I just know how to use it."

"So what's the plan for getting the ID?" asked Rio.

"*You* tell *us*," said Kat.

He gave her a strange look. "What do you mean?"

"It's going to take a magician to get that key," she said. "That means you have to be the alpha."

Rio was stunned. "But I'm not . . ."

"Absolutely," Paris said, reading his uncertainty.

"No question," said Sydney.

Rio scanned their faces, amazed that they'd trust something so important to him. He stopped on Brooklyn, and she smiled.

"We need you," she said. "Tell us what to do."

"But tell us quickly," added Kat. "He's going to be here any second."

Rio grinned, his confidence growing. "It's going to take two of us, and everyone else needs to scatter," he said as he began to explain his plan.

When he was done, Kat gave him a look. "You still have to say it."

He smiled at her and replied, "This operation is hot. We are a go."

Seven minutes later François Fournier walked past the Kashmir Café. Rio and Sydney followed him to the Metro where he boarded line four headed into the city. Just as Kat had predicted.

The train was packed with rush hour commuters. With no seats available, Fournier had to stand and hold on to a strap. Rio was right next to him and spied the photo ID clipped to his jacket pocket. He waited for the movement of the train to jostle them, and when it did, he used his magician's dexterity to snatch the ID.

He palmed it like a playing card, but only for a few seconds until Sydney moved by as if preparing to exit. Then he slipped it into her pocket using a perfectly executed brush pass. The use of two people was vital in case Fournier noticed it was missing before he got off the train. Sydney never came close to him, so he wouldn't suspect her, and Rio stood next to him for a few more stations, which made him seem completely innocent.

Sydney got off at the next station and doubled back to meet up with Paris and Brooklyn at the Gate of Hell.

"Did it work?" Brooklyn asked as Sydney walked up to them.

"Pleased to meet you," Sydney joked, flashing the ID

like a badge. "My name's François Fournier, Information Technology."

The second trip through the catacombs was much easier for Sydney and Brooklyn. They knew what to expect and were able to move faster. Brooklyn even prepared herself for the "Great Wall of Bones," as she called it. Like she'd done the day before, she kept her eyes focused on Paris in front of her.

The main difference this time was that they encountered three groups as they went along. Two looked to be young adventurers out for fun while the third was a tour led by an underground guide.

Normally spies didn't want to be seen on the way to a black bag job, but they weren't particularly worried. Anyone down here was already breaking the law, so they were far less likely to volunteer information to the police if anything happened.

Still, the trio waited and made sure no one was around when they reached the hidden door leading to Asgard.

"You ready?" Paris asked Brooklyn before he pried it open.

"Yes," she said. "We've got this."

He smiled at her. "That's what I like to hear."

They climbed the spiral staircase silently and came to

the security door. Everything hinged on whether Kat was right about the electronic keys. If François Fournier's ID didn't open this door, the mission would be over before it even started.

Sydney took a deep breath and pressed the ID against the electronic card reader. There was silence for a moment and then a *click*.

"Abracadabra," Sydney whispered as she pulled the door open. "Welcome to Asgard."

They entered through the basement and moved cautiously down the darkened hall.

"This way," Brooklyn said, motioning toward a corridor.

"How do you know?" Paris asked in a whisper.

She pointed to the blue-and-yellow data wires that ran in a clear tube along the ceiling. "All roads lead to Rome, and all wires lead to the server."

The hallways and offices were empty, and the building was dark except for the occasional security light.

"Good thing no one's working late," said Brooklyn.

"It's because of the summit," said Sydney. "Juliette mentioned that Sinclair employees are helping out at the evening events."

They followed the data wires to a room one level up.

Once again Sydney held her breath as she pressed the ID against the card reader, and once again they were rewarded with the click of a door unlocking.

"Gotta love Kat," said Brooklyn.

Sydney handed the ID to Paris and whispered, "You stand lookout and let us know if anyone's coming."

He nodded, and they went into the server room.

"This room is huge," Brooklyn said. "It's at least twice as big as the one we had for practice at Pinewood."

"Cold, too," Sydney added with a shiver.

The room was dimly lit except for the glow of blue, red, and green lights on computers that whizzed and whirred with activity. They filled nine rows of black metal cabinets arranged like the aisles of a grocery store.

"We need a crash cart," said Brooklyn.

"What's that?" asked Sydney.

"It looks like one of those things you see in a hospital that holds IV bags," she said. "It should have wheels at the bottom with a keyboard in the middle and a monitor up top."

They found it in the third aisle. Brooklyn quickly studied the tangle of wires that ran to the back of one of the computers and patched in the crash cart. Her fingers danced on the keyboard as code streamed across the monitor. Sydney had no idea what Brooklyn was doing, but she could tell she was doing it well.

Once Brooklyn accessed the system, she pulled out a flash drive containing the virus created by the computer techs at MI6. She plugged it into a USB port, copied the program, and activated it.

"Done," Brooklyn said with a smile. "We did it."

"No," Sydney said. "*You* did it. We just got you here."

"Well, now let's get out."

They put the cart back the way it was and were headed toward the door when Paris rushed in.

"We've got a problem," he said.

"How big a problem?" Sydney asked, unsure she really wanted to know.

"Two guards headed this way," he replied. "And I heard one of them mention François Fournier."

"Okay," Brooklyn said, trying to wrap her brain around this bit of information. "That's pretty big."

29. The Sinclair Collection

AT THE SAME TIME KAT WAS LAYING OUT her plan to use François Fournier's ID to access the server room, Mother was across town in Montmartre visiting the Sinclair Collection.

The more he thought about it, the more he believed Stavros Sinclair was actually Le Fantôme. Both were shadowy figures who oversaw global organizations. Both had seemingly endless supplies of wealth and influence. And both were obsessed with art, specifically French impressionism.

Mother was so convinced, he'd sent an encrypted message about it to Tru at MI6 headquarters. Now he was hoping to find clues among the art collection that might prove him right.

As he approached the unmarked building, Mother saw Sinclair's personal curator pacing the sidewalk.

"*Bonjour*, Gilles," he said, rushing over to him. "I'm sorry I was delayed."

"That is fine, Monsieur Archer," said Gilles. "But I am on a tight schedule, so we must 'chop-chop,' as they say."

"Of course," replied Mother. "I just want to double-check a few things before I go back to Scotland. I think they'll be amazed when they hear what I have to tell them."

What Mother hoped to find was more art of dubious origins. If there were other paintings among the collection that came from the black market, then he might be able to match that criminal activity with Le Fantôme.

Once again, they went through the various layers of security. But this time when they stepped off the elevator, things were different. The wall that held the works by Van Gogh, Monet, and Renoir was now empty.

"Where are the paintings?" asked Mother.

Gilles didn't answer.

Workers in blue jumpsuits were carefully taking down some artworks and placing them into narrow crates. Gilles seemed dismayed but did his best not to appear flustered as he approached a woman supervising them. She had long brown hair tied up in a topknot and wore a matching jumpsuit that somehow looked stylish on her.

"Marie," said Gilles, still trying to keep a brave face, "what's going on?"

"Did you not receive word?" she asked.

The man chuckled, reluctant to show confusion in front of a guest. "What word?"

"Stavros decided to move some art," she replied.

Mother noticed that she called the boss by his first name, while Gilles always referred to him respectfully as Monsieur Sinclair.

"*Pourquoi?*" asked Gilles. "Why?"

Marie shrugged. "I never ask why. I just do what he tells me."

Mother knew his visit was about to be cut short, so he quickly surveyed the scene, trying to figure out what was happening. He looked at which paintings were being crated and realized each had an identification label with a red dot. Sinclair was leaving the art owned by the company but taking the pieces that belonged to him. Two workers passed by carrying a crate, and Mother saw it had a sticker reading LBG, the code for Paris-Le Bourget Airport. These paintings weren't just going across town.

He's packing up his toys to go, Mother thought to himself. *I think he's leaving Paris with no plans to come back.*

The Guards of Asgard

TWO SECURITY GUARDS HAD AN ANIMATED discussion as they walked through the Asgard building. One, younger and more gung ho about his job, was determined to check on something he thought was suspicious. The other, older and more interested in watching football on television, thought they were wasting their time.

The problem lay in the system that tracked employees as they moved through the facility. Like Olympus, Asgard was designed to be an "intelligent building."

Only, now it claimed François Fournier was currently in the server room, which didn't make sense because he'd clocked out and left the building nearly three hours earlier.

"He can't be here if he already went home," complained the reluctant guard.

"Exactly," replied the other. "That's why we're checking it out."

"But it's just a mistake," said the older man. "A glitch."

"Impossible," said his partner. "This system doesn't have glitches."

They reached the server room, and the young man opened the door and called out, "Monsieur Fournier!"

When there was no response, the other replied, "See? I told you."

That's when the younger guard saw the footprint. It was dirt from a shoe. Brooklyn's shoe, to be precise. And in a room that was otherwise spotless, it was impossible to ignore. He nodded toward it, and his partner was no longer reluctant. They stopped talking and used hand signals to communicate.

They also drew their weapons.

The servers continued to work, their fans humming, drives periodically spinning and then stopping. Despite this, however, there was an eerie calmness to the room.

Brooklyn and Sydney were both hidden beneath the false floor. The base of the room was raised to prevent possible flood damage and so that cables could run beneath the computers.

Paris had lifted two of the floor panels so they could nestle down among the wires, a high-tech version of the wormholes they'd used to get into the catacombs.

But he was too big to fit, so he'd searched the rows desperately looking for someplace to hide. He finally found a spot. There were empty racks built into the cabinets at the end of the eighth row, space for when Sinclair wanted to add more servers.

Paris managed to squeeze his body into one, but there was no door to the cabinet. If the guards stood at the end of the row and looked down the aisle, he'd be out of sight. But if they walked even halfway down, there'd be no way they'd miss him.

He tried to listen to their progress, but it was hard to hear anything above the din of the machines. He could see a shadow on the wall that let him know they were getting closer. He could also see the outline of a gun.

Meanwhile, under the floor, Sydney held her breath as the larger guard stepped onto the panel directly above her face. It dipped slightly, almost pressing against her nose.

Paris was paralyzed as he saw the shadow grow and realized one of them had almost reached his aisle. Even though the room was kept cold for the servers, he could feel droplets of sweat forming on his forehead. Then he had an idea. He wasn't sure if it was good or if he was just desperate, but it was his last hope.

He waited for one of the larger drives to engage and spin, letting the noise cover the sound as he tossed François Fournier's ID down the aisle.

When the older guard reached the row, Paris kept perfectly still. His mouth was beyond dry, and his heart was racing a thousand beats per second.

"*Regardez là-bas!*" the man called to his partner. "Look there!"

He took two steps down the aisle, but before he was close enough to spot Paris, he leaned over and picked up the ID.

The man let out a roaring laugh and put his pistol back in its holster. "Here is your François Fournier!" He held up the ID for the other man to see. "It must have fallen off while he was working."

The younger man wasn't completely convinced, but

that was probably because he'd actually been excited about the chance to come face-to-face with criminals.

"Come on, let's get back," said the older man. "Maybe we can see the end of the PSG match."

Reluctantly, the younger man holstered his weapon and followed his partner out of the room. He did stop momentarily at the door to look at the footprint again, but then left.

"I told you it was not a glitch," he called out to the other guard. "It was a mistake by the employee. The computer never makes mistakes."

The Eiffel Tower

IT WAS ELEVEN O'CLOCK AT NIGHT, AND the lights on the Eiffel Tower twinkled as they did at the beginning of every hour. The area was still packed with tourists and would stay that way well past its midnight closing. That's why Mother had picked this as their rendezvous point. No matter what time they met or how long they talked, they wouldn't look out of place. Especially with the Youth Summit in town. Young people were everywhere.

While they waited for Monty and Kat, Brooklyn

walked over to a gift kiosk that sold official Eiffel Tower souvenirs. Everything from T-shirts and posters to models and bookends.

"How much is this?" she asked, holding up a plastic snow globe.

"Six euros," said the woman behind the register.

Brooklyn dug into her pocket to get the money, but Mother swooped in and beat her to it. "My treat," he said, handing the woman the cash.

"Thanks," said Brooklyn. She shook the globe and watched the snow fall on the miniature tower. "I thought I'd add it to my collection."

"You have a snow globe collection?" said Mother.

She smiled weakly. "Well, now I've got two, so that's kind of a collection."

"What other snow globe?" he asked, and then it dawned on him. "Ahhh, the shoebox . . ."

"You're pretty smart," she said. "You should be a spy."

Just then Monty and Kat arrived, each carrying a white paper bag.

"We come bearing macarons!" Monty said cheerfully. "They are *magnifique*."

Brooklyn had never heard of macarons before, but was a fan from her very first bite. They were colorful little cookies shaped like miniature hamburgers. They passed around the bags and retold the story of the hack at Asgard. Although Paris downplayed how close they came to being caught by the security guards.

"Know this," Monty said proudly. "If we're right and Sinclair Scientifica is linked to Umbra, then what you accomplished today is one of the biggest achievements for British Intelligence in years."

Next, Mother told them about Stavros Sinclair packing up his paintings. He was more convinced than ever that Sinclair and Le Fantôme were one and the same. However, it seemed as though every bit of information they uncovered raised more questions than answers.

"Let's break everything down into three groups," said Mother. "The things we know; the things we think we know but don't know for sure; and the things that totally baffle us and are driving us bonkers."

"I know that tomorrow Sydney is going to get up there and deliver a speech," Paris said, pointing to the stage that had been constructed at the base of the tower. "What I don't know is whether she's going to get scared and forget all her lines."

"You'll know it's an emergency if you hear me say,

'I'm here for queen and country, and I'd like to . . . um . . . um . . . what's my line?'"

Everybody laughed.

"What else do we know about tomorrow?" asked Rio.

"We know that if the pattern continues, the Purple Thumb will do . . . *something*," said Kat.

"And we think we know that they'll attack Sinclair Scientifica," added Sydney. "At least they have every time before."

"We know Stavros Sinclair is packing up his paintings," offered Rio. "Although we have no idea why."

"You know what's baffling me?" said Mother. "We have no idea if or how the stolen virus fits in with all of this."

"I find that particularly worrisome," said Monty.

They sat there for a moment considering all of these, and then Kat broke the silence when she said, "I'll tell you what troubles me most," she said.

"You mean other than people touching your stuff?" said Rio.

She ignored him and continued, "We know virtually nothing about Leyland Carmichael's thumb."

This brought more laughter.

"That wasn't a joke," she said. "In this pattern he's

the constant. How does a dead man's thumbprint keep winding up at crime scenes?"

"The police have been asking themselves that for years," said Mother.

"What do we know about him?" asked Brooklyn.

Rio did a quick search on his phone. "He was an attorney who turned into an environmental activist who then became a self-proclaimed 'ecoterrorist.' He was primarily opposed to logging companies," he said, reading. "He felt guilty because he grew up rich in a family that made millions cutting down forests in Washington and Oregon."

"How rich?" asked Sydney.

"Exceptionally," said Kat, reading from another article she'd pulled up on her phone. "He attended St. George's International School in Switzerland, one of the most expensive boarding schools in the world, and went to Stanford for college and law school."

"He was a lawyer turned terrorist," Paris said, shaking his head.

"Where have we seen that before?" asked Brooklyn.

"Lawyers turned terrorists?" Paris asked, confused.

"No, St. George's International School," she answered. "Are they one of the teams in the competition?"

"Nope," said Sydney. "There aren't any teams from Switzerland."

Brooklyn thought hard for a moment, trying to place it before she remembered. "Oh, I know where I saw it. . . . That's interesting."

"What's interesting?" asked Monty.

"I read about it last night," Brooklyn said. "St. George's is where Stavros Sinclair went to school."

"And didn't he get his PhD at Stanford?" asked Paris.

"He sure did," she said.

Now all of them were on their phones searching for any articles or reports that might shed some light on the relationship between the two.

"Stavros was seven months older," Kat said. "Even if they were a grade apart, they'd almost certainly know each other."

"So are we saying that Stavros is Le Fantôme and the Purple Thumb?" asked Sydney, confused.

"Listen to this," Rio interrupted. "It says that Carmichael was severely injured in an explosion when he tried to use dynamite to blow up a bulldozer at a logging site. The fuse was faulty, and it exploded when he was still too close. He lived another nine months but died because of the injuries from the explosion."

"So you think that's where he lost his thumb?" asked Brooklyn. "If so, it would've been too damaged to leave a print. How does it connect to Sinclair?"

Kat smiled. "Stavros already told us the connection," she said as she slid her phone into her pocket.

"He did?" said Paris.

"Today, during his speech," she answered. "'We're developing prosthetic limbs so lifelike, they . . .'"

"'. . . re-create a person's fingerprints,'" said Sydney, finishing the line. "You are so right."

They considered this for a moment. "So we're thinking what?" said Mother. "Leyland Carmichael accidentally blows up his hand, and his old school buddy Stavros gives him a state-of-the-art prosthetic."

"Yes," said Brooklyn. "That's exactly what we're thinking."

"But wouldn't the FBI have found that when they dug up his body?" asked Sydney.

"They wouldn't have buried him with it," said Kat. "It wouldn't make sense. It's new and experimental technology. Once he was done with it, Sinclair would want it back to study its durability."

"And if they got it back . . . ," said Paris.

"Then they'd be able to use it during the burglaries," Brooklyn said.

"But that still doesn't answer the biggest question," said Monty. "If Stavros is the one who has it, and Sinclair Scientifica is the target of all the crimes, that would mean he's breaking into his own company. Why?"

"For the same reason a magician uses misdirection," answered Rio. "He wants everyone looking at one hand, so nobody notices what he's doing with the other."

The Rally

AMELIE BOUHADDI WAS ONE OF THE chief organizers of the Global Youth Summit on the Environment. Twenty-four years old, she was the daughter of Algerian immigrants, spoke four languages fluently, and sometimes performed as a soloist with the Paris Opera. That is, when she wasn't too busy saving the world.

She'd achieved so much at such a young age because she was obsessive about making precise schedules and following them to the last detail. That's why she was in charge of the biggest and most important rally of the summit. Over the next three hours and forty-seven minutes, there would be a steady stream of pop singers, movie stars, activists, celebrities, and other notables committed to protecting the environment who would take their turn at the microphone.

Each was allotted a specific amount of time, and Amelie had been deadly serious when she told them the microphone would be turned off if they went so much as one second over. Likewise, they would be silenced if their speeches veered off topic.

"I don't care how famous you are," she said. "Today you are the orchestra, and I am the conductor." Then she softened her tone, flashed a winning smile, and added, "And together we will make wonderful music."

Sydney, who was standing at the rear of the group of speakers, turned to Mother and whispered, "I'm torn. Part of me is terrified of her, yet part of me wants to be just like her."

Mother chuckled and whispered back, "Just for the record, you already are."

Sydney was among the fifteen students whose speeches would be sprinkled among more famous names. They were given the least amount of time: one minute and forty-five seconds. The combination of the time constraint along with Sydney's desire to say something significant and inspirational was what had caused her to rewrite her speech so many times.

Every word has to count, she'd told herself repeatedly.

The stage faced the Champ de Mars, a public park that stretched out from the base of the Eiffel Tower. When Sydney peered out from behind the curtain, she saw an endless sea of faces.

"That is a lot of people," she said, slightly overwhelmed.

"You've got no worries, Olivia," Mother said, using an Australian accent.

She looked up at him, stunned. "You haven't called me Olivia since . . . I don't know when . . . back at Wallangarra."

"The day you blew the head off that statue."

They both laughed at the memory.

"Mrs. Hobart, racist cow," joked Sydney. "What a sorry lot we were. Me with my purple hair. You with your phony copper's badge."

"That girl with the purple hair," said Mother. "She had something to say. Something important. She still does. Just go out on that stage and be yourself. For a minute forty-five, forget Sydney and MI6, and just be Olivia."

She smiled at him. "I can do that."

The speaker onstage was a French actor Sydney didn't recognize, but when he finished, the crowd cheered.

"I don't know what he said, but it must've been good," she told Mother. "Maybe I should give my speech in French too."

"I'm not sure that's the best idea," he replied. "Especially since you only know about a dozen French words."

"Good point," she said. "Although, on the plus side, I could say them all and still finish under my time limit."

A singer-songwriter with a guitar was now at the microphone, and she started to perform a song.

"You're up next," Amelie told Sydney. "As soon as she finishes the song and the audience begins to applaud, start walking across the stage."

"Got it," Sydney said, her voice a blend of fear and admiration.

Sydney and Mother stood listening to the song for a moment.

"I'm gutted that I'm not with the team today," she said. "I hope they're okay."

"At this point they're just doing a Devon Loch," he said. "They don't need any help for that."

"What's a Devon Loch?"

"Devon Loch was a racehorse owned by Queen Elizabeth, and he was about to win the Grand National," he said. "He was in the final stretch with a big lead, and for no apparent reason he did a belly flop and lost the race. It's pretty much what the team's doing right now as they make sure to finish sixth or lower."

"And if the Purple Thumb attacks?" she asked.

"The place is loaded with secret agents," he answered. "They couldn't be more protected."

"Why is it loaded with secret agents?" asked Sydney.

"Didn't I tell you about the press conference?" he said.

"No," she said.

"Out of the blue, Stavros Sinclair decided that he's going to hold a press conference immediately following the conclusion of this rally," he said. "That's when he's going to announce the winner of the Stavros Prize."

"Why does that make the team safe?" she asked.

"Because it's the first time he's done something truly public in years," he said. "Every intelligence officer who can make it is going to pretend to be a reporter and attend the press conference. I just spoke to Tru, and she said that MI6 has sent at least seven undercover agents. It got so crowded, they had to stop letting people in."

"What about the actual press?" she asked. "Won't they be mad if there's no room for them?"

"Not really," he said. "I think most reporters are far more interested in movie stars and singers talking about the environment in front of fifty thousand kids than they are in some crackpot billionaire talking about making fake rain."

"Crackpot billionaire?" she scolded. "I thought you preferred the term '*eccentric philanthropist.*'"

This made him laugh.

"You're right, *eccentric philanthropist*," he said. "Fitting, when you think about it. This press conference is about as well planned as the one Big Bill Maxwell scheduled to coincide with the queen's coronation."

Sydney smiled. "Big Bill, the original magician's misdirection."

Onstage, the singer was nearing the end of her song, and Sydney could feel her heart rate pick up. She tried to calm herself by taking a deep breath and holding it for a moment before exhaling. She did this again. And then she thought of something that really made her heart race.

"Big Bill," she said to Mother, worried.

"What about him?"

"He was a fraud," she said. "An actor hired to play a role by MI6."

"So?"

"What if Stavros Sinclair isn't Le Fantôme?" she asked. "What if he's just like Big Bill? What if he's a fake used to keep us looking in the wrong direction?"

Mother considered this.

"Brooklyn said that in his biography, everyone who ever knew him and all of his teachers are completely surprised he's been so successful," she continued. "They said he was just an average student, not someone you'd expect to revolutionize the tech world."

"Which would make him perfect for the part," he said.

"What do you mean?"

"If Sinclair Scientifica is a cover for Umbra, they'd need someone to be a figurehead," he said. "It would have to be someone who'd gone to the right schools and knew how to talk the talk."

"But not someone who actually had the talent and drive to change the world," said Sydney. "Someone like that would get in the way."

"Right. They'd want a human puppet like Big Bill," he continued. "That would explain why he never appears in public or talks to the press. If he talked publicly, then people might figure it out. Just like MI6 didn't want Big Bill to talk to anybody."

Sydney thought about this for a moment. "But if they don't want him to answer questions, why schedule an actual press conference?"

The singer was in the final moments of her song.

A look of total dread overtook Mother. "He's the nugget."

"What do you mean?" asked Sydney.

"We tricked Brooklyn's foster parents to get them on the roof by making them think there was money hidden there," he said. "They've just tricked top spies from around the world to come into their headquarters."

Now she knew why he looked so nervous. "The virus," she said. "If they're all together, they can all be exposed to the virus."

"It would devastate intelligence agencies across the globe," he reasoned. "MI6, CIA, DGSI. All the agents who've been pursuing Umbra for years could be wiped out."

"Not just them," said Sydney. "Brooklyn, Kat, Paris, and Rio would be wiped out too. You've got to get over there."

"There may not be time," he said. "Besides, they stopped letting people in. We've got to call them and tell them to get out."

"We can't," said Sydney. "Security confiscates all phones when you enter the building."

Onstage the singer was done, and the crowd was cheering. Sydney was not where she was supposed to be, and Amelie Bouhaddi was very unhappy.

"You need to be out there," she said as she put a firm hand on Sydney's back and helped move her in the right direction. "I'm taking this out of your time."

Her mind was racing as she walked up the steps onto the back of the stage.

"Sydney!" Mother called out.

She turned toward him, but Amelie kept her pushing toward the microphone.

"*You* can tell them," he said, raising his voice over the crowd. "They'll be watching."

33. A Change of Plans

THE TEAM FROM KINLOCH ABBEY WAS upset. Twenty-four hours earlier they'd had good reason to believe they might win the Stavros Prize and with it a million euros. But for the second day in a row, that chance was being undermined by a series of unexplained computer problems. No matter what Charlotte tried, the weather models that worked so perfectly back home in Scotland failed here.

It reached the point that one of her teammates took her spot at the keyboard. For Charlotte, this was the ultimate insult. She had unwavering confidence in her computer skills. She was certain that she was better than anyone else in the room.

And that was her undoing.

There was in fact one person who was better. Brooklyn sat across the room and smiled as they tried to solve the problems that she was secretly sending their way. They wouldn't be able to do it. She'd written this code with the help of a supercomputer, and it would take a supercomputer to unravel it.

She tried not to smile when Charlotte came over to her.

"I know you did this," Charlotte said angrily. "I don't know how, but I know it was you."

Brooklyn smiled innocently. "I have no idea what you're talking about."

"Sydney's coming onstage," Paris called.

The rest of the team was watching the rally, which was being broadcast throughout the Olympus building.

"She doesn't look so good," Rio said with concern as Sydney approached the microphone.

"It's a huge crowd," Brooklyn replied, coming to her defense. "She'll be great once she gets started."

"I don't know," said Kat. "She looks like she's going to hyperventilate."

"Come on, Syd, you've got this," Paris said, willing her to succeed.

Sydney took a deep breath and started. She had one minute and forty-five seconds to try to save the lives of her four best friends as well as those of countless intelligence officers.

"My name is Sydney, and I'm fourteen years old," she said. "I come for queen and country, and I need to . . . um . . . um."

"Oh no!" said Brooklyn. "This is not good."

"I represent a group called the Foundation for Atmospheric Research and Monitoring, which was created by a remarkable man named William Maxwell, the twenty-fourth baron of Aisling."

"What's going on?" said Paris. "This wasn't part of any of her speeches. And believe me, I had to listen to every one."

"This is a train wreck," added Rio.

"When he founded FARM, which is what we call it, he delivered an important speech about his vision for the future," Sydney continued. "And I think there will be a very similar speech delivered today by Stavros Sinclair."

Charlotte had been watching on a different monitor but came over to ask the others, "Is this some sort of joke?"

"Shh," said Kat, trying to quiet them. "I want to hear this."

"Why? Do you take glee in other people's misery?" asked Rio.

"No," Kat replied. "I think she's sending us a message."

"In fact, even though Mr. Sinclair is famous around the world and William Maxwell was not," Sydney continued, "I think they are *exactly* alike. Big Bill was worried about the pollution that poisoned our oceans. He said it was like a *virus without an antidote* and called on all of us to keep that virus from spreading."

Sydney looked down at the clock on the podium. She had only seventeen seconds to go.

"And so I call out to all my brothers and sisters around the world, in places as far away as Rio, New York, and Kathmandu. Just as I call out to all of you here in Paris. You have to stop this virus before it spreads. You have to act now!"

She had three more seconds.

"Save the Earth. Save yourselves."

She stopped, and there was polite applause. Her speech didn't make much sense to the fifty thousand young people who filled the Champ de Mars park. It may not have inspired them, but she'd made sure that every word mattered.

The team knew that Sydney was sending them a message even if the details weren't immediately clear.

"Somehow they're going to release the virus unless we can stop them," said Paris.

"Maybe they're going to let it loose in the ballroom when Stavros announces the winner of the prize," offered Rio.

"But they can't do that," said Brooklyn. "If they released the virus in the ballroom, then Stavros would be infected too. He wouldn't infect himself."

They considered this, and then Rio said, "Unless he doesn't know."

"What do you mean?" asked Kat.

"Sydney just said he's *exactly* like Big Bill," answered Rio. "Big Bill didn't know anything. He was just some actor put up by MI6. Maybe Stavros is a fake too. And if that's the case, Umbra wouldn't hesitate to kill him."

They stopped talking when Juliette came over to them. "Your friend's speech was very . . . interesting," she said, trying to pay a compliment but struggling to do so. "Tell her I said congratulations."

"Thank you, we will," said Paris. "When are we going to the ballroom to see Mr. Sinclair?"

"There's been a change," she replied. "The announcement has been moved to the Workshop. The auditorium where Mr. Sinclair spoke the first day."

"Why did it relocate?" asked Kat.

"Mr. Sinclair decided to open the announcement to the media," she explained. "We needed more room, so we'll be heading there in a few minutes."

She left, and they tried to figure out the plan of attack.

"So we're not going into the ballroom, which means our mission plan is useless," said Rio. "We're just going to have to make this up as we go."

"How do you think they'll do it?" asked Paris. "How do you spread the virus without exposing yourself in the process?"

They stood quietly, trying to think like Umbra. Then Kat felt a blast of cool air from an air-conditioning vent. It was refreshing, but it was also more than that.

It was informational.

"I know how they're going to do it," she said excitedly. "They're going to use the air climate control system. It's designed to control the temperature and flow of oxygen throughout the building. It's perfect."

"I think you're absolutely right," said Paris. "It's the ideal delivery system."

"Do you know what that means?" said Brooklyn.

"No, what?" asked Paris.

Brooklyn thought about it for a moment and realized there was only one way to reach the climate system.

"It means I'm going to have to climb that wall after all."

The Climb

EXECUTIVE ELEVATOR—OLYMPUS BUILDING

ONLY A HANDFUL OF PEOPLE HAD ACCESS to the executive elevator located in the rear of the Olympus Building. One of them was Stanislav Rada, who'd been known as "The Professor" since his days as a top chemistry student at the University of Prague.

Rada was tall with friendly eyes and a booming laugh. He loved to bake, and his specialty was a type of fruit pastry called a kolach, which he made from a recipe passed down from his grandmother.

In addition to his baking skills, he was very talented at killing people.

Paris had first seen Rada five years earlier outside the factory fire and then again seen him with Stavros Sinclair during the competition. According to Rada's business card, he was the worldwide chief of security for Sinclair Scientifica. In reality, he was the person who took care of Le Fantôme's dirty work.

A few weeks earlier, the Professor had killed two French secret agents and dumped their bodies in the Seine. Now he was about to unleash the deadly virus he'd stolen from them. He pressed the button for the fifth floor, and the elevator began to climb.

According to the software that monitored everyone inside Olympus, the elevator was empty. Rada had programmed it to ignore his movements. There would be no record of where he was today.

EXTERIOR WALL—OLYMPUS BUILDING

Brooklyn couldn't ride an elevator to the fifth floor. She'd have to climb twenty-two feet up a wall. First, though, she needed to crawl out a narrow ladies' room window and stand up on the sill. As she got into position, she made the mistake of looking down at the courtyard below.

That looks really far, she thought to herself.

During her training at Pinewood, Brooklyn's instructor told her to break down the climb into separate sections. She said it would be less intimidating if she thought of it as several manageable parts instead of one complicated procedure.

The first step was to make it seven feet up from the window to a small ledge called a cornice. As she looked at the bricks in the wall, it dawned on her that they formed a pattern. She thought about Kat and tried to view them the way she would.

Brooklyn looked for any bricks that didn't quite fit the pattern and noticed that several were slightly uneven and out of place. Each of these stuck out about half an inch farther than the others. These would become her hand- and footholds. She reached for the lowest one and began to pull herself up from the window.

THE WORKSHOP—OLYMPUS BUILDING

Of the sixty-three reporters who filed into the small auditorium for Stavros Sinclair's press conference, more than thirty were actually operatives working for various intelligence agencies around the world.

Unlike the actual reporters who rushed to the front rows so they'd be able to ask questions, the agents preferred seats near the doorways where they'd have a vantage point to watch for possible threats.

It never occurred to any of them that the real danger would come from the air-conditioning vents above their heads.

COMPUTER LAB—OLYMPUS BUILDING

The team from FARM was standing around the television monitor pretending to watch the rally when Juliette approached them.

"Where's Brooklyn?" she asked.

There was a momentary pause before Paris answered, "I thought she was right here."

"Well, she's not," Juliette said, irritated. "And she's supposed to be. We're scheduled to head to the press conference in three minutes."

"Maybe she went to the loo," said Kat. "I'll go check."

"Quickly," said Juliette. "We cannot be late."

EXTERIOR WALL—OLYMPUS BUILDING

Brooklyn's fingertips burned with pain. The coarse granules of the cement mortar cut into her skin as she grasped for the small ledge just beyond her reach.

You cannot achieve what you cannot believe, she said to herself, her sweaty cheek pressed against the bricks as she hugged the wall. *You cannot achieve what you cannot believe.*

She reached again, this time lunging a bit, and managed to grab on to the cornice. She let out a sigh of relief and counted this as a small but significant victory. One step was complete; now she had to cross the cornice over to a drainpipe.

PONT DE L'ALMA—ALMA BRIDGE

Because the Metro stations near the rally were closed for security, Mother and Sydney had to run from the Eiffel Tower toward the Olympus building. As they sprinted across the Alma Bridge, Mother called Monty on his cell.

"Get to the embassy," he said breathless. "Tru will be waiting for you. Tell her everything we know."

CLIMATE CONTROL ROOM—OLYMPUS BUILDING

Originally the plan had been to set off an explosion

during the press conference. That would've been big and made headlines. But Rada was the one who thought of using the virus instead. Perhaps it was because of his background in chemistry.

"It will not kill anyone immediately," the Professor said when he pitched the idea to Le Fantôme. "In fact, they will not even exhibit any symptoms for five or six days. This is good because they will be infected when they return to their intelligence agencies to report on what happened. They will spread the virus at CIA headquarters in Washington and at MI6 headquarters in London. It will spread wherever we have enemies. And then, when the people start to get sick, it will be too late for them to stop it."

Before he could inject the virus into the climate control system, Rada had to put on a special BSL-4–positive pressure suit. This was more commonly known as a "spacesuit" because it looked like something an astronaut would wear. He needed to make sure no part of him was exposed to the virus. If a drop of it touched his skin, it would almost certainly be fatal.

EXTERIOR WALL—OLYMPUS BUILDING

Brooklyn had worked her way uneasily along the cornice

and reached the copper drainpipe. For this stage she was supposed to shimmy up the pipe to the next floor, but found herself frozen with fear. She tried not to think of what was at stake, but it was overwhelming as her mind flooded with thoughts of people in danger and her difficulties during training. It only got worse when she looked down at the ground more than thirty feet below.

She tried to repeat the Motherism, but she couldn't even do that. She just stood there on the ledge, clinging to the drainpipe, the copper cool to her touch.

Then she thought about the catacombs. When she was frozen with fear, Paris had told her what to do. *Point yourself in the right direction, and follow your eyes,* he'd said. *You are much braver than you realize.*

COMPUTER LABORATORY—OLYMPUS BUILDING

Juliette's frustration had grown. It was time for the team to head to the auditorium, but there was still no sign of Brooklyn.

"She's not in the restroom," Kat said when she returned. "She's got to be here somewhere."

"That's it," said Juliette. "I'm calling security. I'll have them locate her by her badge."

"Wait a second."

They turned to see that it was Charlotte.

"Are you looking for Brooklyn?" she asked.

"Yes," answered Juliette. "Do you know where she is?"

Charlotte looked at the team and read their angry expressions, which she ignored. "I saw her going someplace she shouldn't," she said.

Paris couldn't believe that Charlotte would turn on them like this. She'd been a part of the team for years, and now she was selling them out. "Are you sure it was her?" he asked, giving her one last chance to change her mind.

"Positive," said Charlotte. "Come with me. I'll show you."

Charlotte set off with Juliette, and the others followed close behind.

"She walked over toward the bathroom," Charlotte said. "But then she went in here."

They reached a utility closet.

Juliette used her electronic key to open the door, and when she did, Charlotte shoved her into the closet, trapping her inside.

"Hold the door closed," Charlotte instructed Paris.

A stunned Paris pressed his body against the door and kept it shut while Juliette protested from inside, her cries muffled by the door. Charlotte started typing on the electronic keypad.

"What are you doing?" asked Kat.

"Overriding the system and locking the door," she said. "I bet your friend Brooklyn can't do this."

The pad made a beeping noise, and Charlotte smiled.

"It's good," she said to Paris. "She can't get out."

"But . . . ," Paris said, confused.

"Tell Mother this is my way of apologizing," said Charlotte. "Tell him I said I was sorry."

PARIS-LE BOURGET AIRPORT

Le Fantôme stood in the hangar and watched as his paintings were carefully loaded onto a private jet. Included among them was the Renoir of the young girl. When he reached his new home, he would hang it over his desk again, so that she could watch over him and he could remember his sister.

CLIMATE CONTROL ROOM—OLYMPUS BUILDING

Now fully protected by his spacesuit, Rada was ready. He opened the silver case and pulled out a vial marked XUHET.

He took out a syringe to extract the virus from the

vial and inject it into the clear plastic tube that delivered extra oxygen into various rooms each afternoon. He'd already overridden the program so that all the oxygen would be delivered to the Workshop, where the virus would become airborne.

He wasn't used to wearing the spacesuit and found it cumbersome to move around. The thick rubber gloves made it difficult to manipulate the syringe, and the helmet made it hard to hear, which was why he didn't notice Brooklyn coming up from behind.

She used the element of surprise, and a kick she'd learned one summer in a YMCA karate class, to momentarily stagger him. This gave her just enough time to grab the vial.

"Put that down," Rada commanded once he regained his balance.

"Back off," she said, waving the vial like a weapon. "Or I'll release this."

The plastic helmet of the spacesuit muffled his booming laugh.

"It will do me no harm," he said. "This suit will keep me safe." Then he held up the syringe, its silver needle reflecting in the light. "You, however, have no such protection."

Brooklyn's eyes opened wide at the sight of the needle. He moved toward her, and, in a fit of panic, she flung the vial across the room.

"You'll have to get it first," she said, waving the fingers of her now-empty hand.

"Stupid girl!" he yelled. "If that breaks, everything is ruined!"

"Not my problem," she responded as she sprinted toward the door.

He was torn for a moment, uncertain if he should go after her or the virus. It didn't help that he was wearing the spacesuit. Maybe if he wasn't, he would've noticed the vial was now in her left hand.

All that practice with Rio had paid off. She'd swapped it from one hand to the other with a perfectly executed French Drop. Now she had to get out of the building before Rada figured out what she'd done.

The Three Lions

IT TOOK RADA LONGER TO GET OUT OF the spacesuit than it did for him to realize Brooklyn still had the virus. This gave her enough time to find the stairwell she needed to take in order to escape the building. Even though she'd studied the layout of the fifth floor during her training at Pinewood, in her nervousness she took a couple of wrong turns before she finally found the right way.

She ran down the stairs so fast, she almost tripped twice and needed to grab onto the handrail to keep from wiping out. One time this caused her to bobble the vial, and she had to snatch it in midair before it hit the second-floor landing and shattered.

Stay cool, she said to herself. *Stay cool.*

When she reached the emergency exit on the ground level, she could hear Rada rushing down the stairs above her. The alarm sounded as she flung open the door and started sprinting down the sidewalk. It was three blocks to the Three Lions. If she could make it there, she could get to the tunnel and the British embassy.

An angry driver honked at her when she darted across the street, and the sound helped Rada spot her as he emerged from the building.

Brooklyn knew he was behind her, but she didn't turn to look. She just ran as fast as she could, careful to hold the vial tight enough so that she didn't drop it, but not so tight that it might break open in her hand.

She thought back to the beach in Aisling, where she and Sydney ran every morning.

"This isn't just exercise," Sydney had told her that first day. "We need to get you in spy shape."

This was what she meant. This was "spy shape."

The memory put a smile on her face, and she tried to pick up her pace.

Finally the Three Lions came into view. But, as fast as she was running, Rada was going faster—and getting closer.

She burst through the door and yelled for help. "Reggie!"

Then she looked up and saw the most unexpected thing: a sign on the counter that read BACK IN FIVE MINUTES.

"Reggie!" she called frantically.

She spun around and saw that Rada had almost reached the door.

"Reggie!" she yelled one more time as she rushed to the linen closet so that she could reach the tunnel.

She went to type the code into the lock, but couldn't remember it. "What is it? What is it?" she asked herself. "When did England win the World Cup?"

"1966," said a thickly accented voice.

It was Rada. He'd caught up with her, and there was still no sign of Reggie. There was no sign of anyone else.

"They didn't deserve to win, by the way," he added. "West Germany were the better team."

"Back off," Brooklyn said, holding the vial up for him to see. "If you take one step closer, I will throw this against the floor, and we'll both be dead. You don't have your fancy suit to protect you anymore."

"I don't fall for that twice," said Rada. "You're not going to throw the vial. You are going to hand it to me."

"Are you willing to take that risk?" she asked him.

He took a step toward her, and she motioned like she was going to throw it against the ground, but she didn't. She couldn't.

His smile grew bigger.

He took another step, and just as he was about to reach for her, the smile disappeared and his substantial body crumpled to the floor, landing face-first with a loud thump.

Brooklyn didn't realize what had happened until she saw what was sticking out of his neck: a feathered dart from Reggie's tranquilizer gun.

She almost collapsed with relief.

"I didn't think you were going to make it," said Brooklyn. "I kept calling for you."

She looked up expecting to see Reggie, but instead a woman she didn't recognize was holding his cane.

"Good thing Reg keeps a couple of extras around," said the woman. "By the by, England totally deserved the Cup in sixty-six."

Brooklyn didn't know what to make of her. Was she a

friend? An enemy? She stood motionless, and then both of them looked at the vial in Brooklyn's hand.

"You better hurry up and get that to the embassy," she said.

Friend.

"Thank you," answered Brooklyn.

She typed in the code, and the door opened.

"But before you go," said the woman, "take this." She handed Brooklyn a thumb drive. "Give it to Mother, and tell him to stop looking for the kids."

"You know Mother?" Brooklyn said, confused. Then she looked at the woman again. "Wait a second. You're his wife, aren't you? You're Clementine!"

The woman didn't answer the question. Instead she said, "Tell him Robert and Annie are healthy and happy and that he has to stop looking."

"But . . ."

"Quickly," the woman said. "This situation is about to get worse, and you don't want to be here when he wakes up."

Brooklyn paused for a second and realized she was right. She studied the woman for a moment more and then ran toward safety.

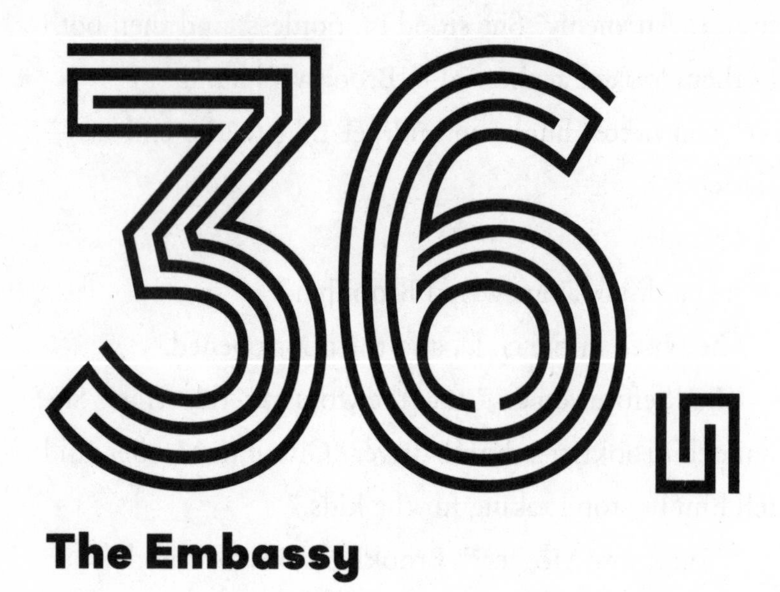

The Embassy

BROOKLYN WOKE UP IN A COMFORTABLE bed located in a section of the British embassy known as the Residence. She wasn't exactly sure how she got there. She remembered running through the tunnel, the sound of an alarm going off, and someone taking the vial and telling her everything would be all right.

She thought that that someone was Monty, although she didn't know why Monty would've been at the embassy. So that part might have been her mind playing tricks on her.

Either way, once she'd handed over the vial, she'd

collapsed from a combination of mental and physical exhaustion. She had no idea how long she'd been asleep, but when she woke, the first thing she saw was Sydney sitting at her bedside looking down at her.

"Well if it isn't Brookie the Rookie," Sydney said sweetly. "Why am I always having to wake you up?"

They both smiled.

Brooklyn sat upright. Everyone was there.

"I think I told you that you didn't have to climb the wall," joked Mother.

"I think I told you that I could do it," Brooklyn replied proudly. "And I did!"

"Yes, you most certainly did," he said.

"How'd you sneak the virus out?" asked Paris.

"The French Drop," Brooklyn said. She turned to Rio and added, "You're a good teacher."

Rio looked at her and smiled. And, though it was brief, for the first time the two of them had a connection as he answered, "You're a good student."

"French Drop's appropriate, I guess," said Monty. "Considering this is Paris."

Kat sat down on the edge of the bed, her eyes full of emotion, and without saying a word wrapped Brooklyn up in a big hug.

Brooklyn was caught so off guard that she didn't know how to react at first. But after a second, she hugged Kat right back and said, "I'm glad to see you, too."

"When we get back to the FARM," Kat said, "you can come into my room and borrow any items of mine that you want."

This elicited hoots from the others.

"Now I have seen everything!" exclaimed Paris. "Absolutely everything!"

Kat laughed through her tears.

"You'll have to tell us what she has in there," said Sydney. "She's never let any of us see."

They talked for a few more minutes, and Mother stepped into the hallway. When he came back, he said, "There is a very tall woman with a limp and nine fingers who'd like to speak to you. If you're ready."

"Let her in," said Brooklyn.

Tru entered the room and had each member of the team tell her their version of what happened. She informed them that Stanislav Rada had been taken into custody and was being flown to a secret location somewhere in the north of France.

"We're going to work together with our French partners to see what information we can get out of him about

Umbra," she said. "But I think it's safe to say he'll never see the light of a free day again."

"What about Stavros Sinclair?" asked Paris.

"As far as we can prove, he's done nothing illegal," said Tru. "We're keeping an eye on him, but that's it for now."

"And the prize?" asked Brooklyn. "Who won?"

"That school you like in New York," said Rio.

"The Metropolitan Institute of Science and Technology?"

"That's the one," he answered.

"Nice," said Brooklyn. "It just goes to show you, New Yorkers got mad skills."

They all laughed.

"Yeah," said Sydney. "We've kind of seen that firsthand."

"It's too bad they get all that money, though," said Rio. "A million euros. We could've done a lot with that."

"Don't feel too jealous," said Tru. "You may not have won the Stavros Prize, but your performance here in Paris has more than guaranteed MI6 will continue to fund Project Neverland for quite some time."

"Project Neverland?" asked Brooklyn.

"Yeah," Sydney said unenthusiastically. "That's our official name."

"I don't like it," said Brooklyn.

"Nobody does," she replied.

"Well, I think it's clever," said Tru. "Mother's Peter Pan. Monty's Tinkerbell. And the FARM is Neverland."

"What does that make us?" asked Brooklyn.

"The Lost Boys," Kat said with disdain.

"What?!" said Brooklyn. "That can't be right. First of all, we're not lost. And second of all, three of us are definitely not boys!"

"Well," Tru said, scrambling. "Code names aren't meant to be literal."

"If I'm being honest," said Monty, "now that we're talking about it, I don't much care for Tinkerbell. She was pretty scatterbrained, and a spoiled brat."

"I don't mind it," said Mother.

"Of course not," said Monty. "Peter Pan's the hero. The boy who never grew up. That *is* you."

As the tone of the conversation reached near mutiny, Tru held up her hands to silence everybody. "All right, all right," she said. "Just out of curiosity, what would you like to be called?"

All eyes turned to Brooklyn, who'd started this.

"Well . . . we all use our hometowns as our names," she said, thinking out loud. "And we're spies. So . . . how about . . . the City Spies."

"Ooh, I like it," said Sydney. "I like it a lot."

"Me too," said Paris.

"I like the fact that it uses a pattern," said Kat. "I approve."

"I'm sold," said Rio. "Call us the City Spies."

Tru looked around the room and saw that everybody was in agreement.

"I'll see what I can do," she said.

As the celebratory mood continued, Brooklyn got up and walked over to Mother.

"Can I speak to you alone for a moment?" she asked.

"Of course," he said. "Come with me."

They walked into an adjoining room, which was set up as a home office with bookcases, a desk, and a computer.

"What's the matter?" asked Mother.

"There's something I left out," she said. "I didn't want to say it in front of anybody else. At least not until I told you first."

"What is it?" he asked, concerned.

"Reggie didn't save me," she said. "A woman did. She gave me this." Brooklyn took the flash drive out of her pocket and handed it to Mother. Then she looked up at him and said, "I think it was Clementine."

The color drained from his face.

"What makes you say that?" he asked, stunned.

"She told me to tell you that the kids are fine. That they're happy and healthy but that you have to stop looking for them," said Brooklyn. "And here's the weird part." She paused for a moment. "She knew about Reggie and the tranquilizer gun. She knew about the tunnel and the code for the door. It felt like she was still part of MI6, not Umbra."

Now Mother's eyes narrowed, and he looked through the doorway into the other room. Everyone was laughing and having a good time, but he focused on Tru. He studied her and wondered what she might know and what she might have kept from him.

He tried to hide his emotions, but he desperately needed to see what was on the drive. He went to the computer but realized it needed a log-on username and password.

"Can you take care of this?" he asked Brooklyn.

She smiled. "No problem."

It took her about thirty seconds.

He plugged in the flash drive. There was only one file on it. He clicked it open to reveal a photograph.

"Is that them?" asked Brooklyn. "Are those your kids?"

On the screen was a picture of a boy and a girl on the sidewalk of a city street. They were five years older than the last time he'd seen them, but he knew without question that it was Robert and Annie. Both were smiling. Both looked happy.

He didn't answer her. He just stood there looking at them with tears in his eyes.

The Snow Globe

IT HAD BEEN THREE WEEKS SINCE THEY'D returned from Paris, and Brooklyn was finally getting a glimpse of normal life at FARM. That is, if you could call demolition practice and martial-arts training normal.

She'd enrolled in Kinloch Abbey and was trying to adjust. The school was unlike any she'd ever known, and she was pretty certain Charlotte was going to make her life there as difficult as possible. But she had some classes with Kat and Rio, and they all sat together at lunch. Ever since the hug, she and Kat had been steadily building a friendship, and, while she wouldn't yet say that Rio considered her a mate, there were times when he was at least friendly.

Brooklyn hadn't told anyone about Mother's wife. He'd asked her to keep it secret. If there was any chance she was some sort of double agent for MI6, that information needed to be closely guarded.

She worried about him, though. Keeping the secret meant she couldn't ask anyone else to look out for him. She needed to do that, which is why she went to the air traffic control tower to visit him one Sunday afternoon. She was carrying the pale blue shoebox from her closet. The one she retrieved during her first alpha test.

She climbed up the stairs to the top of the tower and found him lost in thought as he looked out the window, an untouched cup of tea sitting on the table next to him.

"What's wrong?" asked Brooklyn, startling him.

"Nothing," he said. "Just looking out at the ocean and enjoying a cuppa."

"Liar," she said. "Do you want to know how long I was standing there without you noticing me?"

"Okay, you got me," he admitted. "What can I do for you?"

"You've got that backward," she answered. "I'm going to do something for you. I'm going to help you."

"How do you mean?"

"I know what goes on here," she said. "At night, when everyone else is sleeping, you're searching for them, aren't you?"

"What makes you say that?" he asked.

"Beny," she replied. "You're using his computing power. I can see the spikes in his usage every night. Where are you looking?"

He shrugged. "Anywhere I can think of," he said. "Social media accounts, school attendance rolls, hospital records. Anything with a list, anywhere around the world. Robert has asthma, so I check pharmacy orders. Annie's an excellent swimmer, so I look at race results. I even check police arrest reports."

"Like when you found me?" she asked. "You were looking for them in New York City arrest records?"

He nodded.

"I'm sorry I wasn't her," she said.

"Don't be," said Mother. "That's ridiculous." He paused for a moment before adding, "By the way, I was right."

"When?" she asked.

"When I told Tru that you were a natural," he said. "Already better than the other four. I didn't want anyone to hear it. But I was right."

She didn't know what to say, so she didn't reply at all. She just looked out at the sea.

"It doesn't let you off the hook," he said. "You're going to have to work twice as hard because you have twice the potential."

"I know," she said.

She saw the picture of Robert and Annie on the table. "Has it given you any clues?"

"A few," he said. "I'm studying the reflection in this store window, trying to identify which city they're in."

Brooklyn looked at the flash of color in the window. There wasn't much to go on. "I'm going to help you find them," she said.

"How?" he asked, perplexed.

"In case you haven't noticed, I'm pretty good with computers," she answered. "I can write some algorithms to help your search. I can create a visual recognition program to see if their faces pop up in anyone else's social media. I can help a lot."

"I appreciate it," he said. "But this is my obsession. You've got plenty to worry about on your own. It's hard enough being twelve years old, much less a twelve-year-old spy."

"Back in Brooklyn, when you busted in on the meeting with my attorney, did you ask me if I wanted help?"

"No," he said with a chuckle.

"Right, and just now I wasn't asking you," she said. "We're going to work on this together."

He looked at her and sighed. "That sounds very good to me." He motioned to the shoebox she was carrying. "What's in there?"

"A present," she said. "Your room needs a little decorating help, so I thought I'd give you this." She reached into the box and pulled out the old snow globe of the Brooklyn lighthouse. "The water's missing, and the plastic's been taped back together, but it seems to fit in with the decor."

She handed it to him, and he studied it.

"Whenever I'd move into a new foster home, I'd put it up on a shelf near the window," she said. "I think some part of me thought that the lighthouse would guide my family back to me."

The memory of this caused her to pause for a moment.

"Then one time, a boy in one of the houses was mad at me, so he threw it against the wall and shattered it."

She wiped a tear out of her eye. "My foster parents threw it away, but I went out to the trash and found it. I taped it back together and hid it in my shoebox."

Mother was touched. "I can't take this from you."

"I want you to have it," she said. "Put it by the window, so it can guide your children back to you."

"No," he said, near tears. "This is yours. This is for your family."

Brooklyn turned and looked out the window back toward the FARM. The rest of the team was playing soccer in the yard. They were kicking the ball back and forth, laughing. Monty was watching and shouting encouragement. Everyone was happy.

"I don't need it anymore," she said, turning back to him. "I found my family."

UK EYES ONLY

Secret Intelligence Service/MI6

Vauxhall Cross, London, UK

Project City Spies (aka Project Neverland)

Dossier prepared by A. Montgomery

BROOKLYN

NAME: ~~Sara Maria Martinez~~

AGE: 12

BIRTHDAY: November 20

BIRTHPLACE: Vega Alta, Puerto Rico

RECRUITED: Kings County Family Court, Brooklyn, New York, United States

SPECIAL TALENT: Computer hacking—used an outdated laptop to hack into the computer of Dr. Serena Ochoa to wish her a happy birthday. At the time, Dr. Ochoa was an astronaut on board the International Space Station.

LIKES: Enjoys graphic novels and writing code.

DISLIKES: Hates that spies never get to sleep in.

LANGUAGES: English, Spanish

CURRENT ASSIGNMENT: FARM-Crypto Unit, Aisling, Scotland, United Kingdom

PARIS

NAME: ~~Salomon Omborenga~~

AGE: 15

BIRTHDAY: January 13

BIRTHPLACE: Kigali, Rwanda

RECRUITED: 14th arrondissement, Paris, France

SPECIAL TALENT: Survival skills—youngest person ever to pass Special Forces Survive, Evade, Resist, Extract (SERE) Training at RAF St. Mawgan. Graduated top of class.

LIKES: Has three great loves: chess, *Doctor Who*, and Liverpool FC.

DISLIKES: Convinced the fall of the British Empire was due to its food, which he calls "a culinary crime against humanity."

LANGUAGES: English, French, Swahili (partial)

CURRENT ASSIGNMENT: FARM-Crypto Unit, Aisling, Scotland, United Kingdom

SYDNEY

NAME: ~~Olivia Rose~~

AGE: 14

BIRTHDAY: July 15

BIRTHPLACE: Bondi Beach, New South Wales, Australia

RECRUITED: Wallangarra School for Girls, Sydney, New South Wales, Australia

SPECIAL TALENT: Field ops—highly resourceful and creative. She once saved a mission by disabling an Indonesian passenger train using only "some rando stuff I found in the snack bar."

LIKES: Describes both surfing and explosives as "Bonzer!"

DISLIKES: Practically allergic to following rules.

LANGUAGE: English

CURRENT ASSIGNMENT: FARM-Crypto Unit, Aisling, Scotland, United Kingdom

KAT

NAME: ~~Amita Bishwakarma~~

AGE: 13

BIRTHDAY: December 8

BIRTHPLACE: Monjo, Nepal

RECRUITED: UNICEF Transitional Learning Center, Kathmandu, Nepal

SPECIAL TALENT: Cryptography—uses off-the-charts code-breaking skills to decipher encrypted communications. Also used them to determine which candy bars held the winning pieces for a £5,000 sweepstakes. (Donated prize money to UNICEF efforts in Nepal.)

LIKES: Secretly maintains a social media account focused on yetis and the Loch Ness Monster.

DISLIKES: Most people.

LANGUAGES: English, Nepali

CURRENT ASSIGNMENT: FARM-Crypto Unit, Aisling, Scotland, United Kingdom

RIO

NAME: ~~João Cardozo~~

AGE: 12

BIRTHDAY: November 3

BIRTHPLACE: Rio de Janeiro, Brazil

RECRUITED: Copacabana, Rio de Janeiro, Brazil

SPECIAL TALENT: Street magic—incredible sleight-of-hand skills allowed him to gain access to high-security area at the Russian embassy by picking the pocket of ambassador Anatoly Morozov.

LIKES: Despite his small size, has a voracious appetite and once won a £20 bet by eating ten hot dogs in ten minutes.

DISLIKES: Homework. He's very intelligent but struggles academically.

LANGUAGES: English, Portuguese, Spanish (partial)

CURRENT ASSIGNMENT: FARM-Crypto Unit, Aisling, Scotland, United Kingdom

Acknowledgments

Writing is a solo endeavor, but publishing is most definitely a team sport. I'm beyond lucky to have a book family made up of remarkable people, including a few who I'd like to thank for helping *City Spies* come to life.

Fiona Simpson edited this book, just as she edited my previous six, which is a testament not only to her talent and skill but also to her incredible patience and good humor. She's a superb collaborator whose only notable flaw is that she roots for the Yankees.

Not only is Mara Anastas a wonderful publisher, she was the first person other than my wife to hear the concept for *City Spies*. We were at the ALA convention in Orlando when I blurted out my idea for the opening chapter and the basic premise. She responded with a big smile that told me we might be onto something.

Mara and Fiona are joined by the amazing Aladdin all-stars. This group includes Tricia Lin, Rebecca Vitkus, Brenna Franzitta, Kathleen Smith, Chelsea Morgan, Tiara Iandiorio, Caitlin Sweeny, Alissa Nigro, Savannah

Breckenridge, Nicole Russo, Cassie Malmo, Anna Jarzab, Lauren Hoffman, Michelle Leo, Amy Beaudoin, Sarah Woodruff, Chriscynethia Floyd, and Yaoyao Ma Van As. They are smart, funny, and dedicated. They're also tons of fun to hang out with and always make me feel welcome when I visit New York.

Rosemary Stimola is equal parts Sherpa, spirit guide, and literary agent. She's also a great friend. I'm so fortunate to be part of the Stimola Literary Studio and have her guiding the way. I'd also like to give a huge shout-out to Peter Ryan and the rest of the crew at SLS.

One of the greatest treats of writing middle-grade fiction is getting to know others in the kid-lit community. Among those I'm lucky enough to call friends are a host of great writers who are even better people, a group of coconspirators called the Renegades of Middle Grade; my wonder twin, Rose Brock; the dynamo that is Donalyn Miller; and a multitude of librarians and educators who work every day to put books into the hands of young readers. To all of you, who are too numerous to name, know that you are my heroes.

Finally, I'd like to thank my family. You give me purpose. You give me inspiration. And you fill my heart with love and joy.